I0574325

A Mystery Yarn

AN OMNIPODGE MYSTERY

Novels by Mike Befeler

Unstuff Your Stuff
Death of a Scam Artist
The Back Wing
The Front Wing
Mystery of the Dinner Playhouse
Court Trouble
Paradise Court
The Tesla Legacy
Murder on the Switzerland Trail
The V V Agency

Paul Jacobson Geezer-Lit Mysteries

Retirement Homes Are Murder
Living with Your Kids Is Murder
Senior Moments Are Murder
Cruising in Your Eighties Is Murder
Care Homes Are Murder
Nursing Homes Are Murder

The Omnipodge Mystery Trilogy

Old Detectives Home
Last Gasp Motel
A Mystery Yarn

A Mystery Yarn

OMNIPODGE TRILOGY • BOOK 3

Mike Befeler

Encircle Publications,
Farmington, Maine, U.S.A.

A Mystery Yarn Copyright © 2024 Mike Befeler

Hardcover ISBN:-13: 978-1-64599-517-3
Paperback ISBN-13: 978-1-64599-516-6
E-book ISBN-13: 978-1-64599-518-0

Library of Congress Control Number: 2024932959

ALL RIGHTS RESERVED. In accordance with the U.S. Copyright Act of 1976, no part of this publication may be reproduced, distributed, or transmitted in any form or by any means, or stored in a database or retrieval system, without prior written permission of the publisher, Encircle Publications, Farmington, ME.

This book is a work of fiction. All names, characters, places and events are either products of the author's imagination or are used fictitiously.

Editor: Cynthia Brackett-Vincent

Published by:

Encircle Publications
PO Box 187
Farmington, ME 04938

info@encirclepub.com
http://encirclepub.com

To my wife, Wendy,
who helped me with all the cozy tropes.

Chapter 1

THE DOORBELL JANGLED, AND BART Cunard stormed into Driftwood Creatives.

"Rats," I muttered under my breath from behind the counter. I had no desire to see him here or anywhere.

Bart hitched up his red, white, and blue striped Bermuda shorts, tried to suck in his stomach beneath his bright orange Hawaiian shirt, and waggled his eyebrows at me. "Well, if it isn't the cutest little shopkeeper in all of Omnipodge Village Center. Sure is quiet in here. Most of the other stores play music. How come you don't?"

"I have tinnitus."

"What's that?"

"It's a condition that means music and other sharp sounds cause a crackling noise in my right ear. It's very distracting. So, while I'd love to listen to music, I avoid it."

Bart clapped his hands together right next to the side of my head. "Like this."

I put my right hand over my ear at the sound of a runaway popcorn machine. "Yeah, like that."

"You're weird. Well, you have one other problem."

I knew what was coming but held my tongue.

He pointed a meaty finger at me. "You're a month behind on rent. Time to pay up, sweetheart."

He had a huge diamond ring on his hand that, in the light,

sparkled blue. I felt the urge to jam that ring down his throat. Good thing I was a lady.

With a resigned sigh, I launched into my planned spiel. "It's like this, Bart. I've been spending money on preparing for the Spring Break rush. You'll notice that my shop is freshly painted and chock-full of driftwood pieces to sell. In two weeks, college kids and families will be stopping in Omnipodge as they travel between Los Angeles and San Francisco. I'm going to sell oodles of my driftwood creations as I did last Spring Break. Then I'll pay what I owe you."

He shook his head. "Not good enough, little lady. I need the money now." Then he waggled his eyebrows again. "Or we could settle for something other than money."

I resisted the urge to puke on his sandals. "Not going to happen. But what I'll do is this. After the Spring Break rush, I'll pay what I owe you plus an additional month in advance."

"Make it two months and we have a deal."

I did a quick mental calculation and gritted my teeth. "Okay, two months."

He reached out to try to tweak my chin, but I ducked out of reach, and his arm swung past me like a batter who had tried for a home run and missed the ball completely. Instead, he tapped his forehead. "I have it locked in here. Pru Pendergast owes me back rent plus three month's advance rent."

I put my hands on my hips. "We agreed on two months."

"The extra month is for interest. I have one other idea on how you can repay me. I've heard from a reliable source that Willie Woburn hid gold under this cottage when he built it in the nineteenth century. You find any to share with me?"

"That's a myth."

"I don't know. Could be gold around here. You going to be in your shop all day?"

"Not that it's any of your business, but I intend to visit the other shops in a little while and go out to lunch with Herb."

"That fruitcake."

"Don't you dare call him that."

"I'll say what I want to." He spun on his heels and stomped out of the shop. I pictured a large piano falling from the sky and smashing Bart to smithereens on the sidewalk. Unfortunately, it didn't happen.

Although the shop was now empty and had no windows open, a breeze rushed past my cheek. "Okay, Wrong Way Willie, I know he's a descendant of yours, but what do you think of that jerk, Bart Cunard?"

The breeze angrily shook the curtains and then ruffled the fur of Boopsie, lying on her pillow in the corner. Boopsie, my rescue Persian, let out a loud "meow" to indicate her indignation at being disrupted from her usual four-hour morning nap.

That brought Spools from the back room, tangled in fishing line. He raced around the room as if chasing a squirrel before the trailing fishing line got caught under my stool. I reached down to free him. "What am I going to do with you? Can't you stay out of my work material?" He had once again lived up to his name by becoming entangled in a spool of fishing line.

He gave my hand a Shih Tzu bath before prancing over to sniff Boopsie's tail. She responded by swishing it into his face.

I took a moment to scan around the shop. I had a dozen driftwood mobiles hanging from the ceiling, and the display cabinet vibrated with the latest driftwood creations of gnarled wood, imbedded colorful stones and attached seashells. That was the beauty of my business. The raw material was free: driftwood, shells and rocks I had collected on beaches along the coast. For stringing my mobiles, I had a lifetime supply of fishing line. I only had to buy glue and lacquer, a small investment. Every time I sold a driftwood mobile or creation, ninety-nine percent profit accumulated in my coffers. Well, except for the rent to the slimebag Bart Cunard, utilities and various overhead expenses.

Not expecting any customers at this slow time of year, I headed to the back of the store to check on my workspace. My shop and home had originated as a house in the nineteenth century. What was once the living room now served as my retail space with an added door to the outside. The long-ago dining room had been converted into my workshop area. The downstairs also had a nook, being used as my small dining area, a kitchen, and a tiny bathroom. My bedroom, a guest bedroom and another bathroom filled the second story. The basement provided ample storage space. This was the extent of my domain.

I had left everything in order in my work room, but after Spools once again had tangled himself in the fishing line, pieces of driftwood had been knocked across the floor and a jar of moonstones had been overturned. Between Spools and the ghost of Wrong Way Willie, I had to constantly clean up. Boopsie rarely got into my stuff unless I had accidently dropped some catnip in a box. She was a certifiable addict.

I regarded the two framed pictures above my work bench. The first showed a bewhiskered gentleman with his hand inside his peacoat. Wrong Way Willie Woburn had arrived in Monterey during the height of the California Gold Rush. Apparently, he caused some sort of ruckus on a clipper ship and was unceremoniously thrown into Monterey Bay. After he swam to shore, he had a little problem with direction and instead of turning left toward San Francisco, went right, down the coast. When he discovered his mistake, he decided to try his luck at fishing instead of mining. Other people came to fish, and after tiring of living in a tent, he founded the town of Omnipodge and built the house that had become my shop and residence.

Some people claimed Willie actually found gold in Omnipodge, but I doubted the stories. One previous owner of my cottage even went to the effort of tearing up the floorboards to look for gold underneath. The result—nothing, other than my floor still squeaked in places. But the rumors still persisted, as evidenced by Bart's earlier comment.

The second picture showed a bare-chested hunk who could have been a model for the cover of a steamy romance novel. Sigh. Kurt Whelan. Kurt worked as a dispatcher for the Omnipodge Police Department and was a volunteer firefighter with Omnipodge Fire and Rescue. Last year the fire department had issued a fundraising calendar with pictures of their best masculine specimens, of which Kurt was a leading example. Kurt and I had been *kind of* seeing each other—the *kind of* being because he had taken me out to dinner once at Dina's Diner, not much of a date. We hadn't even held hands yet.

The picture bore an inscription, "Best wishes to Pru from Kurt." He was a real romantic.

At least things were better than when I dated that putz, Nate Dupres. We had gone through a long, on again, off again relationship starting at UC Santa Cruz. He was the consummate frat boy, ready to party night and day. I thought I loved him, but little things began to irritate me about him. Such as he always ate candy bars but never put on any weight, whereas I'd sniff one and put on five pounds.

But the real kicker—Nate chased anything wearing a skirt, or for that matter, any feminine attire. I finally realized the relationship was doomed. Fortunately, Nate was long gone. Good riddance. So much for my love life.

I stared at Kurt's picture again, as my heart went pitter-patter. Maybe someday things would develop between us.

I had another thought. Maybe I could sic Kurt on Bart Cunard.

Kurt had enough brawn to beat Bart into a bloody pulp. The problem—Kurt couldn't hurt a fly—literally. When on duty at the fire station, he caught flies in his hand and released them outside the building. My gentle giant, *sort-of* boyfriend.

Maybe Wrong Way Willie could do something about Bart. My local haunt didn't approve of Bart, but he could only cause a breeze. Maybe if Bart were standing on a cliff, the breeze could knock him into the ocean. But I didn't know if Wrong Way Willie could go anywhere other than float around inside this building.

I'd have to try an experiment. I stepped to the front of the shop and opened the door. "Come here, Willie." The breezed ruffled the back of my head. Boopsie, apparently intrigued, wandered over and plopped down inside the doorway. I went outside. "Okay, Willie. Come join me." No breeze on my face or the back of my head. I peered at Boopsie. Her fur raised in places on her back, imitating a crowd of people in a football stadium executing a wave.

"Come outside, Willie."

No dice. Boopsie purred as her fur continued to fluff out, up and down her back and tail. No amount of coaxing would bring Wrong Way Willie outside.

"I guess you're a captive spirit, Willie. We'll make do with that. Looks like you won't be able to push Bart off a cliff."

No, I'd merely have to stay out of Bart's way, earn a good amount of money from Spring Break sales and pay the rent. Of course, I could continue to wish for killer bees to attack Bart. I shivered. I hated bees.

Chapter 2

SINCE THE SUN HAD COME out from behind the morning fog bank, I decided to visit some of my fellow merchants in the Omnipodge Village Center. We occupied what had once been old homes now converted into a shopping area with a central commons area that served as a park. I put Spools on a leash for his morning constitutional. Then I turned the sign around that had clock hands and set them to show I'd be back in an hour. That way any visitor dying to buy a driftwood creation could stop by other shops and know when to return to mine.

We had gone no more than a dozen paces before Spools decided he needed to fertilize the grass. I reached for the poop bag dispenser on his leash. No more bags. I tied Spools' leash around the armrest of an emerald green bench and raced back to the shop to grab a plastic bag.

When I returned Bart Cunard stood glaring at Spools. When he saw me, he gave a snort. "No unattended animals allowed here. Your beast has desecrated the pristine lawn. Do you know how much I pay to have this area kept clean?"

"I know. I know. I had to go back to get a bag. I'll clean it up."

"You do that." Bart shook his clenched fist at me and waddled toward Yalley's Jewelry shop.

I took care of my civic responsibility and deposited Spools' "present" in the nearest garbage can. I proceeded along the walkway next to Jake Yalley's shop but came to a screeching halt when I heard raised voices. I knew I should ignore the loud argument but couldn't resist the urge to snoop since this ongoing confrontation was better than any soap opera. And besides, none of the combatants had bothered to close the door that Jake had left wedged open with a doorstop. What did it matter if their conversation could easily be heard a block away and the three people inside were too occupied with themselves to notice Spools and me outside? Through the large plate glass window, I could see arms waving.

Sally Midge Cunard, Bart's ex, shouted, "What are you doing here? I'm going to get a restraining order if you keep stalking me."

"I happen to be checking the shops this morning," Bart replied. "I didn't even know you were in here. It's not all about you, Smidge."

"And quit calling me that demeaning name, you fat, sleazy runt." Sally slapped Bart.

"I'll have you arrested for assault and battery. And I'll call you Smidge if I want to. Smidge. Smidge. Smidge."

I wondered if this was the kids' playground rather than a business establishment.

Jake Yalley joined the altercation. "G-get out of my shop."

"It happens to be my shop, and you lease it, stutter boy. And since your lease runs out next month, I think you'll be needing to find a new place to sell your cheesy jewelry. It's as worthless as the stones in Pru's driftwood disasters."

What the fig? I had half a mind to go in and join the fray and tell Bart what I thought of him. Fortunately, Sally Midge took care of it for me. "All you do is insult everyone. I don't know why I ever married you, you piece of bat snot."

Whoa. Sally Midge practically had steam coming out of her ears.

"You had it good, Smidge. I never heard you complain when you spent my money."

"Speaking of money. You're four months behind on alimony."

"I'll pay you once my tenants catch up on their back rent."

Sally stamped her foot. "You've got plenty of cash, most of it from illegal sources like the scams you're pulling with Larry Ludwick."

Hmm. This was getting interesting. Sally Midge had fingered our local development tycoon. I wondered what was going on.

"Smidge, you like to take the moral high ground, but now you're shacking up with stutter boy here. You deserve each other."

"And you deserve to be six feet under."

"Yeah, who's going to do it? You and stutter boy?"

"O-out." Obviously, Jake had had enough because he shoved Bart hard enough that the slimebag shot out of the shop, tripped over Spools' leash and landed head first in a hydrangea bush with his large tush in the air. I only wished I was competent enough to take a cell phone picture of him.

"Are you inspecting the vegetation?" I asked in my sweetest voice.

Bart extracted himself and dusted off his Bermuda shorts. "You're a bunch of pissants."

"You were looking for ants in the bush? Such a thoughtful landlord. You might also try the rose bushes. They might be infested as well."

Bart limped off toward the parking lot without another word. I didn't think I had ever before encountered him speechless.

With my curiosity piqued, I entered Jake's shop, catching Jake and Sally Midge in a fierce embrace. She wore a tie-dye hippie dress, and Jake had on his usual Dockers and white button-down shirt. "Sorry to interrupt, but Bart came flying out as if auditioning for the Omnipodge ballet company. What gives?"

Sally Midge disengaged from the clench and gave a loud sigh. "He's up to his old tricks. Harassing me and Jake."

"I overheard something about Larry Ludwick."

"Yeah. Bart has some kind of illegal operation going with Larry. The two of them have been cooking up deals for years and are trying to put together some sort of new real estate fraud. Typical."

"L-Larry plans to develop the old fish processing plant site. Turn it into townhouses."

I held my nose. "I sure wouldn't want to live there. It was a dumping ground for years' worth of discarded fish parts."

Sally smoothed her dress. "That's the irony of their operation. They're going to call it Lilac Acres."

"It would t-take acres of lilacs to overcome the lingering aroma."

I resisted the urge to roll my eyes. "If Bart is involved in illegal activities, maybe the police will arrest him and he'll be locked away."

"H-he's not a very arresting personality."

Sally Midge gave Jake a playful swat, not the head snapper she'd delivered to Bart. "Cut out the dumb puns. I wish the police would put him away permanently, but they aren't doing anything. I even spoke to Detective Moriarty once. He told me not to be an emotional female. Can you believe that? Me?" Her voice went up an octave. "Emotional?"

I decided to change the subject. I pointed to a hand grenade resting on one of the shelves. "You collect armaments, Jake?"

"That's a practice grenade, not a real one. I kept it as a souvenir when I left the army."

"Jake was quite the army man at one time," Sally Midge said. "Did some hush-hush work, rumor has it."

"N-nothing special. Just a grunt."

Then Sally Midge fixed her eyes on me. "I'm sensing something about you?"

"Huh?" was all I could muster.

Sally Midge put her right index finger against her slightly rouged cheek. "Yes. I'm definitely getting a vibe from your aura."

"S-sally Midge is psychic, you know."

That's all I needed. A psychic analyzing me.

"I'm picking up very strong signals from you, Pru. You're in touch with a spirit from the other side."

"The other side of what?"

"You know. Someone who's dead."

I flinched. No one but my Granny Mulligan knew about Wrong Way Willie, and Granny would never tell anyone, particularly a gossip monger such as Sally Midge.

"My parents are dead, but they haven't communicated with me."

Sally Midge bit her lip for a moment. "No, it's not a relative of yours. It's someone from farther in the past who isn't part of your family."

I gave my best casual shrug. "Don't know what you could be picking up."

"We should have a séance some time."

"S-sally Midge helped me speak to my great uncle Howard."

"I appreciate the offer, but I'm too busy getting ready for the Spring Break rush. Maybe another time." Like the next millennium. I checked my watch. "I need to stop at a few of the other shops, and then I'm going out to lunch with Herb."

Sally Midge let out a heartfelt sigh. "I'm so tired of these run-ins with Bart."

Jake gave Sally Midge another hug. "D-don't let him get you down, sweetie. He'll get his comeuppance."

Chapter 3

I LEFT YALLEY'S JEWELERS, HAVING RESISTED the urge to buy new dangly, gold **lamé** hand-painted earrings, the urge suppressed by the fact that I had only three dollars and forty cents in my purse, an overextended Visa account and forty-six dollars in my checking account.

Next on the list—a visit to Flo Florrest's Flowing Yarn shop. This was Spools' favorite place, other than the fire hydrant on the far side of the commons.

Flo also had her door open to let in the pleasant ocean air. Our entrance was greeted by a loud blast of rap music. I put my hand to my right ear as a cacophony of crackling kept rhythm with the pounding beat coming from a speaker mounted over the counter where Flo stood snapping her fingers. She had her head wrapped in a blue silk scarf that matched a blue blouse tucked into black slacks.

"Can you turn that music down?" I shouted.

"Sorry." Flo reached under the counter and the music dropped fifty decibels.

"Why so loud?" I asked after the crackling in my right ear descended to a minor roar.

Flo graced me with a huge smile. "I'm in a good mood because I received my shipment of Vicuna yesterday. Come take a look." She came out from behind the counter and led me to a bin full of luscious brown yarn.

I picked up a skein and felt the soft texture. "Yum."

"You should use yarn instead of fishing line for your mobiles."

"I considered yarn at first, but, fortunately, I found a supply of fishing line in my basement. Must have been left over from the days of Wrong Way Willie, but it's strong and holds my mobiles together. Uh-oh."

The bin of Vicuna lay on its side, and Spools raced around the shop with a skein of yarn tangled in his paws. I reached down to grab the leash before he knocked over any other bins. "Cussed dog. How do you get into things so fast?"

He rolled over, kicking his feet in the air, obviously taking pleasure in the havoc he had caused.

Flo laughed. "Here, let me untangle him."

Between the two of us we rescued a skein of once pristine yarn.

"I'll pay you for the damage done." I sucked on my lip, thinking over how much the skein would cost. It would have to be a very good Spring Break to cover this plus the money I had to pay Bart.

"Oh, posh. No harm done. I'll rewind it, and it will be as good as new."

I let out a loud sigh of relief. "Thanks, Flo. You're the best."

"I wouldn't say that," came a voice from the doorway.

Oops. In came Bart Cunard.

He waggled his eyebrows at me. "We have to stop meeting like this, prurient Pru. I think you're following me."

I gagged loudly. "It seems to be the other way around. I came here first." Seeing Bart a third time today was four times too many for me.

Fortunately, he turned his attention back to Flo. "Even if you're the local communist you still need to pay rent. This isn't a welfare state, floozy Flo."

"The check's in the mail, you Nazi."

"Right." He held out his hand. "As if you have to mail it. You can give it to me now." He wiggled his fingers in a come here fashion.

Flo crossed her arms. "You'll get it when the United States Postal Service decides to deliver it to you. Why don't you go back to your right-wing fascist buddies and leave this shop in peace?"

"Oh, you won't get rid of me that easily, pinko lady. Pay up and you can stuff the rest of your left-wing rhetoric in your autographed copy of Mao's *The Little Red Book*."

Flo shook her fist at Bart. "I'm surprised you even have the word rhetoric in your vocabulary. You must have been reading *Mein Kampf* again."

Spools chomped down on the heel of Bart's sandal.

He shook his foot. "Get this mangy mutt off me."

This made Spools bite down harder, growling ferociously. As the saying goes, the smaller they are, the louder they growl.

Flo picked up a broom and swatted Bart. "Leave that poor defenseless animal alone, you despotic pig."

Bart backed away toward the door, and Spools must have decided to let the giant squirrel escape because he released his grip.

"You come in here again, and I'll sic more than a dog on you." Flo thrust the broom at Bart again.

He tried to avoid another assault by backing out the door but tripped on the doorsill, waved his arms in an unsuccessful attempt to regain balance and landed in a wagon being pulled by a young girl in braids.

"Mommy, he crushed my dolls."

A woman in a billowing flowered dress walloped Bart on the side of the head with a large black purse. "Get out of my daughter's wagon, you pervert."

Bart dodged the second time the purse swung his way, blocking the assault with his forearm. The woman prepared for the third attempt, when he rolled out of the wagon, picked himself up and stumbled away.

Flo cupped her hands and called out, "Have a nice day, Adolf."

I waved at the departing figure. "Jeez, what a pain in the fanny he's become. He definitely is having trouble staying on his feet today."

Flo dusted her hands together. "Couldn't happen to a nicer guy."

I nodded. "He and my ex-boyfriend, Nate Dupres, who I told you about, are two of a kind."

"Speaking of Nate, I heard he's in town."

"What?"

"Yeah. Don't be surprised if he shows up on your doorstep."

I smacked my forehead with the palm of my hand. "That's all I need." I picked up Spools, and he licked my hand. "I take it you and Bart still don't see eye to eye on politics."

Flo gave Spools a scritch. "Of course not. He's to the right of Genghis Khan, whereas I'm a realistic liberal. I can't stand his bigoted and demeaning comments. If it weren't for the shopkeepers I like here, I'd go somewhere else."

"And the check in the mail bit?"

"I actually did send him a check." Flo gave me a wink. "But I conveniently forgot to put postage on it."

That caused me to have the giggles. "I owe Bart rent as well, and he was harassing me earlier. I'm waiting for the Spring Break rush to earn enough to pay him."

Flo put the broom back in the corner. "I could give him the money now, but I like to tweak him a little. He gets so uptight when not paid on time. If enough of us delay payments, maybe he'll have a conniption fit or a heart attack. Either that or someone can feed him to the sharks, although I think he'd give the sharks indigestion."

Chapter 4

I TORE SPOOLS AWAY FROM ANY further attempts at becoming entangled in yarn and returned to my shop since I knew he wouldn't be welcomed at my next stop. Back inside my place, I unleashed him, and he immediately went over to nudge the sleeping Boopsie who responded by lashing him with her fluffy tail. Ah, all was well in the animal kingdom.

Still no signs of customers, so I reset the hands of the clock on my door to indicate I'd be back in two hours and continued my tour. Next stop, Bea's Bookstore.

I loved books, and Bea's was one of my favorite places in the whole world. I could spend hours perusing the shelves or snuggling down in a beanbag chair in a corner to read the latest Agatha-award-winning mystery. And Bea had a wonderful bookstore cat named Jane Austin.

The problem was that Jane Austin and Spools didn't get along. Spools wanted to play, and Jane Austin, the aloof Siamese, considered such behavior as being beneath her level of dignity. She corrected the situation with a swat to the nose. To prevent any veterinarian bills I couldn't afford, I didn't bring Spools along to the bookstore.

A thought occurred to me, and I wondered how Boopsie and Jane Austin would get along, but both were inside cats and never ventured out to encounter the other. They had in common the desire to sleep twenty hours a day with the other four hours made up of eating, grooming, coughing up hairballs and allowing humans to pet them.

I double checked to make sure Bart wasn't in sight and headed over to Bea's. Her window displayed a collection of children's books and some of the latest teen supernatural adventures. She was obviously getting ready for Spring Break as well. Families would have to buy at least one book for their children or hormone-infected teen on a trip along the coast.

Bea stood on a ladder dusting between the top of the wall and the ceiling. She had a cute upturned nose and a figure to die for, which attracted its fair share of male attention. Fortunately, Kurt Whelan seemed more interested in my pedestrian curves, *sort of.* Today she wore shorts, which showcased her legs, and a T-shirt that read, "Books are better than booze."

"Find anything interesting up there?"

"Oh hi, Pru. No, only a few cobwebs. You looking for anything in particular today?"

"I want to peruse your cooking books."

She descended the ladder and waved me over to her cooking section. "I have just the thing for you. The latest in French cuisine."

I gulped. "Um. As you know I need something a little more basic. How about simple American meals?"

"After you complete the cooking class, you'll be ready for all kinds of culinary adventures. Here are several new cooking books that might interest you." She grabbed a heavy tome and handed it to me.

"Speaking of the cooking class, I'll be here tomorrow night. What's the subject?"

"Sauces."

"Goody. I could use something besides a jar of mayonnaise."

"That's the purpose of tomorrow's session—to introduce you and the others to Béarnaise, Hollandaise and Mornay."

I rubbed my hands together. "Those sound scrumptious." Then I slumped. "But last time I burned the chicken Marsala. Did you ever get the pan cleaned?"

"Nope. It was a lost cause. I had to throw it out."

I put my hand to my suddenly warm face. "Oh, dear. I'll reimburse you."

"Not to worry. It was an old pan I found in the cupboard when I moved in here." She winked at me. "I wasn't going to trust you with a new one."

Heat pulsed along my neck. "I have a long way to go with my cooking."

"You merely need to pay more attention to the temperature and the length of time you're cooking."

"That's the problem. I got distracted worrying about measuring the right amount of sherry and Marsala wine and when to add the mushrooms and didn't notice the chicken turning black."

"Didn't you smell it?"

"There were so many aromas in your kitchen that I missed the telltale sign. I apologize again."

"You'll do better tomorrow."

Jane Austin spotted me, stretched, pranced off her pillow and padded over to rub against my leg. I tucked the cookbook under my arm, reached down and chucked her under the chin, producing a loud, gravelly purr. She gave me a final fuzz-by before returning to her majesty's roost.

I leafed through the cookbook. Most of the recipes had ingredient lists a page long. More than five ingredients confused the heck out of me. The dessert section caught my attention. Maybe I could bake a pie or cake for Kurt. He loved sweets. I bit my lip at the thought of the cooking class two weeks ago when I had burnt the oatmeal cookies. No one else in the class had any problems, but mine turned out the color of brownies.

The doorbell jangled, and I cringed when Bart Cunard entered. "Rats."

"No," Bea replied, "only one large rat."

Jane Austin arched her back, hair standing up, and hissed.

He gave a bow, displaying the top of his bald pate. "Oh, good. Two sexy ladies here together. I don't know which one is my first choice."

"Too bad you're not on either of our lists," Bea said. "What do you want, Bart?"

"Checking on my chattel." He guffawed. "All sexual favors will be reciprocated."

"You're a chauvinist, sexist pig, Bart."

"You're saying I'm charming, sexy and big?"

Bea picked up a used paperback and flung it at Bart, hitting him in the chest. "Get out of my shop."

"You don't seem to be making many friends today," I said. "You might want to cut your losses and take a long drive… and never come back."

"Aw, you know you'd both miss me."

"Like missing a snake." Bea reached behind the counter and pulled out a shotgun, which she leveled at Bart.

His eyes widened to the size of silver dollars, and he thrust his arms into the sky like the bad guy being arrested by the sheriff. "No violence."

"Out."

This time he got the message and skedaddled.

I shivered. "Would you have shot him?"

"Nah. It's not even loaded. But I keep it under the counter in case I have any unruly visitors, and Bart is as unruly as they come."

"I wish there was something we could do about Bart. I love the Omnipodge Village Center, but with him as the owner, he makes our lives miserable. He harassed me a little while ago over the rent I owe."

"Maybe we can enact a plot like in *Murder on the Orient Express* and all stab him. I don't know a shopkeeper who likes him."

I put the cooking book back on the shelf, realizing it was way over my ability level. "We all agree on that—Bart is sewer scum."

"No, sewer scum can be used for fertilizer. Bart has no redeeming qualities whatsoever."

Chapter 5

I PROCEEDED TO DINA'S DINER FOR my regular lunch with my best friend, Herb Hanover, who ran Herb's Herbs, the best herb and spice shop in the state of California. I had purchased a whole rack of condiments from him for my ill-fated cooking attempts. Hopefully the class at Bea's would improve my cooking skills so I could take advantage of the herbs that had run my checking account dry. In the past whether I added oregano or basil to food, it tasted the same—burnt.

Herb greeted me with a flick of the wrist, "You look lovely, simply lovely, Princess. Your azul blouse shows off your eyes perfectly."

Actually, he was the one who looked lovely in his paisley silk shirt, tight jeans and wavy blond hair.

I scooted into the booth and took his hands. "Thank you. It's good to see you. I need this break with someone I can speak with. I've had a rough morning—too many encounters with Bart Cunard."

"That cad. What did he do this time?"

"He was up to his usual tricks. Sexual harassment and insulting everyone in sight. But you'll get a kick out of this. Jake and Flo both threw him out of their shops, and he exited none too gracefully."

Herb clapped his hands together. "Oh, that sounds delightful. Do tell me the gory details."

I recounted Bart's header into the hydrangea bush and the tumble into the little girl's wagon.

Herb giggled. "Oh, I wish I could have been there. That would have been a sight for sore eyes."

Speaking of eyes, Herb's misted over at that point.

"What's the matter?" I asked. "One minute laughing and the next crying."

He sniffed and wiped away the tear. "I had a dreadful encounter with that horrid Bart yesterday. He came into my shop, to complain that I hadn't paid my rent. It had slipped my mind. I told him I'd have a check to him today. He knocked over a bowl of turmeric, which caused me to sneeze." He rubbed his nose. "You know how sensitive I am. Then he called me 'weird' and said they should have laws against 'my kind.' Can you image what a Neanderthal he is?"

I patted his hand. "There. There. We all love you. Bart treats everyone that way. Don't take it personally."

Herb sniffled. "Yesterday was the one-year anniversary of that unspeakable event… last night I even had a nightmare of Carl in his mauve wetsuit being drowned in the kelp bed. There he was going out to catch the perfect wave, and he met his demise. I'll never find another partner as loving as he was."

Now a tear rolled down my cheek. Herb and Carl. I only wished that I could have as close a relationship with someone. Images of Kurt Whelan surged through my mind. Would that ever be us? I pictured myself curled up in Kurt's arm, leaning against his chest, him reaching for me, me reaching for him, and then…

"Are you all right, Princess? You had a goofy look on your face. Kind of as if you'd found a mountain of chocolate."

"Oh, it was nothing." That was the problem. It definitely was nothing so far. I knew Kurt liked me, but for all his brawn, he didn't take much initiative in moving our relationship forward. Would I have to be the one to get things started? No. After my disastrous relationship with Nate Dupres, I would let things take a natural course. No sense rushing anything. We'd get to know each other slowly and see what happened.

"I know. You're thinking of Kurt."

I smiled. "You're a mind reader."

"It's obvious. You had that Sleeping Beauty waiting for the prince's kiss look on your puss. One of these days Kurt will wake up."

"I hope you're right."

"He is a hunk, but not my type. Definitely for you. Maybe I should whisper in his ear: Pru, Pru. It's time for Pru and you."

I swatted his hand. "You do nothing of the sort. It's up to Kurt to do this on his own."

"Even if it takes months?"

"Yes. Even if it takes years."

Herb waved at the waitress. "Oh, Alice, dear. We're ready when you have a moment." He turned back to me. "All this talk of romance makes me hungry. I think I'll have the Cobb salad with an extra order of croutons. What about you?"

"I'm ready for a large greasy cheeseburger."

Herb stuck out his tongue. "Yuck. How can you stand eating cow?"

"Humans are carnivores."

Herb rearranged his silverware. "Not all of us. Some are more refined and can get along very nicely on flora instead of fauna."

"I still like nice red, dripping meat."

Herb turned pale. "How can my best friend be such a beast?"

"We can't agree on everything. That would be boring."

"I guess you're right."

Alice appeared and took a pencil out of her Marge Simpson beehive. I flinched thinking of bees.

I placed my order, and while Herb explained the details of how his lettuce should be arranged, I watched a family having a meal at a nearby table. Mother, father and two kids: a girl approximately ten and a boy maybe eight. Well-behaved and neatly dressed. Would that be Kurt and me someday? I resisted the urge to slap my cheek. Get real. Was my biologic clock sending these messages? Tick. Tick. Get going, girl. I stuffed the mythical clock back into my imaginary cupboard. I'd deal with that later.

"You've gone off into your little world again," Herb said.

"Sorry, I'll try to be present."

"You do that. I can't have you slipping off into some netherworld."

"We have to do something with Bart. He's getting worse. We have such a wonderful group of shopkeepers in Omnipodge Village Center. It's a shame that we have to put up with such an atrocious landlord."

"Maybe we could hire a hit man."

"You've been watching too much television."

Herb sighed loudly. "I know. I used to go to art festivals and trips up and down the coast. But ever since… the awful event, I've done nothing but watch television when not working."

"You need a diversion. I'm going on a driftwood, shell and moonstone expedition in a few days. You're coming with me."

"But who will watch the shop?"

"You and I can both close our shops for one day. Neither of us has that much business right now. Fortunately, we'll then have the Spring Break rush."

"True. I guess I can be talked into an expedition. I have my chartreuse reef walkers. They will be perfect for combing beaches."

Chapter 6

HERB NEEDED TO GET BACK to his shop because he was expecting one of his best customers to stop by to stock up on herbs and spices for a snazzy restaurant, but I had no pressing appointments, so I decided to take a walk down to the sea cliffs. The day remained mild, with a slight breeze off the ocean. I stood and stared out to sea imagining the many boats that had sailed or motored along this coastline. Down below the waves broke on rocks sending plumes of spray skyward. Much of this area was rugged, with imbedded beaches where locals would gather for picnics and campfires and where I could collect driftwood, shells and rocks. Today the hunting mood did not seize me. My feet remained planted on the high ground. Instead, my mind wandered to the events of the morning, mainly the negative people in my life.

It was definitely not good news that Nate Dupres had reappeared in town. There could only be one reason he came here. Me. I shivered. That gave me a queasy sensation in the pit of my hamburger-clogged stomach. Maybe I should have had a salad as Herb did. I punched my gut and let out an unladylike belch. There. That felt better.

Nate and I had met at the University of California at Santa Cruz while I pursued a degree in Marine Biology and he studied girls. For some reason, we hooked up. He caught my attention with his chiseled face, quick smile, and great sense of humor. I should have known better, but at the time I didn't. We got together, and

I thought everything was wonderful until I discovered that on nights we weren't in each others' arms, he shared his favors with three other coeds. What a rodent. He professed his love for only me, but his actions proved otherwise on numerous occasions.

We broke up right before graduation. Then I took my nearly useless degree and ended up working as a waitress in Monterey for three months before my own dreadful event—my parents were killed in an auto accident on the Grapevine, north of Los Angeles. I entered a deep funk, only to be revived when Granny Mulligan invited me to come stay with her here in Omnipodge. She nursed me back to this world with her no-nonsense approach to life, her typical statement being, "Your parents are dead. I miss them, too, but you need to get a life. Go out and meet people."

With her prodding, I entered society again. The one mistake—I got back together with Nate. That lasted two months before I found him in a clench with another waitress. He took a job in San Jose, and I headed to Los Angeles for a few years. Being a clerk in too many different retail stores proved to be not financially lucrative, but it did spawn the idea of running my own store. After much thought and consideration, I decided I'd try my own business and returned to Omnipodge. Granny staked me for a loan to get Driftwood Creatives started.

Granny accused me of being driftwood myself, but she supported my entrepreneurial desire. Now, I was ensconced in Omnipodge with a thriving business—not thriving at the moment, but soon to be with the Spring Break rush.

My mind turned to my other problem—Bart Cunard. What a piece of yuck. Too bad he hadn't been the one to drown in kelp rather than Herb's partner, Carl. Every time Bart appeared, I wanted to haul off and sock him. Only one thing held me back— as the landlord, he could kick me out, and I liked my shop. The combination of finding treasures on a beach and then crafting them into creative works of art appealed to me. And on top of that, people forking over their hard-earned cash to buy one of my creations warmed my heart. Nothing like the validation of money in exchange for art.

Not everyone considered my creations to be art, but I did, and that's what mattered. "To heck with the pissants," Granny always said. And she followed with her favorite saying, "Tell them to hit the street on the jackass they rode in on."

I looked out to sea as the wind whipped up white caps on the rolling waves. I had never been an ocean person. Again, the irony of being a Marine Biology major in college. But I liked the things along the shore—the tide pools, the sea urchins, the crabs, the shells, the rocks, the driftwood. One of my favorite books was *Cannery Row* by John Steinbeck, comparing the life of quirky people in pre-World War II Monterey to life in the tide pools. That was my kind of literature.

Time to head back to the shop. I gave one more glance out to sea, twirled in a half-circle, and planted my feet one after the other toward Omnipodge Village Center.

I didn't pass anyone I knew. In fact, I saw few pedestrians before I got to my shop. I reached for the door handle.

Something was wrong.

I had locked the shop, but the door now stood open a crack. No one had a key except me, Granny, and Bart Cunard.

Uh-oh. Had the pus sack invaded my privacy?

Sticking my head inside, I shouted, "Hello. Anyone here?"

No answer.

I called out again.

This time, I heard a plaintive, "*Meow.*"

Instead of being on her pillow, Boopsie stood in the middle of the floor with her fur sticking out like a puff ball and her eyes an angry yellow. Had someone disturbed her space as well as mine?

Spools came charging out of the back room, tangled in fishing line. Nothing unusual there, except for his manic circling and barking. He screeched to a stop at the corner of the counter and pointed. I had never seen a Shih Tzu assume this position. He also wanted to tell me something.

Then I spotted a box of driftwood spilled on the floor. Had that been caused by Boopsie or Spools or Wrong Way Willie? Or by an interloper?

I wondered if my resident ghost had noticed anything. "Willie?" No response.

He must have been asleep upstairs. What a time for him not to be paying attention. He liked sleeping in the guest bedroom down the hall from my room. It surprised me, but even haunts needed their rest.

Boopsie stalked over to the edge of the counter, arched her back and hissed loudly, pawing at the ground like a lion ready to attack.

"What is it, girl? Something back there?"

I pictured an intruder huddled behind my counter, holding a knife, gun, or, as they said in the movies, a blunt object. I decided to arm myself with my own blunt object and picked up a three-foot-long piece of driftwood.

I shifted into my best softball batting stance and carefully tiptoed toward the counter. The first thing I noticed was a strange object resting on the floor. I peered at it. A driftwood handle attached to a twisted cord of yarn. And not any yarn. The same brown Vicuna yarn I had seen in Flo's shop that morning.

I gasped and dropped my weapon.

The twisted cord of yarn was wrapped around the throat of the lifeless body of Bart Cunard. Lifeless, because a bloated purple tongue hung out of his mouth. A second driftwood handle dangled from his neck. He had been garroted right here in my shop.

Chapter 7

I GASPED, THEN STIFLED THE URGE to scream. I would not lower myself to be a shrieking female. Once my stomach decided not to unload lunch on Bart, I studied him more closely. He actually looked better dead than when alive. As if time stood still, I looked at his outstretched right hand. The ring I had noticed earlier was no longer on his finger. I looked around the shop. Could the murderer still be here somewhere?

Not wanting to tempt fate, I dashed outside, took out my cell phone and called 9-1-1. No bars. I'd forgotten I resided in a dead zone. I steeled my nerves and went back inside, picking up Boopsie. I figured I could throw her into the face of any lurking killer. When no one appeared, I put her down on the counter, grabbed the landline and punched in the three digits. A woman operator informed me that someone would arrive soon.

Still feeling nervous being inside, I headed out and paced back and forth in front of my store, interrupted only by a middle-aged, frizzy-haired woman who peered through the window and asked if the shop was open. I informed her that it would not be a good idea to go inside at the moment.

"I love driftwood. I simply have to buy one of these wonderful creations for my sister."

I bit my lip, sad that I would lose an immediate sale. "Tell you what. If you can return tomorrow, I'll give you a ten-percent discount on anything in the store."

"Oh, goody. Since I'm saying here for another day, I'll be back late tomorrow afternoon."

I watched as she headed toward Flo's yarn shop, clutching her purse. Flo's yarn. I gulped. Had Flo suffered enough from Bart and dispatched him with her new yarn? Although she had been angry with Bart, I couldn't see her resorting to murder. Also, how would she have gotten into my shop since I had locked the door? And whoever had done this apparently had used some of my driftwood to make handles for the garrote. None of it made any sense.

Who else could have done this? Since Bart had a key to the store, maybe he had let himself in, and someone had used that opportunity to sneak up and attack him. Then the realization struck me. Everyone knew that I detested Bart, and he had shown up dead behind my counter. Who would be the primary suspect? Yours truly. I'd have to be very careful.

Then another thought whapped me alongside the head. Had someone set me up? Who else besides Bart might be out to get me?

My ruminations were interrupted by the sound of a siren, and an ambulance pulled into the Village Center parking lot. Two EMTs hopped out, and I waved them toward my shop. They jogged up.

I pointed inside. "I found Bart Cunard lying on the floor when I returned to my store. You can take a look, but he's beyond saving."

They dashed inside while I watched a fire engine followed by a police cruiser join the ambulance in the parking lot. I hoped Kurt would be one of the fire fighters responding, but then I remembered that this was his shift on dispatch for the police department, so several of the other volunteers would be arriving instead.

Within minutes a confab took place between the EMTs, fire and rescue, and a police officer. After looking in my shop, the policeman got on his radio and made a call. Then he pulled a roll of yellow crime scene tape out of his pocket and sealed off the front of my store. So much for doing any business today.

But I knew that was the least of my troubles. The crowd increased with the arrival of the coroner's assistant to inspect the body. Then the *pièce de résistance*—Detective James Moriarty. I had encountered him once before when a theft occurred. A kid had run into my shop, grabbed a driftwood creation and bolted. Moriarty came to interview me afterwards and made insulting comments implying that no one would steal one of my "pieces of junk." When a police officer caught the kid, I received my creation back, but Moriarty never apologized. Now he stood here, ready to investigate the murder.

He pushed through the others. "Okay, let me see this dead body in the junk shop." He snorted in my direction and stomped inside. I waited for the inevitable, which took all of ten minutes.

When he came back outside, he strode up and stopped inches from me. I resisted the urge to step back a pace but bucked up my courage and glared at him.

He met my gaze, glare for glare. "You have something to do with this?"

"I returned from lunch and found the body. That's it."

He knifed his hand for emphasis. "You say body so you knew he was dead."

"It didn't take a rocket scientist to determine that he had left the land of the living."

"Pretty convenient that some of your driftwood was used to garrote him."

"I don't know who got a hold of driftwood, but I had nothing to do with his death."

"We'll see."

I put my hands on my hips. "When can I get back in my shop?"

"When we're done."

"And that would be?"

"When we're done." He spun around, slipped under the yellow tape and went back inside.

So much for an intelligent conversation with Detective Moriarty.

By now the crowd had expanded to other shopkeepers. Bea approached me. "What's the commotion?"

"Someone murdered Bart Cunard."

"Couldn't happen to a nicer person."

I whispered in her ear. "Watch what you say. We are apt to be suspects given our dislike of Bart."

Bea sniffled loudly. "I don't care who knows my feelings toward that pus pot. I better get back since I left the cash register unattended."

Next, Herb came over to me. "What's going on?"

"Our landlord met his maker in my shop."

Herb put his hand to his mouth. "My goodness. Were you involved?"

"Only in finding the body."

He took my hand and patted it. "That must have been dreadful."

I sighed. "The only saving grace—we don't have to worry about Bart harassing us anymore."

Moriarty stuck his head out the door. "I heard that." He bent under the crime scene tape and headed our way. "So, you had a problem with the victim. Did you two conspire to kill him?"

Herb turned pale, and I thought he might pass out. I steadied him. "Look, Detective. Bart Cunard wasn't the most popular person in town. A lot of people had trouble with him and disliked him. You better get cracking on finding who the real killer is."

"You trying to run the police department, missy?"

"No, but I hope you're going to do more than track mud into my store." I pointed to his shoes. "I would think an experienced detective would be more careful not to contaminate a crime scene."

He turned crimson and stormed back toward the parking lot.

Herb nudged me. "Good one, missy."

Chapter 8

SINCE MY SHOP HAD BEEN taken over by the storm troopers, I decided to go see Granny Mulligan. I retrieved my red motorized bike, fastened my helmet, fired up the engine and putt-putted away. I had named her Mopsy, because she wasn't quite a Moped. This was the only mode of transportation I could afford. She used little gas and, although slow, got me where I needed to go—eventually.

I headed along Main Street as two bicyclists raced past me. No concern. I was the tortoise, slow and steady.

Turning left on Second Street, I picked up a little speed on the downhill. The wind whipped through my hair at going twenty miles an hour. All of a sudden, a car raced past me, cut in front and slammed on its brakes. I screeched to a stop, missing a collision by inches. Then the car shot off again. It happened so quickly, I didn't even notice anything other than a flash of black.

I pulled over to the curb, shaking. I should have paid closer attention to the type of vehicle and got a license plate number of the jerk. After several deep breaths, my heart rate returned to normal, and I resumed my journey.

I found Granny Mulligan out in her garden tending her roses. At the ragged sound of Mopsy, she looked up. "Dang aphids. Where are the ladybugs when you need them?"

I turned off the motor, hopped down and set the kickstand. "I'm sure they'll be here when it gets a little warmer."

She stood and gave me a hug. "Speaking of ladybugs, how's my favorite ladybug?"

"Oh, Granny. I'm too old for that."

"You're never too old for nicknames, hugs and ice cream."

She gave me another hug. I guessed ladybug was better than being called missy.

"Come on in, and I'll brew us some green tea."

Granny had her own special concoction that she swore added years to one's life. So far it had worked for her. She had passed eighty-nine with a full head of steam toward ninety without a heart murmur, mental glitch, limp or tumor in sight.

After we sat down at her dining room table, she took a sip of tea and smacked her lips. "Since you haven't been over here for a week, I'm ready to hear a full report on what my ladybug has been up to."

I leaned closer. "The big news. Bart Cunard showed up dead in my shop this morning."

"About time. Someone blow him away with a nail gun?"

"Garrote."

"I'll be danged. How'd he end up in your store?"

I put my cup down. "That's the big question. I had lunch with Herb, took a walk and when I returned, I found Bart purple and spread out behind my counter."

She chuckled. "That must have been a sight for sore ears."

I stamped my foot under the table. "It's not funny. It happened in my shop. That awful Detective Moriarty practically accused me of murder."

"Don't get your knickers in a snit. I know you didn't do anything to Bart. But I'm sure half the town would love to take credit for his demise. Now, the important stuff. How's that new boyfriend of yours?"

My cheeks grew warm. "He's not exactly a boyfriend."

Granny rubbed her hands together. "More than that? You two playing bumpy-bump?"

"Granny! Kurt and I have only been on one *sort-of* date."

"One sordid date?"

"No. We only went to the diner. Nothing more."

"Well dang it, Ladybug. Get a move on. That hunk shouldn't go to waste. Don't let the grass grow under your fanny."

"Granny!"

"Back in my day I had a bunch of suitors. Your granddad beat 'em all out. And I didn't waste any time either. I learned that she who hesitates is a loser and the early bird gets the wormhole. Your granddad had a sparkle in his eyes, a huge smile and some other good equipment."

"Granny!"

"Take my advice. You jump that Kurt Whelan. Time to bite the ammunition and get a move on. And he's not like that slime sack, Nate Dupres."

"Rats, that's another piece of bad news."

"There you go cussing again."

"'Rats' isn't cussing."

Granny smacked her hand on the table. "It sure as hell is."

"In any case, I heard that Nate is in town."

"Well, point him my way. I'll give him my two-bits worth—a Mulligan greeting that will send him stuffing his suitcase."

"I'll deal with it. What have you been doing since I last saw you?"

Granny ran her hand through her silver blue hair. "I have a new boyfriend, too."

"You do?"

"Yes. His name is Hercule and he lives in the Old Detectives Home out near the cliff."

I had driven along the cliff road a number of times and knew the place. "That's a retirement community, right?"

"Yup. And my boyfriend is short and a little chubby but has the cutest moustache. It tickles."

"Granny! Too much information."

"Aw, don't be such a prude. He and I are taking a cane fu class at his retirement home."

"What the heck is cane fu?"

Granny Mulligan picked up one of her hiking poles and crouched into a fighting stance. "It's a terrific martial art. No one will mess with me."

"No one has messed with you since I've known you."

"Darn tootin'. Now I can defend myself with a cane or pole, scare the bejabbers out of anyone who tries to snatch my purse and take down the bad guy."

I tried to imagine Granny sparring with her new boyfriend. The guy didn't stand a chance. He'd end up with pole marks all over his body.

She rapped the hiking pole into her left hand. "I have these new Leki Carbonlite Aergon XL Trekking Poles that are hankering to get some exercise. Only cost me $219."

I gasped. "Why pay that much? You could have picked up two wooden sticks from the forest."

"Are you kidding? Look at these babies." She demonstrated the spring loading and contoured handles. "I get a good workout with both my legs and arms."

Not for me. On my budget, if I were going to use walking poles, which I had no intention of doing, I'd go find two fallen branches and pull off the leaves.

She went over and grabbed the second walking pole. "Are you ready to take a trek with me? A rolling stone gathers no mulch."

I knew I needed to do something about the murder and had one idea to follow up on. "Not now. I have some errands to run."

"The busy professional woman. Too bad." She put the poles

back in the corner. "Anyway, my new boyfriend and I met through Facebook. It was love at first click. Speaking of which, when are you going to get with the computer generation, Ladybug?"

Computers and I didn't see eye to eye. "One of these days."

"I showed you how to use Facebook. How's it going?"

I gulped. "I have ten friends."

"What! I have two thousand friends. What the heck are you doing, or should I say, not doing? You need to make more friends. No woman is an atoll."

I waved my hands in a crossing fashion. "As I told you, computers aren't my thing. I stick with a few Google searches, and that's it."

"I'd be happy to give you lessons. I'm also on Twitter, Pinterest, and have a new blog. In my spare time, I've been researching our family history on Ancestory.com. You'll have to try it."

"Right now, I'm focusing on my store."

"You need to get with the computer program, Ladybug. I just updated my web site with animation and video."

"I had to pay to have my store web site developed. Maybe I should hire you to update it for me."

Granny cracked her knuckles. "Be happy to. I can put some pizzazz into your business. Got to protect my investment anyway."

"Speaking of which, after the Spring Break rush, I had meant to start paying you back on the loan. But Bart Cunard made me agree to give him three months of advance rent… wait a minute. That was a verbal agreement we made this morning. Now I won't have to do that. I'll be able to start paying you back."

"See, it's a good thing he kicked the pail."

"With Bart dead, I wonder who will inherit the Village Center."

"He has no children. Maybe his ex, Sally Midge."

I shook my head. "I don't know. They aren't, or should I say, weren't on very good terms."

Granny stood to take our empty cups to the sink. "We'll have to see after all the dirt settles."

"I have a favor to ask."

Granny arched an eyebrow. "What now?"

"I need to make a run to collect driftwood in a few days. May I borrow your car?"

"Sure as honking. Three days ago, I changed the oil, rotated the tires and filled Bessie with gas. She's good to go. You have to promise to take better care of her than you do that motorized bike of yours."

"I've only had a few accidents and some dents."

"Dents, my tush. That thing looks like it had been used as a percussion instrument."

"It still runs fine."

"I won't debate that. But remember, Bessie is dent free. Keep her that way."

"Yes, Granny."

"Maybe you can take that boyfriend of yours to watch the submarine races from the lookout point."

"Granny, cut it out. We're only starting to get to know each other."

"In the Biblical sense?"

"Granny!"

"Where's your sense of humor, Ladybug?"

"I think it went on vacation when Bart turned up dead in my store."

Chapter 9

I DONNED MY BIKE HELMET AND putt-putted away from Granny's, realizing my grandmother was quite a gal. Going full speed at her age. She had more energy and a better memory than I did. I only hoped I lived to be her age with half of her mental ability and dexterity.

On to my next destination.

I motored through town with nothing more than a car's tire shooting a pebble that added one more dent to the front of Mopsy. I stopped in front of the real estate office of Larry Ludwick and chained my bike to a lamppost.

Inside, the receptionist flashed her pearly white teeth at me. Her cleavage was enough to make any male, other than Herb, drool. I hoped Kurt didn't happen to stop by this office.

"I'd like to speak with Mr. Ludwick, please?"

The pearly whites again. "And you are?"

"I'm standing right here."

This time the teeth showed less white. "Your name?"

"Pru Pendergast."

"And the nature of your business?"

"I run the Driftwood Creatives shop in the Omnipodge Village Center."

The teeth had turned to a grimace. "I mean what is your business with Mr. Ludwick?"

I wasn't going to level with this dingbat. "It concerns a real estate transaction."

"One moment please." She picked up the phone and whispered something I couldn't hear. I'd definitely have to get my ears checked. I wondered if my tinnitus indicated some permanent hearing loss. No, I decided the receptionist only had a very soft whisper.

"He'll be with you shortly. Please take a seat."

"Where to do you want me to take it?"

The grimace again. "Please sit right there." She pointed to a padded chair.

"I think I'll use your restroom first. Where is it?"

"Down the hall, second door on the right."

Good. Now she had been trained to be more explicit in her statements. I ambled through the hallway and found the designated door. Inside, I took care of business, washed my hands and looked around for a paper towel.

They only had one of those air dryers. I hated those blasted things. I pushed the button and rubbed my hands together. The loud noise caused my tinnitus to go crazy. Maybe these devices saved trees, but they wreaked havoc with my delicate ear. Me and my weird condition. Most people with tinnitus heard ringing in their ears. My variation had crackling instead. I had to be grateful. Mine wasn't continuous, and was something I could live with.

I returned to the lobby as I listened to the dissonant symphony of crackling in my right ear.

The receptionist click-clacked away on her keyboard while I scanned the outer office. The walls had pictures of Larry Ludwick shaking hands with various dignitaries including our mayor, the governor of California and several aspiring actors.

The "be with you shortly" turned into half an hour, but finally Larry oozed out of his office to greet me. "What can I do for you, Ms. Pendergast?"

"If we can speak in your office."

"Certainly." He ushered me into his inner sanctum that contained more of the celebrity photos as well as several pictures of apartment and business buildings.

I decided to attempt the direct approach. "Mr. Ludwick, a tragedy took place this morning. Have you heard what happened to Bart Cunard?"

He plastered a serious, tight-lipped expression on his face. "Yes. I was saddened to hear that he died."

Right. Word had circulated. "Since I have a shop in his Omnipodge Village Center, and I understand the two of you worked together, I thought you might have some insight into the future of our retail complex."

"Mr. Cunard and I have collaborated on several projects. In fact, yesterday we completed refinancing of the Omnipodge Village Center. I'm now majority owner."

"What?"

He held up his hand. "Mr. Cunard expressed an interest in recouping part of his original investment, and I was only too happy to assist."

Right. One slimebag helping another. I wondered how this would play out. "Will you be taking an active role in managing the Village Center?"

He let out a deep sigh. "Originally, I wasn't planning to, but with Mr. Cunard out of the picture, I guess I'll need to get personally involved. I think there's an opportunity to make some changes that would increase the value of the property."

Great. That was all we needed. "Do you have any idea who will inherit his share of ownership?"

He shrugged. "Don't know. I assume I'll be working with the executor of his estate on what his will specifies."

"You must have an educated guess."

He shrugged again. "It could be his ex-wife. As I said, we'll see once the executor gets involved."

"Does that concern you at all?"

"No. As majority owner, I'll be able to make the changes I want even if the other owner or owners object." He gave me a steely stare. "That's the way business works." He looked at his Rolex. "Now, if you'll excuse me, I have a client to see." He stood and motioned toward the door.

Recognizing I had been dismissed, I headed out the door. Something didn't feel right with this whole situation—the timing of Bart's death and Larry taking over majority ownership of the Village Center. Had there been more to the business transaction that led to a falling out and murder? Larry was certainly a better suspect than any of the shopkeepers. At least I'd like to think so.

Deep in thought, I put-putted back toward my shop. The sound of a loud engine brought me out of my reverie. I looked over my left shoulder and saw a black SUV bearing down on me. I jerked the handlebars to the right as it shot past, clipping my rear tire. I went up over the handlebars and landed on the sidewalk. Stunned, but still conscious, I stared at the black vehicle. It had tinted windows. Then all went black.

Chapter 10

I AWOKE WITH A MAN IN a white coat shining a light in my eyes. He smiled. "Welcome back to the land of the living."

My head felt like someone had slammed it with a two-by-four. I put my hand to my temple. "Ouch."

"You have a nasty bump, but your vital signs are stable. It was a good thing you were wearing a helmet."

I raised myself. My head pulsed followed by crackling in my right ear. You'd think that with an accident it might reset my crazy tinnitus, but no such luck. I looked around the room. Definitely the ER. Then I focused in on the guy attending me. Hadn't seen him around town before. Kind of cute in a doctorly sort of way. "What's the diagnosis?"

"No broken bones. A few minor bruises and a possible concussion. I'd like you to stay here for a few hours under observation."

Great. Like a germ under a microscope.

"I think I feel well enough to get up. I dangled my legs off the bed, and the world began to spin. "Uh-oh."

My new friend put a hand behind my back and guided me back to a reclined position. "Take it easy for a while. Don't rush it."

"Don't worry." I closed my eyes and zonked out.

* * * * *

When I awoke, my stomach rumbled. A good sign. I was starving.

I sat up and noticed a slight dizziness, but nothing like earlier. I swung my legs out of bed and stood. I considered dancing a jig but then thought better of it.

A nurse stuck her head in the room. "How ya doing?"

"I think I've recovered."

"I'll have the doctor come take a look."

I strolled around the room, looking at a picture of an ocean wave breaking on shore and of an eagle soaring over a mountain. No anatomy charts or scalpels in sight. Then I realized I was wearing one of those gowns with the rear air conditioning. I sat back on the bed and suddenly realized another little problem—this trip to the hospital would cost me a bundle given my paltry medical insurance. I watched as proverbial dollar signs flew out the window.

Then to my horror who should appear but my ex-boyfriend, Nate Dupres. He marched into the room holding a bunch of daisies. "How are you feeling, sweetie?"

"Don't sweetie me. What are you doing here?"

"I heard you had a little accident. I wanted to stop by to wish you a speedy recovery." He stepped closer and tried to kiss my cheek.

I evaded the move.

He set the flowers down on a table. "Don't be so bashful. It's me."

"Unfortunately. Why are you here in Omnipodge?"

He spread his arms wide. "To see you, of course."

I rolled my eyes. "You've seen me. Goodbye."

"Is that any way to great an old friend?"

"Old friend, my patootie. We're done, finished, kaput."

"Aw. I can tell you still like me." He tried to move in closer, but I swung around and escaped from the other side of the bed. Then I realized my mistake.

Nate whistled. "Looking good."

I grabbed the back of my gown and pulled it tight. Damn hospital attire.

I glared at Nate. "I'd like a little privacy so I can get dressed and leave this place."

"In that case, let's you and I go out to dinner?"

"Dinner? What time is it anyway?"

Nate looked at his Timex. "Five fifteen."

"I've been in this place that long?"

I was saved when the doctor appeared. He asked Nate to leave the room and then pulled a curtain to give more privacy.

"How are you feeling?"

"Almost as good as new." Except for the nausea from Nate showing up. "I'm ready to head home."

"Let's take a look." He inspected my head and shone a light in my eyes. "Do you think you can walk on your own?"

"Yup. I've already been up. If someone can give me my clothes, I'm good to go."

"I'll have a nurse bring your things."

He departed, and in a few minutes a nurse appeared with a bundle. I quickly dressed. Then I realized I needed transportation. I pulled out my cell phone and called Herb who answered on the third ring. "Can you come pick me up at the Omnipodge Community Hospital?"

"What are you doing there?"

"A little mishap on Mopsy."

"Again?"

"Don't give me any of that. I need transportation."

"Okay, Princess. I'll be there in a jiff."

I quickly dressed, hoping that Nate had taken off. No such luck. His head appeared in the doorway followed by the unwanted rest of him. "Ready for dinner?"

"No thanks. I have someone coming to pick me up."

His lips curled in a snarl. "You're coming with me."

"Not on your life." Then a bad thought occurred to me. "Were you in my shop this morning?"

He snorted. "Why would you ask that?"

"Get out of here!" I found the call button and pushed it.

A nurse quickly appeared. "Is there a problem?"

I pointed at Nate. "Yes. This man is bothering me."

"Sir, you need to leave."

Nate shook his fist at me. "You'll be sorry." Then he spun on his heels and stalked away.

The nurse's eyes went wide. "Should I call security?"

"That's not necessary. He's gone."

I double checked to make sure I had my meager belongings and then headed to the lobby to wait for Herb. Once through the swinging double doors, I scanned the waiting area to make sure that Nate wasn't lingering. No slimeball in sight.

Shortly, Herb came rushing in.

"Am I glad to see you," I said.

He put his hands on his hips and looked me up and down. "And you, Princess, are a sight. You look like you've been through a meat grinder."

I took out my compact mirror, glanced quickly and stuck out my tongue. "Yuck. I see what you mean. I'll need a matching wardrobe of purple and black."

"Not to worry. I have my magic carpet waiting for you outside."

Once in his red classic 1957 Chevy, Herb said, "Now tell me everything, Princess."

"Not much to it. Someone ran me off the road. I did a header and ended up in the hospital. Then you came to rescue me." I patted his arm. "My hero."

After we parked and walked to the front of my place, I could see the yellow tape still strung across the door. Detective Moriarty lurched under the tape and stomped toward me. "We need to talk."

Chapter 11

I LEANED TOWARD HERB. "ON TOP of everything else, I have to deal with the detective."

Herb stepped in front of me and whispered over his shoulder. "I'll run interference for you, Princess."

But Moriarty brushed Herb aside like a discarded cigarette and faced me. "Why'd you kill Bart Cunard?"

I winced. "I did nothing of the sort."

"Care to explain why your fingerprints were on the driftwood handles of the garrote wrapped around his neck?"

"Fingerprints? How do you even have my fingerprints on file. Oh… from when I volunteered at the Omnipodge Elementary School."

"Exactly. And a perfect match."

"I assume someone took some driftwood I had handled to use for the garrote. It certainly wasn't me."

"Let's review." Moriarty held up a finger. "First, you report the murder." He added a second finger. "Then it turns out to be in your shop." A third finger. "And your fingerprints are on the murder weapon." A fourth finger. "And all kinds of people have heard you expressing your negative opinion of the victim. Are you ready to make a confession?"

Now he had my undivided attention. Rather than being hungry, I had a lump that felt like lead in my stomach. I decided to hold my ground. "Sure. I confess that I had nothing to do with the murder.

I only found the body. That's it."

"I should take you down to headquarters."

I sighed. "Do what you want, but I'm innocent."

Herb tried to insert himself between us. "Everyone here hated Bart. Pru had nothing to do with the crime."

Moriarty eyed Herb. "Maybe you killed him. I understand you also had some bad feelings toward the deceased."

Herb pulled himself up to his full five foot ten. "Neither Pru nor I had any involvement. I can assure you of that, Detective."

"I think I'll keep you as number two on my suspect list."

"What?" Herb turned white then red.

Moriarty focused on me again. "I'll be watching you, missy."

At least he hadn't arrested me. "When can I get back in my store and residence?"

"It's a crime scene, and we're still investigating. You can't go in until tomorrow."

"But where am I going to sleep?"

"You can come to my place," Herb said.

"Thank you. But I also have a cat and dog in there that need to be fed and taken care of."

"You can't go in," Moriarty said, "but I'll bring them out." He disappeared into the shop.

I whispered in Herb's ear. "I hope Boopsie claws him."

"And I would love to see Spools pee on his shoes."

Neither happened, so after Moriarty turned them over to me, I carried Boopsie and Spools to Herb's Chevy. Boopsie merely tolerated being in cars, but Spools loved rides, which he didn't have an opportunity to take very often given my limited mode of conveyance. Then I remembered. "Mopsy. I wonder what happened to my bike."

"Show me where the accident took place, and we'll take a look."

I directed Herb to the block where I had done my acrobatics and found Mopsy leaning against the wall of Buck's Bakery. "I don't know if she's in running condition."

"It is hard to tell since you've accumulated so many dings and dents. I'll put her in my trunk, and we'll take her to my bungalow."

Herb hefted the bike into the trunk compartment and dusted his hands. "My car may get horrid gas mileage, but it has lots of room."

I thought of Boopsie and Spools staying at Herb's for the night. "We better make one more stop on the way. I need to get some cat and dog food and a disposable litter box."

"And let's add some pasta, and I'll make you a scrumptious dinner."

At FoodForYou, I went in to pick up the necessities while Herb entertained the animals. They always got along well. I paid with my credit card, wondering how I would make a payment when the next bill came due. Hopefully, Spring Break would solve my financial difficulties.

When we reached his place, Herb unloaded Mopsy and took the groceries into the bungalow. Boopsie shot inside on his heels. Spools sniffed every inch of Herb's garden, while I fired up Mopsy's engine, and she sputtered to life. No flat tires. I surveyed the dents, checked the gears and brakes. She had survived the accident better than I had.

Herb cooked us a luscious dinner using his exotic spices. He had tried to teach me some of his secrets, but as Granny said, "It was like water off a goose's back."

With a full tummy, I sauntered past Herb's room and peeked in to see a bright patchwork knit quilt on the bed. And the many pictures of Carl on the wall and nightstand. I hoped that Herb would find someone new one of these days. I hoped I would find someone to be with. What a bummer. Things going slowly with Kurt and Nate back in town.

In the guest bedroom, I picked up a stuffed elephant, one of the dozen Beanie Babies that covered the bed. I would have company with these, Boopsie and Spools for the night. After I returned to the living room, Herb, sensitive to my tinnitus, put on some soft instrumental music, and we ensconced ourselves on the couch to chat.

Herb adjusted himself much like Boopsie finding the right position. "That dreadful detective made such nasty accusations. How could he even consider you or me suspects?"

I shrugged. "The circumstantial evidence. We need to do something to get him off our backs."

Herb rubbed his hands together. "Goody. We can become amateur sleuths and solve the crime."

"I don't know about that, but we can certainly find some evidence that points toward the real murderer. Who do you think killed Bart?"

"All the other shopkeepers detested him as much as we did, but everyone here is so nice. I can't picture Bea, Flo or Jake as the culprit."

"What about Sally Midge?"

"Well, she certainly had a lot of gripes about Bart as well. She doesn't strike me as the killing type."

"She gave Bart a good slap today."

"Which I've been tempted to do as well. Who else could it be?"

I thought back over my day's activities. "I have another candidate. Larry Ludlow. He told me that he had bought majority interest in the Omnipodge Village Center from Bart yesterday."

"Oh my." Herb put his hand to his cheek. "Someone almost as bad as Bart."

"As good a suspect as anyone, but why would he kill Bart the day after they consummated a business deal?"

"Doesn't make sense."

"And although there's no connection to Bart, someone who

might have wanted to give me grief is back in town. Nate Dupres showed up at the hospital to see me."

"My goodness. This has not been a good day for you."

"No. And there was my accident. Do you know anyone who drives a black SUV?"

"A dark mysterious car?"

"Yeah. I had one near miss earlier that might have been the same vehicle that clipped me later."

"Enough of the catastrophes." He rubbed his hands together. "Now I want to hear the latest scrumptious details about your new boyfriend."

"You're as bad as Granny. Things haven't progressed very far with Kurt and me. In fact, I haven't heard from him since you and I talked at lunch yesterday."

"Maybe you should give him a call."

"No way. I'm not going to force things. He has my phone numbers. It's up to him to call."

Herb gave me his scrunched eyebrow thoughtful look. "Maybe he called your landline. You haven't been home recently."

My eyes went wide. "Maybe." I pulled out my cell phone, called my landline voice mail and listened to two messages.

"And?" Herb asked.

"Nothing but two robocalls. I hate those."

"I'm sure he'll contact you soon. You need something to help you unwind. Let's knit sweaters for Boopsie and Spools." Herb retrieved his knitting basket and doled out the yarn.

I started with gray for Boopsie since she liked mouse colors. I had a small patch completed when Herb snuffled.

"What's the matter?"

He wiped away a tear. "Knitting reminds me of Carl. We had so many pleasant evenings sitting here crocheting a quilt together. It's the one on my bed."

"I noticed it earlier. It's lovely."

Herb stood and went over to his cabinet. "I purchased some new yarn that we can use." Here." He returned and displayed a skein of brown Vicuna yarn.

My mouth must have dropped open because Herb said, "Don't look so surprised. It's great yarn."

Right. And the type of yarn used in the garrote that killed Bart Cunard.

Chapter 12

MY MIND WAS A JUMBLE. I certainly didn't think that either Herb or Flo could have been involved with the murder, but someone had used Vicuna yarn to dispatch Bart, and Flo had received a new shipment.

"Um. When did you buy this yarn?"

Herb tapped the skein. "Yesterday morning when I went to Flo's shop. She had it out on display. It looked simply scrumptious, and I had to have some. Here, you can use it first."

"No thanks. I'll stick with what I'm working with." I didn't want to have anything to do with that type of yarn. I could picture Detective Moriarty finding the sweater I was knitting for Boopsie and use it as evidence against me. For that matter, I didn't want it to appear in the sweater Herb was knitting for Spools. "Also, please don't use it for Spools. It would be a waste of such fine yarn for a dog's sweater."

Herb eyed me warily. "That's not like you, Princess. You usually want the best for your animals."

"Use it to make a sweater for yourself."

"All right." He put the Vicuna into his knitting basket. "I'll save it."

A half hour later, we called it a night. I snuggled up in the guest bedroom and after reviewing the day, fell into a fitful sleep.

* * * * *

I awoke with a pounding headache and the memory of some crazy dream with flying motorized bikes, black SUVs turning into submarines and yarn falling from the sky. Herb had breakfast cooking, and I indulged in scrambled eggs, toast and two Advil. Whereas eggs I cooked ended up too runny or as hard as plastic, his were firm and delicious. Also, he didn't suffer from my knack of burning toast.

Herb was anxious to get to his shop, and I wanted to check to see if the police had taken down the yellow tape.

"Do you want me to give you a ride?" Herb asked.

"No. I need to get back in the saddle on my bike."

"I'll follow you to make sure no black SUVs try to run you off the road."

I gave his arm a pat. "I appreciate that, but you'll have to go pretty slowly to stay behind me."

"I'll handle it. Like one of those presidential motorcades."

I fired up Mopsy, and our cavalcade took off. I noticed the handlebar had a little more give than before and detected a slight wobble when I exceeded twenty miles an hour, but other than that, she ran fine. She would need a tune up, but that would have to wait until after Spring Break.

I heard honking behind and checked my mirror. A car shot around Herb's Chevy, but it wasn't a black SUV. It continued past me fast enough to make Mopsy vibrate. I wanted to shake a fist at the aggressive driver, but decided not to risk taking a hand off the handlebar.

Without any further disturbances, we pulled into the parking lot at the Omnipodge Village Center, where I chained Mopsy to a lamppost. We sauntered across the commons and to my dismay found my shop still costumed in yellow tape with a police officer standing outside. I approached him and asked, "Any idea when I'll be able to get into my store?"

"Let me check." He stooped under the tape and disappeared inside.

In a moment Detective Moriarty rather than the police officer appeared. "You here to confess, missy?"

"I'm here to run my business and return to my home."

"Not yet. It will be a few more hours."

"Rats."

Moriarty glared at me. "Are you insulting the police with animal names like calling us pigs?"

I hung my head. "No, it's only an expression." Then I had an idea. "Say, Detective, there's a guy who has been bothering me, Nate Dupres. You might want to check for his fingerprints inside."

"You trying to interfere with police business, missy?"

"Only a suggestion. Someone else was in my shop. You might want to follow up on that lead. Could be a suspect for you."

"An attempt to divert attention from your own guilt? Maybe we should have a further chat at police headquarters."

"No thanks."

I decided to cut my losses and leave. I crossed the commons and returned to the parking lot. I wanted to see Kurt but knew he would be on duty today at the police department. If Moriarty took me in as a suspect, I might see Kurt, but I preferred a more benign encounter. Next choice, Granny.

I putt-putted away, constantly checking my mirror for any sign of a black car behind me. Fortunately, nothing threatening other than another pebble striking Mopsy's front fender, which now resembled a cratered moon.

Granny was out fighting the aphids again, but when I appeared she insisted that we take a walk. She went inside to retrieve her walking poles, and we took off toward the cliffs.

After a block I gasped for air. "Slow down, Granny. You act like you're in the Olympics."

"That's the best pace for a good workout, Ladybug. If you can't stand the heat, get out of the kitchenette."

"But if we go a little slower, we can carry on a conversation. I have some things to tell you."

"Oh, all right." She slowed her pace to a mere jog, and I was able to keep up without passing out. "What's the news?"

"I've been thinking about the yarn I saw on the garrote that dispatched Bart Cunard. I saw that same kind of yarn in Flo's shop yesterday, and Herb also bought some of it. I'm concerned that either of them could be arrested."

"Better them than you."

"That's the problem. Detective Moriarty has me in his sights as well, but I don't believe Herb or Flo would kill someone. I can't figure out who did it."

"That's up to the police, Ladybug."

"Still, I'm worried."

"As they say, there's nothing to fret about but fretting itself. Don't stress until you or one of your friends gets locked in the slammer."

We reached the overlook and sat down to admire the ocean.

Far away thoughts pulsed through my brain, momentarily pushing aside my worries. "One of these days I'd like to go to Hawaii."

"Well, go for it."

"Can't afford it. I have to make some money this Spring Break, start paying you back and get financially solvent. My ocean travel will be limited to looking from here. Speaking of which, I'm getting thirsty."

"Me, too. Liquid, liquid everywhere but not a drop to guzzle. Let's go back and have some green tea."

* * * * *

After lunch and a gallon of green tea, I headed back to check on the shop and, to my delight, found the yellow tape had been taken down. I corralled Herb, and he agreed to close up for half an hour and take me back to his place to retrieve Boopsie and Spools.

When we returned, Herb headed to his store, and I carried Boopsie and Spools to my shop. I looked forward to getting up to my room and changing out of the clothes I had worn for over a day. When I unlocked the door and stepped in, the floor was covered with pieces of driftwood, shells, rocks, and tangles of fishing line.

Chapter 13

I KNEW THAT SPOOLS HADN'T CAUSED the mess in my shop because he had joined me for the sleepover at Herb's. Did the police trash my store or had it been Wrong Way Willie? Only one way to find out.

"Willie!" I shouted. "I know you're in here somewhere."

The curtain puffed out.

"I thought so. Tell me. Did you make this mess?"

The curtain shifted from side to side.

"Did the police do this?"

The curtain bunched up and then dropped.

"Was it Detective Moriarty?"

The curtain briskly waved up and down.

"I'm going to have some words with him the next time I see him." I considered siccing Granny and her cane fu walking poles on Moriarty. What a mess.

Spools was in seventh heaven. He scampered around rolling in the fishing line and kicking his feet in the air. Boopsie sniffed one piece of driftwood and retired in dignity to her pillow in the corner.

I looked behind the counter, expecting to find the chalk outline of a body but, fortunately, discovered nothing. That was a relief.

I headed upstairs to find my bedroom also in a mess. The contents of my dresser drawers had been dumped on the floor along with the bedding. "That detective should be hung by his thumbs."

The bedroom curtain danced up and down.

"I'm glad we agree on that, Willie. Maybe you can be a help with this murder. Were you downstairs when it happened?"

The curtain blew side to side.

"Did you hear anything?"

Again, a lateral motion.

"Were you asleep?"

The curtain bounced up and down.

"That's what I was afraid of. What a time for you to be taking a nap. And since Spools and Boopsie can't talk, there are no witnesses to who killed Bart. I have to find a way to solve this so Moriarty will quit accusing me. Willie, I want you to pay careful attention when people come in the shop. See if you can pick up any clues."

The curtain danced a little jig, up and down.

"Good. We're a team on this."

I began cleaning, and it took me a good two hours to get everything in order—the bed made, my clothes in their proper places, my artwork materials back in bins and jars, and the floor upstairs and down vacuumed. The good news. Nothing broken. Downstairs, I surveyed my supply of driftwood, rocks and shells. It was a good thing I had a replenishment trip planned for the next day. I had run low on pebbles, especially moonstones. I would remedy that.

I sat on the stool behind the counter contemplating all that happened. "Willie, I'm going to review the possible suspects I can think of with you, and you can give me your opinion."

The curtain bobbed.

"Okay. First, my ex-boyfriend Nate Dupres is at the top of the list. I don't know why he would kill Bart, but he might have wanted to get back at me. What do you think?"

The curtain flipped up and down.

"Okay. We keep him on the list. Next, the sleazy developer, Larry

Ludwick. He now owns a majority interest in the Omnipodge Village Center. Maybe he wanted his minority partner out of the way. Do you agree?"

The curtain waggled from side to side for a moment and then jostled up and down.

"Okay. You concur but don't feel as strongly as with Nate. Then there's Sally Midge. She has quite a temper with no love lost toward her ex. What do you think?"

The curtain swayed back and forth before springing up and down.

"Okay. Again, yes but not as strong as with the previous two."

Our conversation was interrupted by a woman tapping her fingernails on my counter. I jumped. Deep in discussion with Willie, I hadn't noticed her entering through the open door. She was the fuzzy-haired woman I had seen outside my shop the day before.

"You always talk to yourself? I thought you might be on a cell phone but don't see any device or ear buds."

Heat went up my throat. "Only thinking out loud. I'm glad to see you came back."

"I'm looking for an anniversary present for my sister. She loves knickknacks. I'm hoping to find the right thing for her here."

I came out from behind the counter. "I'm sure you can. Are you interested in a mobile or a stationary sculpture?"

"I think something she can put on her mantel."

I led her over to my reassembled display cabinet and took out several driftwood creations that I particularly liked, one with the gnarled wood in the shape of a dolphin and the other that resembled an eagle.

"Do you carve these?"

"No, ma'am. The beauty of driftwood creations is finding natural shapes in driftwood and augmenting the wood with stones and shells."

She dismissed my two suggestions but settled on another piece that I considered more mundane. Maybe she didn't like her sister very much. I gave her the promised ten-percent discount and rang it up, grateful for a sale. I now had enough money to pay for gas when I borrowed Granny's car the next day.

After my customer departed, I closed the door so Willie and I wouldn't be interrupted since I wanted to continue the conversation with him. "Now the difficult part. Every shopkeeper here in the Village despised Bart. They have to be on the suspect list, but I'm hard pressed to picture any of them as killers. Let's start with Jake Yalley. He certainly has a motive since he wants Sally Midge all to himself without any interference from Bart. Your opinion?"

The curtain bunched up, then waved from side to side, then bunched, then waved.

"Okay. You're somewhat ambivalent. So am I. I don't know Jake as well as the other shopkeepers, but he seems like a nice guy. Sally Midge sure likes him. Let's move on to Bea Potter. When I went in her bookstore yesterday, she and Bart had an altercation. He was such a sexist pig anyway. Your thoughts?"

The curtain flapped in a circular motion.

"Okay. We can't take her off the list, but I concur that she doesn't appear to be as good a suspect as some of the others. She doesn't have a bad bone in her body. If she can handle my cooking mistakes in the class, she could put up with Bart without resorting to killing him. Okay, next is Flo Florrest. Her yarn appears to have been used on the garrote. She and Bart had a knockdown argument over their political differences. What do you think?"

The curtain bulged, oscillated left and right, jounced up and down, then undulated again and ended with a small wiggle.

"I can see you're of a mixed mind. Sounds like you'd keep her on the list, though."

The curtain sprang up and down.

"I can't see her as a killer, but I can't eliminate her either. Then there's my friend, Herb Hanover."

The curtain jerked a little and then swished back and forth.

"No, although Bart certainly picked on Herb, I can't see him resorting to murder." I paused to think. "That exhausts my list. The only other shopkeeper is me."

The curtain flew up and down.

I put my hands on my hips. "That's not funny, Willie. You know it wasn't me."

The curtain made a circular motion.

"Right. But Detective Moriarty doesn't know that, does he. That's why we have to keep working on this. We have to point him in the right direction."

Chapter 14

I TRIED TO THINK OF SOME ways to focus Detective Moriarty on someone other than me, but my ruminations were interrupted by a soft rap on the door. Maybe another customer?

I opened the door to find Kurt Whelan standing there, his San Francisco Giants ball cap in his hand and his eyes focused on the ground. Warmth spread through my chest at the sight of his curly locks. "Kurt, come on in."

He raised his gaze to me and graced me with his smile. Other parts of my body gained heat.

"How ya doing, Pru?"

"I've missed seeing you the last few days, Kurt."

He rubbed one foot against the welcome mat like a bashful little boy. "I missed seeing you, too, Pru." At least he didn't say, "Aw, shucks."

Since he didn't move, I motioned him inside my shop and pointed to a chair. "Have a seat."

He dropped onto the chair, and I pulled my stool out from behind the counter so we could be closer together. I waited. Finally, he glanced at me. "I heard that Bart Cunard died here. I was worried about you."

"Aw, what a nice thing to say, Kurt. Yeah, I found Bart lying behind my counter. He had been killed with a garrote wrapped around his throat."

Kurt's dark complexion turned white, and he put his hand over his mouth.

"Are you going to get sick?" I asked.

He took in two deep breaths. "I'm okay now. The thought of a dead body made my tummy rumble."

Great. This was the guy who wanted to become a police officer? "Umm, Kurt, if you pass the police exam, you'll have to deal with dead bodies."

His lips quivered. "That's the problem. I failed the police exam again."

I reached over and patted his arm. "That's okay. You'll pass it next time. Tell me what happened."

He sniffed. "The chief told me I needed to study up on probable cause. I didn't write a good enough answer."

"What did you put down?"

"I could arrest someone when it's probable 'cause I think he did it."

I grimaced. "You need to work on that one. I could help you study to get you prepared for the next time you take the test."

He looked at me with his large brown doe eyes. "Thanks, Pru. You're the best."

"Any other problems with the test?"

He let out another sigh. "I missed too many questions on the written test and had a little trouble with the interview. The chief and lieutenant asked me a bunch of questions. I kinda froze. The lieutenant asked me what I'd do if I came upon a kid stealing a candy bar from Hank's Groceries. My mind went blank. All I could think of was, 'Go ahead, make my day.'"

"I see the problem."

"Then the chief asked how I'd handle a bag lady who started swearing at me. I wanted to give a thoughtful answer, but I blurted out, 'Shoot first and ask questions later.'"

We had a lot of work to do. "When can you take the test again?"

"The chief suggested I do more studying and could try again in three months. I bought *Police Officer Exam for Dummies* at Bea's Bookstore. I'm going to work real hard to get ready."

"You do that." I snapped my fingers. "Tell you what. I'll quiz you, and you'll be so familiar with the types of questions that you'll ace it next time."

His eyes lit up. "You'd do that for me?" He leaned toward me. Would this be our first kiss?

From the corner of the room came a loud sputtering, gagging sound. I looked over, and Boopsie heaved several times and coughed up a hairball.

I grabbed a tissue from the counter and went over to clean it up. After pitching the remains in the trash, I washed my hands and returned to my stool. The mood had been broken. Kurt had a frown on his puss.

"Something else bothering you?" I asked.

He scuffed his shoe on the floor. "Yeah. I heard you spent the night at Herb's."

I giggled. "Are you jealous, Kurt?"

He scrunched his brows, looked at the floor for a moment and then raised his head. "Uh… I… ah… don't like you being with other guys."

"What a sweet thing to say. You do know that Herb isn't interested in women."

"Huh?"

"Herb is gay."

Kurt scratched his ear. "As in happy or the other thing."

"The other thing."

"Oh."

"You don't have to worry about Herb and me. He's a good friend, nothing more."

"That's a relief."

I had an idea. "If you're hungry, I can whip up something to eat."

A glint appeared in his eyes. "That would be great."

I headed into the kitchen. Success. As Granny would say: the way to a man's heart is through his gizzard. Then the realization struck me. What could I fix? I searched though my cupboard and found some hamburger buns. I knew I had some lean hamburger in the fridge. I could fry some burgers. No one can mess that up. I heated the frying pan over the burner. Using all the hamburger on hand, I formed four patties and dropped them in to sizzle.

At that moment, Spools came dashing into the kitchen, entangled in fishing line. I turned the hamburgers over and reached for Spools. He dashed out of reach and headed into the shop where Kurt waited. I followed and finally corralled him where he had come to rest sniffing Kurt's tennis shoes. I grabbed my little furry friend and unwound the line. He had really enmeshed himself this time. I shook a finger at him. "I'm going to have to put the fishing line on a higher shelf." When I finally freed him, he scampered over to sniff Boopsie who ignored him.

Kurt stood up. "Something's burning!"

His fire fighter's instinct was better than mine. I raced into the kitchen. The frying pan was spitting grease into the air. I pulled the pan off the burner and lifted one of the patties out with a spatula. It was the color of coal. I tried scraping the black off with a knife, but it was too thick. Maybe Kurt wouldn't notice when it was inside the bun. I disguised the burnt hamburger with plenty of lettuce, tomatoes, ketchup, mustard and pickle relish, put two on the plate for Kurt and one for me, and the fourth on an extra plate in case either of us wanted another, as highly unlikely as that seemed. I put the plates and two glasses of iced tea on the dining nook table.

Then I invited Kurt in and we sat. He took a big bite from one of the hamburgers, and a strange expression crossed his face. He chewed, swallowed and coughed. He pounded on his chest, guzzled half the glass of iced tea and in a high falsetto spit out, "Good."

I took a bite of my hamburger and thought I might imitate Boopsie with a hairball. I peeked inside the bun. Burned on one side and raw on the other. I decided it wasn't worth a second bite.

I heard a pounding on the front door and then a stomping sound as someone crossed the floor toward the back area where we sat. Granny stuck her head around the corner. "There you are. And you got company." She stormed into the room like the troops landing on the Normandy beaches in June of 1944.

"Granny, you know Kurt Whelan. Kurt, you've met my Granny Mulligan."

"How do, Mrs. Mulligan."

Granny eyed him up and down as if selecting a steak at the butcher's. "When are you going to make Pru an honest woman?"

"Huh?" was all Kurt could reply.

"When are you two going to get hitched?"

"Granny!"

Kurt choked, and it wasn't from the hamburger.

Granny put her hands on her hips. "You two need to get a move on. You should be practicing to make babies."

This time I choked. "Granny!"

"Oh, you saved me something to eat." She grabbed the hamburger from the third plate, took a bite, chewed for a moment, and spit the contents onto the plate. "Yuck. You can't make hamburger without breaking a few cows, but this is gawd awful." She stomped into the kitchen.

I followed with the plates and watched Granny rinse her mouth with water in the sink. Then I noticed the clock on the stove. "Phooey. I need to get to my cooking class."

Granny wiped water off her mouth. "You better pay close attention, Ladybug. You need all the cooking help you can get."

Chapter 15

I SHOOED GRANNY AND KURT OUT and raced to Bea Potter's bookstore for the cooking class. As usual I was the last to arrive.

"Nice of you to finally join us." Bea waved a large stirring spoon at me, but I noticed a twinkle in her eyes. "Tonight, we're going to explore and experience sauces."

I looked around Bea's kitchen to find the usual group of Flo Florrest, Jake Yalley and Herb Hanover, with the new addition of Sally Midge Cunard. Many of the suspects gathered here tonight. In addition to improving my cooking skills, I might gain some clues to the demise of our despised ex-landlord.

Why a cooking class in a bookstore? This had once been a small café before being converted into Bea's Bookstore, so it had a large kitchen. And Bea loved cooking and was eager to share her expertise with the local incompetents, that meaning me, since the others had begun to master cooking.

Bea pointed to the stove. "Since we have only four burners, I'll need two of you to double up."

"I'll go with Pru," Herb said. "I know she needs coaching."

Everyone snickered.

I put my hands on my hips. "And I thought you were my friend."

"I am. That's why I'm volunteering to work with you to prevent any explosions or fires."

"Y-you better accept Herb's assistance," Jake said. "We don't want the fire department called tonight."

I started to protest but knew Jake and Herb were right. I was a walking disaster area in a kitchen, so it was best if I had someone working closely with me.

"Does anyone know the history of sauces?" Bea asked.

"To make dishes taste better," Sally Midge said.

"That's part of it. Before refrigeration, meat could spoil. Sauces were used to hide the taste of tainted meat."

"Yuck." Flo stuck out her tongue.

"Not to worry," Bea continued. "We're not going to have anything bad to disguise tonight, but I want you to know the background. In the modern world sauces are used to complement good meat, not hide something that's spoiled. We'll start with one of my favorites—Hollandaise sauce. Always good on vegetables, fish and eggs. All the ingredients are on the table—eggs, butter, lemon juice, dry sherry and tarragon vinegar."

"I wouldn't mind a little of the sherry to get in the right frame of mind," Sally Midge said.

"Hey, s-stay off the sauce until we're finished." Jake gave her a friendly elbow to the ribs.

Ignoring the comments, Bea continued. "First separate the yolks of three eggs. You can crack each egg into the funnel. The white will drain out, leaving the yolk."

We stepped over to the table where Bea had set out small bowls and funnels.

"I'll let you crack the eggs," Herb said. "You should be able to handle that."

"Thanks for the vote of confidence." I took the first egg and cracked it on the side of the bowl and dumped the contents into the funnel. Peering inside, I saw more egg shell than egg. The yolk had broken and was mixing with the white and draining away.

Herb let out a loud sigh. He took my mess and dumped it into the sink. "Let me crack the eggs." He proceeded to neatly complete the task with no egg shell and no broken yokes.

Next, we melted butter, which I burned. Once again, Herb completed the task correctly. I succeeded in heating the other contents, and we took turns whisking the sauce in the double boiler. We ended up with a result that looked edible. I raised my fist in the air. "Victory." When I lowered my arm, I knocked our concoction onto the floor.

Herb gave me a wan smile. "Princess, you've succeeded in snatching defeat from the yaws of victory again. I don't know how you do it."

Heat shot up my neck. I grabbed a dishrag from the sink and dropped onto my knees to clean up the mess.

Once everyone else had oohed and aahed over their results, Bea explained that we would next try a related sauce, Béarnaise. "This is especially tasty on steak."

We added white wine, shallots, peppercorn and chervil. Herb was in his element because he had provided the necessary herbs. With Herb's assistance I avoided burning or spilling the results.

"I think you're getting the hang of it, Princess."

"Only because you're holding my hand. If I were on my own, it would be a disaster."

"Hold your head high. Good things come from practice."

We took a break and had cheese, crackers and cranberry juice for a snack. I decided to use this opportunity to quiz my fellow suspects. "Anyone hear anything more about the murder investigation?"

"That Detective Moriarty has been harassing me," Sally Midge said. "He thinks I did in Bart to get his inheritance."

"Well, did you?" Flo asked.

"Of course not. It turns out he was heavily in debt and probably had changed his will to give anything left to the State Institute for Nincompoops."

Jake patted Sally Midge's hand. "And Moriarty thinks I w-wanted to get him out of the picture since Sally Midge and I are seeing each other." Jake winked at Sally Midge. "S-seeing is believing."

I expected they were doing more than just seeing each other.

"And he gave me a bunch of crapola because yarn like mine had been used for the garrote," Flo said. "I told him anyone can get their hands on Vicuna yarn."

But I hadn't seen it anywhere else besides in Flo's shop, that is other than what Herb had purchased from her.

"W-what about you, Pru?" Jake asked. "Are you getting the treatment too?"

"In spades. Since the body was found in my shop and the garrote had driftwood handles, Moriarty's bugging me."

"The detective had heard about the argument I had with Bart right before he died," Bea said. "I told him Bart had arguments with half the population of Omnipodge. Let's get back to work. Next, Mornay."

Once again, we separated egg yolks, which I succeeded in doing. I didn't attempt any victory dance this time. Herb added the Parmesan and Gruyère cheese. "You take over, Princess, I need to use the facility." He dashed off to the restroom.

I kept whisking the mixture, taking in the savory aroma. I looked at the other chefs, who were busily mixing their sauces. Could one of these be a killer? I tried to imagine whether anyone here would be capable of murder. I pictured hands thrusting a garrote around Bart's neck and pulling it tight until he collapsed. Flo intently stirred her sauce. Hard to imagine her. Sally Midge had her tongue sticking out from between her teeth as she briskly whisked away. Jake held his whisk in his fist as if stirring cement. Who could it be?

"Pru!" Bea shouted.

"Huh."

"Your sauce is burning."

I looked into the pan. My concoction had turned into a smoking, brown coagulated blob.

I wasn't any more successful at cooking than at finding out who killed Bart Cunard.

Chapter 16

I TRUDGED HOME AFTER MY LATEST cooking debacle and considered drowning my sorrows in drink, but I never touched anything stronger than Italian soda. Inside, I found all copasetic—Boopsie asleep on her cushion in the corner, so relaxed she lay on her back with her feet in the air. Spools looked up at me with eager eyes, fishing line dangled around his front paws, and the curtains dancing a little jig from Wrong Way Willie.

"Spools, how did you get into the fishing line again? I put it up on a shelf." Then something occurred to me. "Willie, did you blow the fishing line off the shelf?"

The curtain jounced up and down.

"A big help you are. Oh, Willie, I wish I could cook and figure out this murder."

The curtains bounced in agreement.

"I know, you'd help me if you had any information. Keep your invisible eyes open, though. We may find some more clues."

I sat down at the desk in my work area, pulled out sheets of lined paper, licked my pencil and began writing notes on the various persons of interest. I quickly ran out of creative ideas and retired for the night.

*　*　*　*　*

The next day I arose, fed the animals and ate a bowl of raisin bran while Willie entertained me with a dancing window curtain. The good news—I looked forward to a day of hunting for treasures on the beach, and today was the day.

I mounted Mopsy and putt-putted over to Granny's to retrieve Bessie.

I must have slumped into her house because she immediately accosted me. "You look like something the rat dragged in. Square your shoulders, Ladybug."

I sighed in resignation. "I botched another cooking class last night."

"When the going gets tough, the tough kick heiny. You'll get the hang of it."

"Thanks, Granny. I'm ready to borrow Bessie for a beach expedition."

"You going with that hunk boyfriend of yours?"

"No, Kurt has to work. Herb's going to join me."

"He's kind of cute in a swishy short of way."

"Granny!"

She waved her hands in the air. "I know. I'm not politically correct. Two rights don't make a wrong. Get out of here and have a good time. Every cloud has a golden lining."

I got in Bessie, turned on the ignition, and she let out a loud explosion.

"Are you going to give me problems, too, Bessie?"

She backfired again and then settled in to a rattling hum.

"That's better." I shifted Bessie into gear, thankful that I had learned to drive a stick shift as a teenager. Here I was holding the steering wheel of this blue 1952 Studebaker that only had 82,000 miles on it. Granny drove it once a week to the grocery store, but wanted to have a car to maintain her independence. Maybe she'd be putting more miles on it now that she had a boyfriend at Old Detectives Home. I'd have to check the odometer to see it she racked up more miles.

I stopped to pick up Herb, and he ran his hand over Bessie's fender. "What a lovely old car."

"Granny keeps it in as good working order as you do with your Chevy."

"Classic cars beat all these modern machines."

We headed down the coast, and I tuned Granny's radio to the oldies station. "Nothing like old music and old cars."

"You got it, Princess. And you can add old friends."

Herb and I had known each other for two years. For me that was an old friendship.

"Thanks for trying to help me with the cooking last night. I guess I need the remedial class."

"Don't worry your curly head over it. With lots of practice you'll be able to… break an egg without getting eggshell in the bowl."

I tried to punch him in the arm, but he flattened himself against the passenger door. I missed and almost ran off the road.

"Please, no violence. And I do want to return without any car-accident-induced injuries."

I kept my eyes on the road ahead. I would have to be careful. Granny would skin me alive if I put a dent in Bessie. I periodically peered in the rearview mirror. No black SUV in sight. I had become paranoid but with good reason.

We sang along to Billie Joel's *Piano Man*. Herb had a vibrant tenor voice, and I belted out the words with exuberance.

At the end of the song, Herb nudged me. "I won't say your singing is worse than your cooking, but I did enjoy your enthusiasm."

"Volume over quality any day."

*　*　*　*　*

We arrived at Moonstone Beach with nary a scratch on Bessie.

Herb gave me a salute. "What are my marching orders, oh captain, my captain?"

I handed him a garbage bag. "First, we're going to scour the beach for moonstone, driftwood and shells. Put everything you find in here."

He clicked his heels together. "Aye, aye."

I unfurled another garbage bag, and we set to work. The tide was out so I took off my shoes and ventured along the water line to find anything that had recently washed in. Herb combed the beach higher up because he had forgotten to bring his chartreuse reef walkers and didn't want to take off his shoes, insisting that his feet were too tender.

I found a pearl sized moonstone and admired its grainy quartz flecked with white. Once imbedded in a piece of driftwood and lacquered, this would shine as part of one of my creations. I pushed aside a clump of kelp that had washed ashore and found a piece of entangled wood. It had a nice gnarled shape, perfect for a creation once it had dried out. That got added to my sack.

A wave broke and caught me unaware, splashing my hiking shorts. I needed to pay closer attention. I moved a little farther away from the surf so as not to get wet again.

Herb waved from his position out of the reach of waves. "I'm finding lots of shiny stones for you, Princess."

"Keep at it. You do a good job, and you'll earn lunch."

"Good. Slave labor in exchange for a turkey sandwich."

"You're not griping already, are you? We're just getting started."

He yawned. "Here I am giving up my beauty rest to be bit by sand fleas and have my skin scoured by salt spray."

"Suck it up, big guy."

* * * * *

We collected for two hours. I could do this all day, but I looked up the beach and saw Herb stretched out, flat on his back. I strolled over to where he lay.

"Did you pass out from all the work?"

He fanned his face with his left hand. "I think I'm suffering from heatstroke."

"Don't give me that. It's fifty-five degrees."

"My body has a sensitive thermostat."

I kicked sand at his feet. "Up and at 'em. Give me thirty more good minutes of work, and then you get that sandwich."

He stood and dusted himself. "Slave driver."

While Herb staggered in an imitation of a drunken sailor, I returned to the car to get two large glass jars. I filled these up with the sand consisting of colorful, ground up pebbles. I could use this later to adorn some of my driftwood creations. I had a good supply of material to make final preparations for Spring Break.

I ambled up to Herb.

"Ew. What's that?" He pointed to a black and purple blob on the beach.

"Looks like a dead sea creature of some sort. Same complexion as Bart Cunard when I found him lying on my shop floor."

Herb put his hand to his head. "Don't remind me. That awful detective stopped by to harass me again this morning right before you picked me up."

"He say anything new?"

"Only that he considered me one of a handful of suspects, including you. He hasn't made much headway other than spouting out unfounded accusations. He had the audacity to also imply my shop was a front for drug dealing and that I was illegally growing marijuana and distributing it."

"I need to find some useful clues so he will quit bothering us."

"You do that, Princess. That detective gives me the willies."

Speaking of that, I hoped that Wrong Way Willie could help me solve this mystery.

We packed up, stopped at a small restaurant in Cambria to grab a bite and then headed back to Omnipodge. I belted out my dissonant but loud accompaniment to Bruce Springsteen's "Born to Run."

My reverie was interrupted when I looked in the mirror and saw a black vehicle bearing down on us.

"Look behind us. Is that a black SUV?"

Herb craned his neck. "It's black but looks smaller than a SUV."

"I hope so." I kept alternating glances between the road ahead and the rearview mirror. The vehicle came closer. I finally could see that it was a sedan. I led out a loud sigh of relief.

"A little psycho over black SUVs, Princess?"

"Yeah. One tried to run me off the road. Twice."

I dropped Herb off in front of his shop because he wanted to open for part of the afternoon.

"Thanks for your help."

"I will probably fall asleep in my store after how hard you worked me."

I gave him a wave as I drove to the gas station and car wash before returning Bessie to Granny.

She was in the garden when I pulled up. She circled Bessie. "Looks as good as a rose in heat."

"Yup. Bessie had a full lunch of gasoline, followed by a bath and shampoo. She's good for another month."

"I may lend her to you again if you take this good care of her."

I didn't mention that I had almost run off the road while swatting Herb. "Thanks. I appreciate your willingness to entrust Bessie to me. I may want to take another trip after Spring Break to get ready for summer."

"That's good, Ladybug. Never look a gift mule in the mouth."

*　*　*　*　*

After an uneventful ride on Mopsy back to my shop, I reached to unlock the door and found it ajar.

"Here we go again."

I entered expecting to find the place trashed. Fortunately, everything appeared in order. Boopsie lay on her pillow, and Spools scratched an ear without a strand of tangled fishing line in sight.

Then I went to my work area in the back. The notes on murder suspects I had made earlier were strewn all over the floor.

Chapter 17

"WILLIE!" I SHOUTED.

No answer. Was my resident ghost upstairs taking a nap? And more importantly could there be an intruder upstairs? Should I call 9-1-1? That would look pretty silly if a police officer responded, and the mess had been caused by nothing more than a spirit having disturbed my papers.

Spools came and licked my ankle, unperturbed by what was going on. I picked him up and tiptoed up the stairs. I figured I could fling him in the face of anyone who jumped out at me. In hindsight, Boopsie would have been more effective. Her claws could do major damage. Spools enjoyed the ride and licked my arm.

I reached the top of the stairs and paused to listen. No sound. I peered in my bedroom. No one there. Next, I checked the guest bedroom.

I gave a loud stage whisper. "Willie?"

The bedspread rippled.

"Did you see anyone come into my workshop?"

The bedspread wiggled, puffed out and deflated. Then the window curtain swayed back and forth.

"You must be getting old. This is the second time I've found you taking a nap when something happened downstairs."

The curtain made a circular swirl.

I set Spools down on the rug, and he went over and sniffed the bedspread. "Maybe I should set up a cot for you downstairs, so you can take your naps there and still be on guard duty."

Willie didn't deem this worth an answer.

"Come downstairs with me. I want to show you what happened this time."

I marched down the stairs with Spools and hopefully Wrong Way Willie following me. In my workspace I pointed to the papers littering the floor. "There. Someone did that while I was out."

One of the pages fluttered in the air and settled again.

"That's right. I don't think it was you, Boopsie or Spools who made the mess. But this is the second time an intruder has entered my shop."

"Who are you talking to?" a loud voice intoned.

I jumped, spun around and dropped into my martial arts stance. I didn't know any fighting techniques, but I had watched enough movies to be able to imitate Bruce Lee, crouching with my legs set apart and my hands ready to strike.

"Cool your jets, Pru. It's me."

I groaned. That was all I needed. My ex, Nate Dupres, showing up again to further darken my day.

"What are you doing here?"

"The door was unlocked, so I came in looking for you."

"You could have knocked or something."

He opened his palms toward me and gave me his flashing smile. "Hey, I entered like any customer would."

I gave him my bug under the microscope squint. "You planning on buying anything?"

He waggled his eyebrows at me. "Depends on what you're selling."

I considered being like Boopsie and coughing up a hairball.

"I'm kind of busy right now. I need to clean up my workshop."

"Yeah. Looks like a whirlwind messed up the place."

I crossed my arms. "Were you in here earlier, Nate?"

"Nope. This is my first encounter with your place today."

"Okay. You've been here. You can leave."

His smile turned to a snarl. "You can't dismiss me like that, Pru."

"Sure I can." I wiggled my fingers. "Bye. Have a nice life."

He took two steps toward me until he stood inches from my face. I winced but didn't backpedal.

Nate's shirtsleeve billowed in a breeze. He batted at it. Too bad Willie couldn't do anything more than ruffle cloth.

Nate grabbed my arm. "I saw you at Herb Hanover's house the night before last. Then you went off with him today."

"Are you spying on me?"

"Checking up on my investment."

"What's that supposed to mean?"

He ignored my question. Instead, he jabbed a finger into my arm. "Are you having an affair with Herb?"

I broke out in laughter. "That's rich. Are you dumb enough to ask that question?"

He looked truly surprised. "Huh?"

"Do you know anything about Herb?"

"Only that he runs that ridiculous herb shop that can't be making any money and that he's messing with my girl."

"I'm not anyone's girl, particularly yours. Herb provides a needed product to our community."

"He's probably dealing illegal drugs."

"You really are an idiot."

His eyes flared. "I've had enough of your insults. Maybe I'll make a little hostile visit to Herb and settle things."

I let out a burst of air. "Before you do anything even more stupid than you already have, you might want to learn a few things. For example, here's a little fact concerning Herb's sexual orientation. He's gay."

Nate's mouth dropped open, and he blinked rapidly three times.

"Yeah. Next time don't make assumptions about my relationships and threaten me. Herb's a good friend. That's more than I can say for you. Get out of here, you ignorant jerk."

Apparently, I had surprised him enough that he didn't have anything else to say. He pivoted and stormed out the door, slamming it.

"Good riddance."

The window curtain bobbed up and down.

"But I still don't know who has been getting into my shop and going through my papers. Any new thoughts, Willie?"

The curtain shook back and forth.

Then another thing struck me. Whoever had been here could have read the notes I made. If that person was the murderer, he or she wouldn't be too happy that I was analyzing the suspects.

Chapter 18

I HAD NO TIME TO CONSIDER who might have invaded my shop and seen my abortive attempts to solve the crime because someone banged on the front door. It wasn't the friendly rap of a customer enthusiastically seeking one of my works of art. I shuffled over to grab the door handle and found Sally Midge standing there, a scowl on her puss.

"We need to talk," she announced and then barged into my store, almost knocking me over.

I regained my balance. "By all means. Make yourself at home. But first, what's on your mind?"

She closed the door behind her, none too gently. I hoped it would survive this recent rough treatment from both Nate and Sally Midge.

She swiveled and faced me. "You and I have a bone to pick."

"Well, good morning to you, too, Sally Midge."

Undeterred, she shook her fist at me. "By your killing Bart, you've caused me big problems."

I winced. "I had nothing to do with Bart's death."

"He showed up dead here, in your shop, with your driftwood being part of the garrote. Don't get me wrong. I don't care that Bart is dead, but it wrecks havoc with his alimony payments."

"Nice to see you're not being overly sentimental about his demise."

"We know Bart was a slimebag. No great loss there, but he still owed me four months of alimony. How do you expect me to collect that?"

"I don't know. I guess you'll have to work with the executor of Bart's estate. But get this straight." I stared directly into her eyes. "I did not kill Bart."

"Detective Moriarty hinted that you and I are his two prime suspects. Since I didn't kill Bart that means it must be you."

"It seems the detective is trying to breed discontent among us. He told Herb that he and I are under suspicion."

Sally Midge crinkled her nose. "That makes you the common denominator."

"I think Detective Moriarty's trying to force one of us to say something to incriminate one of the others. I'll repeat this again and read my lips. I didn't kill Bart. Understand?"

Sally Midge sagged like a collapsing balloon. "I'm sorry. I guess I got carried away. I jumped to a conclusion."

"Let's hope the detective finds the real killer rather than continuing to harass us."

I heard a crash, and Spools came running from the back room, entangled in fishing line.

Sally Midge bent over and picked him up. "Isn't he the cutest? What's this stuff he's stuck in?"

"That's what I use for my driftwood mobiles. Spools always gets into it."

She pulled Spools out of his tangles and dropped the mass of fishing line on the floor. "This reminds me of reading tea leaves. Since I'm psychic, and this is where the murder took place, maybe I can figure out something. I'm going to read your fishing line."

Hook, line and sinker. I felt like telling her where she could stuff her so-called psychic skills, but after she set Spools down, she remained focused on the tangle of fishing line, put her hands to the sides of her head and closed her eyes. "Something is happening. Yes. I'm getting a strong vibration."

I watched as Wrong Way Willie ruffled her hair.

"I hear a voice. I can see a faint image. It's getting clearer. The fishing line is communicating with me."

I wondered what frequency she was on.

"I'm getting the image of someone coming into your shop. Bart is standing there. Suddenly, a garrote is thrust around Bart's neck. He struggles, collapses behind the counter and dies."

Duh. We knew that. "Who did it?"

Sally Midge opened her eyes. "I couldn't tell. It was only a dark shape. Very wispy and uncertain."

"Man or woman?"

Sally Midge sucked on her lip for a moment. "Not sure."

"Don't your vibes give you some hint?"

Wrong Way Willie was wrecking havoc with her hair, but she seemed not to notice. What more in the way of vibes could she ask for?

She scrunched her eyes tight. "Could be a short man or a tall woman. I can't get a clear image."

A gagging sound emanated from the corner of the room, and Boopsie coughed up a hairball. My sentiments exactly.

Sally Midge's eyes shot open. Rather than being put off, she dashed over to examine the cylinder of hair and gook. "I can also read hairballs. This could be significant." She repeated the hands to the head and closed eyes bit, this time rocking from side to side. "Yes. I can hear an argument. Bart and someone are having words."

"And the words?"

She put her hands behind her ears like someone eavesdropping. "Something concerning money."

"And the person confronting Bart?"

"A gray shadow. No features."

I rolled my eyes. Her psychic skills rivaled by ex-boyfriend Nate's ability to be couth and act like a human being.

"You're welcome to take the hairball and tangled fishing line with you for further analysis if you like."

She waved her hand. "It's not necessary. I've received all the communication I'll get at this point."

Right. Psychic censorship at its best. She was more full of it than Boopsie right before disgorging. "You mentioned several days ago that I might be in touch with some spirit from the past. Any vibes on that right now?"

Willie caused her hair to flip and twirl.

Sally Midge smoothed out her rat's nest hairdo and closed her eyes. "Nope. Nada. Nothing."

"I thought my house might be haunted. Are you sure there's nothing here?"

She opened her eyes and regarded a mobile hanging above her head. "If there was a ghostly presence, I'd pick it up. You're spirit free."

So much for her knowledge of Willie. As a psychic she was useless. Maybe I'd get her *Psychic for Dummies* for a present.

Willie continued to stir up her hair, the curtains and Boopsie's tail, but Sally Midge remained oblivious to it all.

"If you're done with your reading, I need to get back to work. I'm preparing for the Spring Break rush."

"Oh, right. Jake has the same objective. He's expecting a new shipment of jewelry in today. I better go take a look. He hinted he might have a present for me." She held out her ringless left hand. "You never know when things will change for the better."

I knew things would change for the better when she left my shop.

Chapter 19

ONCE I HAD MY SHOP to myself, that is except for Wrong Way Willie, Boopsie and Spools, I shook my head to rid myself of any dingbat cooties Sally Midge had left behind. "Willie, what a fraud she is, claiming to be psychic. She's as psychic as the toenail on the little toe of my left foot." My foot twitched. Maybe the toenail on the little toe of my left foot was more psychic than Sally Midge.

She had charged into my shop accusing me of killing Bart. Had that been a diversionary stunt on her part? Could she really be the killer? I used to like Sally Midge, but after this latest episode, I wasn't so sure. Maybe she took out Bart to get him out of the way, then realized that she had cut off her source of alimony. On the other hand, if she planned to marry Jake, and there had been that unsubtle hint of an engagement ring in the works, maybe she wanted to eliminate any future hassle from Bart. I could argue back and forth all day.

I threw my hands up in disgust. "What do you think, Willie?"

The curtain swirled, and I had no idea what he meant.

My thoughts returned to when I first renovated this building, opened my shop and moved into the back and upstairs for my residence. I had heard rumors that the place was haunted by the ghost of Wrong Way Willie Woburn. I found the idea intriguing. When Granny asked me if I was scared of moving into a haunted house, I only laughed and explained that I looked forward to meeting a ghost. She crossed herself and said, "Be careful what you wish for. It might bite you in the buttress."

I spent several days calling Willie's name and asking him to show himself. Then in the middle of the night, I felt a breeze pass over my face. I awoke and turned on the light. The windows were closed tightly. Rather than being scared, I jumped out of bed. "Is that you, Willie?" That was the first time the curtains jumped. I pointed to some dust in the corner I had not yet swept away. "If that's you, Willie, stir up the dust for me." And sure enough, he had produced a small dust devil. From then on, I enjoyed my conversations with Willie, although they were somewhat limited in content.

Today, I made a decision. "Willie, we need to find a way to communicate more clearly." I looked around. Then it struck me like a Mack truck. "I've got it." I went into the workshop where I kept Boopsie's litter box. I cleaned it out and replenished it with fresh litter.

"Willie, are you still here with me?"

The curtain danced a little jig.

"You can hear me when I talk, but I have no way of finding out what's on your mind other than asking simple yes and no questions. Since you can blow things around, why don't you write in Boopsie's litterbox to communicate with me? You can start by writing your name."

I waited.

Then some of the gravel began to jump in the litter box.

I eagerly bent over to see what Willie had written. I found a large "X."

"Willie, you can't read or write?"

Pieces of litter bounced around and some dust rose. The "X" disappeared, and a new one replaced it.

"How are you going to be able to tell me anything?" Then I knew what I needed to do. "Okay, Willie. I'm going to have to teach you how to read and write. You know one letter, although it isn't used that much. We'll start with the alphabet. I'm going to write the letter "A" and you can copy it.

I put my finger in the litter box and drew a large "A."

I waited. The litter smoothed out and a line appeared. Then a second line forming a point and an intersecting third one.

"Good, Willie. You've got the hang of it."

We went through the alphabet, with Willie copying each letter. His penmanship wasn't too bad, other than his "S" being a little wobbly.

We were interrupted when the phone rang. I picked up to hear Kurt on the line. "Uh… Pru… you doing anything this evening?"

"No definite plans."

"You by any chance… uh… would you like to grab a bite to eat?"

What a silver-tongued devil. "Sure, Kurt. Time and place?"

"Uh… maybe seven at the diner? I… uh… can give you a lift."

I pictured his grabbing me around the waist and hoisting me into the air. "That would be great. See you then."

My heart went pitter pat. I had a *sort-of* date with my *sort-of* boyfriend. I stood there picturing Kurt and me holding hands, embracing and then—

A breeze ran through my hair.

"Right, Willie. Back to our lesson."

We went through the alphabet again. Then I said a letter and waited for him to write it. He wrote his "B" backwards, and I corrected it. He proceeded to write it a dozen times the right way.

"You're getting the hang of it, Willie. I don't know why you never learned your alphabet before."

The curtain bulged out and returned to normal.

"I guess you didn't have time with getting a town founded and all. In your day someone could get by without reading and writing. Not today. Besides, if you're going to help me solve this murder, we need to be able to communicate clearly. Let's try a word. Here's how to spell your name. I wrote it in the litter.

He imitated it, getting the letters in the right order.

Dust flew into the air. He seemed pleased with himself because he proceeded to write his name six more times.

Then I showed him how to write "YES" and "NO." I figured we could stay with capital letters for the time being.

Maybe I had a new career here. I could teach illiterate ghosts how to read and write. Then I could go on the talk show circuit telling the world of my experiences. I slapped my cheek. Stay focused.

I intended to write my name for Willie, but Boopsie sauntered into the room, having been roused from her nap, and stepped into the litter box. She scratched away the letters, swished her tail to indicate she wanted some privacy and proceeded to desecrate our writing surface. So much for the litter box learning center.

Then I remembered the bottle of colorful sand I had collected from Moonstone Beach. I retrieved a sheet pan from the kitchen and dumped the sand into it. We had a cat proof writing surface.

I taught Willie the names of the suspects for the murder. I quizzed him by saying a name and watched as he wrote it. When I said, "Larry," he wrote in large slashing letters, "LARY."

"Almost right." I made the correction and he rewrote it.

"You don't like him, do you?"

A swirl of wind erased the word and replaced it with, "NO."

"I don't think I do either. He's one of our prime suspects, but I don't have any conclusive evidence to turn over to the police. We'll have to keep working. If you see any of these suspects in the shop, you can write their names here for me. I'll leave the sheet pan with the sand on my workbench for you to use."

He wrote, "YES."

"Good. We have a system. Between you and me, we're going to nail that murderer."

I only hoped reality could match my false enthusiasm.

Chapter 20

ALTHOUGH I STILL HAD NO clue who had killed Bart Cunard, I now had a warm feeling in my chest. I had taken the first steps to help teach a ghost how to read and write. It was nice when you could do favors for people, even if they had been dead for a hundred years.

I sauntered into the retail part of my store to check my inventory. All was in a reasonable semblance of order—enough on display to attract the few customers who might appear before the Spring Break rush. Boopsie lay on her pillow with her feet in the air. Talk about relaxed. Spools rested beside her, having taken a break from his usual Energizer bunny mode. Willie had remained in the workshop to practice writing YES and NO.

So here I was. I only needed to keep from getting run over by a black SUV, avoid my ex-boyfriend, move things along with Kurt and solve the murder. Piece of cake. Speaking of cake, my tummy rumbled. I headed to my kitchen to make a snack. I got out bread, peanut butter and jelly. Even I couldn't ruin a pb&j sandwich. I had finished slathering jelly on a piece of wheat bread and picked it up to mate it with the other piece of bread containing peanut butter, when I heard a loud slam of a door. I spun on my heels, and the bread slipped out of my hand, landing jelly side down on the floor.

Spools came running into the kitchen. Before I could reach down to retrieve the lost half of my sandwich, he wolfed down the bread and began licking up the floor. Knowing that he wouldn't leave a crumb or speck of jelly, I went into the front of the store to see who had come in.

No one there. I returned to the workshop.

"Was that you slamming the door, Willie?"

Wind ruffled through the sand in the sheet pan, and the word, "NO" appeared.

"Did you see anyone?"

The sand danced and another "NO."

"Don't tell me we have another haunt here?" I didn't have to wait for the two letters to appear again. I knew Willie wouldn't put up with a ghostly intruder.

It definitely sounded like the front door had closed. I went into the customer area, opened the door and looked outside. No one in sight. Then I peered down. A sheet of paper. I picked it up and read, "You could be next."

I should have been scared, but instead I felt heat run up my neck. I felt like tearing the note into a thousand pieces. Instead, I took a deep breath and returned inside to call Detective Moriarty.

He must have been having a slow day because he appeared on my doorstep in fifteen minutes. I showed him the note where I had set it on the counter.

He gave an impolite snort. "I supposed it's covered with your fingerprints."

"Well, yeah. I picked it up. But it might have someone else's as well."

He arched an eyebrow. "Trying again to divert attention away from the crime you committed?"

I planted my fists on my hips. "I haven't committed any crime. And I certainly wouldn't waste my time by writing a stupid note like this one. Now, are you going to do something with it?"

He put on some stretchy, blue gloves, gingerly lifted the note and placed it in a paper bag. "We'll take a look. Anything else to confess?"

I reviewed my encounter with Sally Midge, but no sense causing her any more trouble. "That's it for now."

He scanned by display case. "Do people actually buy these things?"

"Yes. Many customers love these *things*."

"You could fool me." Without another word, he departed.

Too bad our town possessed the world's surliest detective. I only hoped he was doing some good on the investigation, but no indication of that so far.

Back to trying to figure out this whole thing. I obviously had caught someone's attention with my snooping. Rather than climbing into a shell, I would have to redouble my efforts. But first, I needed sustenance. I had to re-make my sandwich.

*   *   *   *   *

With a satisfied and sticky feeling in my tummy, I set my sign to indicate I'd be back in thirty minutes and headed to Jake Yalley's jewelry store. Might as well follow up on the Sally Midge encounter.

Jake sat behind his counter with a loupe to his eyes, examining a ring.

"Counting diamonds?" I asked.

He looked up. "Y-you can always count on diamonds."

I groaned. "I heard a rumor that a diamond ring might be in the offing for one recent Omnipodge widow."

He graced me with a huge smile. "That's definitely the c-case. And in the case." He tapped the display case. "I've completed the setting, and tonight is the night. A design-it-yourself engagement ring."

"Don't you think this is all happening a little soon after Bart's demise?"

"No s-sense waiting."

I thought of Granny who would say a watched pot gathers no moss. "But Detective Moriarty might think such a quick engagement is suspicious."

"Sally Midge and I had n-nothing to do with Bart's death. We'd been making plans even before Bart bit the dust. It certainly will be less hassle with him gone. Gone and easily forgotten."

"That's the point. The detective is apt to up his hassle."

"He already h-has. Once a day or so he stops by and accuses me and Sally Midge of the murder, but true love can't be denied nor derailed. He can rail against us all he wants."

I thought of Kurt. Maybe so, but true love sure could be slow in arriving. Now, my other business at hand. "Did you happen to see anyone go into my shop in the last hour?"

"N-nope. I haven't looked outside since I've been here adjusting settings. I'm quite good at adjusting to this setting."

I almost stuck my tongue out but that would really have fed into his dumb sense of humor. "Someone left me a threatening note."

"Struck a b-bad note, huh?"

I resisted the urge to groan again. "It's not a laughing matter. And it could have been one of the other shopkeepers because the person quickly disappeared. I thought I'd check around, and you're the closest shop."

"Not g-guilty. Maybe that detective can figure out something."

"Every time he shows up, he accuses me of killing Bart. It's good to know he's harassing other people as well."

"Yeah, equal o-opportunity harassment in the Omnipodge Village Center."

"Any thoughts on who killed Bart?"

He sucked on his lip for a moment. "S-sally Midge and I have been speculating on that. Sure it's not you?"

"Give me a break, Jake."

"You're into r-rhymes?"

"Purely unintentional. Seriously, you must have some suspicions."

"Since it's not Sally Midge or me and you deny culpability, I'd have to go with L-Larry Ludwick. Sally Midge says Bart and Larry had all kinds of illegal shenanigans going on."

"He's on my list as well. Do you know anyone who drives a black SUV?"

"That's out of the b-blue."

"Someone in a black SUV tried to run me off the road recently."

"Wow, you're really in the crosshairs. Threatening notes and big black cars. You make s-some enemies along the way?"

Other than Nate Dupres? My snooping had definitely caught someone's attention. "I'll have to watch my back."

"Y-you'll need to be a contortionist to do that."

Chapter 21

HAVING HAD ENOUGH OF JAKE Yalley's dumb jokes, I left his shop, wondering if he could have killed Bart Cunard to pave the way for his upcoming engagement to Sally Midge. As they say, two of the main motivations for murder are money and crimes of passion. Maybe he, like the rest of us, had had enough of Bart but took it one step further. Possible, but could someone who had such a weird sense of humor be a killer? I'd have to noodle more on this question.

What next? I checked my watch and still had fifteen minutes before my promised return to the store. On to Flo's yarn shop. I would have to resist the urge to buy anything given my low bank account. Maybe after Spring Break.

The bell tinkled as I entered. No one in sight. I meandered through the shelves, admiring the colorful yarn. Good thing I hadn't brought Spools. I could see him in a gigantic yarn tangle in thirty seconds of sticking his nose into the low storage spaces.

I had wondered how Flo stayed in business. I never saw many people in here, and how many people bought huge amounts of yarn? Probably as many as purchased driftwood sculptures. Talk about the pot calling the kettle black or as Granny would say, the pot yelling back at the kettle.

I tried to picture someone taking some yarn from Flo's and combining it with two driftwood handles from my shop, fashioning a garrote and then—

I jumped at a loud bang. It came from the back of the shop. I raced through the curtain to find Flo standing over a large box that she had obviously dropped.

"That sound scared me," I said.

Flo raised her gaze to me. "I heard the bell ring, but didn't realize it was you, Pru. I was carrying this heavy box, and it slipped out of my hands."

"I'm glad that's all it was. May I help you?"

"Sure. Let's carry it over to the table."

We hefted the box and struggled to move it the rest of the way to where Flo wanted it deposited. A bead of glow dribbled down my cheek. Granny had taught me that horses sweat, men perspire and women glow. "How'd you carry this as far as you did?"

"Part of my daily workout program." She flexed a barely discernible bicep. "Some people lift weights. I lift boxes of yarn."

Still being in tune to Jake's mentality, I thought of someone stealing boxes of yarn. Had the murderer taken some of her yarn or was Flo the killer? I couldn't imagine her slim frame and skinny arms being strong enough to choke Bart to death.

Still, I had to poke at the possibility. "Has Detective Moriarty been grilling you over Bart's murder?"

Flo scowled as if a black cloud had passed over the sun. "That he has. He accused me of using my yarn to kill the slimebag."

"I hope you didn't use those words with the detective."

Flo's good humor returned with a sparkling smile. "I considered it but decided not to give him any more ammunition."

"Moriarty has been accusing everyone including Herb, Jake, Sally Midge and me. I think he's trying to see who gets riled up."

"I maintained my calm when he accused me, although it took all of the control I could muster. And here's the problem." She leaned close to me and whispered. "I'm missing a skein of Vicuna."

"When did you notice it gone?"

"Right after I heard that Bart had been killed. I was taking physical inventory, and it struck me as strange that I would be off on the count compared to what was in inventory when the new yarn arrived the day before. Obviously, someone snuck into my shop and took it. I checked and double-checked. I was off by a count of one skein from what had been sold so far."

"And you're sure of the count?"

"Yup. I counted twice when the shipment arrived and I stocked it. Then the next day I reviewed the sales numbers twice and counted two times what was left in stock. No question that one skein had disappeared."

"And who had been in your shop between the time the yarn arrived and the death of Bart?"

"The shipment arrived late in the afternoon. I unpacked it after I closed the shop for the day. That's when I did the count. The next day I only had half a dozen visitors in the morning. That included you and Spools."

I gulped. Spools had been tangled in a skein of Vicuna, and I helped her untangle him. Did she think I had taken a skein of yarn? She didn't appear to be sending an accusing stare my way.

"Any chance someone broke into your store overnight?"

"No sign of a forced entry and nothing else missing. I can't imagine a burglar picking my lock for one skein of Vicuna."

"And other visitors that morning?"

"All the other shopkeepers stopped by including Jake, Flo, Herb, you and Spools. Sally Midge accompanied Jake. And, of course, Bart barged in, but I think we can rule out suicide."

"Any customers?"

"A women from out of town who bought some Angora, and a man I didn't recognize wandered through briefly."

"I have several male suspects on my list. Do you know Larry Ludwick?"

"Your list?"

"Yeah. Since Detective Moriarty is accusing me of murder, I've been trying to figure out who really killed Bart. Larry is one of my main suspects."

"I've heard of him but never met him."

"Another is my ex-boyfriend, Nate Dupres."

"Doesn't ring a bell."

"Unfortunately, at one time he rang my bell. But that's over. He's back in town, which doesn't please me."

"Why would you suspect him?"

"Nothing specific other than he might be trying to get back at me by staging a murder in my shop. Did you talk to Detective Moriarty about your visitors that morning?"

Flo raised her eyes skyward. "Oh, yes. He grilled me for an hour intermixed with accusing me of the murder. He and Bart would make a good team for most obnoxious people in town."

"I agree. Anyone else come into your shop that morning?"

"That's it. A quiet morning. Until Bart got his."

That was the problem. Nothing concrete yet on the perp and why Bart had met his untimely demise.

Chapter 22

I RETURNED TO MY SHOP AND spent a half hour staring at Boopsie and Spools asleep while ruminating on my fits and starts at solving the murder. No new suspects other than some unidentified man in Flo's shop and no one officially eliminated. Could the unidentified man have been Larry Ludwick or Nate Dupres? And even so, what would that prove?

Then another ugly thought occurred to me. Bart Cunard had duplicate keys to all the shops. He could have snuck into Flo's store at night. She didn't live above her shop as I did. But if he stole a skein of Vicuna, how did it come to be used in his own demise?

I winced. Another worry. Since Bart had a key to my shop, he could have let himself in. I didn't like the idea of a key floating around. With him gone, I wondered what had happened to it. Did I need to change my lock?

Before I could consider doing anything to resolve this concern, a mob of customers descended on me. Within two hours I had a dozen people enter the shop. Was this the first wave of Spring Break?

After selling over two hundred dollars of driftwood creations, I realized I could afford groceries for the week. Over $100 in cash and the rest checks and credit card charges. I felt like I had won the lottery. If this was a portent of things to come over the next few weeks, I would become financially solvent again.

But in the late afternoon, the crowd thinned, and I ended up closing at five to get ready for my big date. Right. A gourmet meal at the diner. Still, I would be with Kurt. Anything might happen.

*   *   *   *   *

I set aside lots of time to primp for my big date. First, a luxurious bath. Willie allowed me to maintain my privacy. At least, I thought he did. I applied a generous dollop of bubble bath liquid and mixed it in to allow the foam to rise to my chin. Then I lay back to soak. I had almost fallen asleep when a thought awoke me. Might I be able to enlist Kurt in my investigation? With his penchant to become a police officer, maybe he'd be willing to provide a little unofficial assistance.

I selected a sexy, red, short skirt, form-fitting knit top, my only pair of high heels and carefully applied mascara and lip gloss. I admired the result in the mirror. I was armed and dangerous.

I heard a horn beep and looked out the window to see Kurt waiting in his pickup truck. Always the romantic. I grabbed my black clutch purse. "Wish me luck, Willie."

The curtain jiggled.

I waved and dashed out the door.

Kurt never bothered to get out to open the passenger's door for me. I sighed. He would require some training.

"Good to see you, Pru."

I attached my seatbelt. "Good to see you, too, Kurt."

He started the engine, and we took off with a loud roar.

"Muffler problem?"

He gave me his sheepish grin. "Yeah. I've been too busy to get it fixed."

"How come you have a pickup truck, anyway?"

"As a volunteer fire fighter, it gives me the flexibility of carrying extra gear to any type of emergency."

102

I pictured myself lost on some mountain trail and Kurt driving through the bush to rescue me. Stay focused.

We arrived at the diner, and this time Kurt actually came around and opened the door for me.

"My knight in shining armor."

He blushed. "Aw, shucks."

Had he actually said that? I shrugged. What could you expect in a small town?

We took a booth, and Kurt handed me a menu. My, he had become quite the gentleman after all.

I scanned the familiar set of selections and chose the meatloaf. You can't go wrong with meatloaf. Kurt ordered the steak, and I pictured the protein surging through his muscles. Not that I had been very close to those muscles yet.

After I munched on a bite of salad and swallowed, I pointed my fork at Kurt. "You hear anything new regarding the Bart Cunard murder?"

"I... uh... shouldn't discuss that with a civilian, Pru."

I winked at him. "I'm not just any civilian. I'm a concerned citizen because the body showed up in my shop."

He reddened. "I... uh... guess I can say a little."

He said nothing so I prompted, "Go ahead."

He leaned toward me. "You're a suspect, Pru."

"That's nothing new. Detective Moriarty has been accusing me and every other shopkeeper in the Omnipodge Village Center. I didn't kill Bart, but do you have any suspicion of who did?"

"Nope." He took another bite of salad and masticated vigorously.

I would need a crowbar to pry anything out of him. I chose another tactic. "Since you want to become a police officer, this might be a chance to practice your investigation skills."

He stopped chewing and actually looked at me.

I gave him my best come hither smile. "We might even work

together to find the killer."

Then his chin drooped. "But that's the responsibility of Detective Moriarty."

"I know, but he hasn't arrested anyone yet. You and I could be a team to assist his investigation. If we helped solve the crime, that might give you the edge on getting hired as a police officer."

His eyes widened. "You think so?"

"Couldn't hurt. With the studying you're doing and a positive boost to your reputation by helping to solve the murder, you'd be a shoe-in."

He scratched his head. "I don't see what we can do to help."

"I've developed a list of suspects. It includes the shopkeepers, Sally Midge, Larry Ludwick and Nate Dupres."

"Who's Nate Dupres?"

"Uh… my ex-boyfriend. He's back in town and causing problems."

"You had a boyfriend?"

"Don't look so surprised. We broke up a long time ago. He's trouble, and I don't want to have anything to do with him."

He nodded and took another bite of salad.

Now I leaned toward him. "My thought is that you could casually stop by Detective Moriarty's desk and see if you can spot any useful information."

"Wouldn't that be like spying?"

"It would help our investigation… and once we solved the crime it would increase the chances of the department hiring you as a police officer. What do you say?"

He bit his lip. "I don't know, Pru."

"Give it a try. See what you can pick up. Then we'll take it from there."

"Don't you have someone else who can help you, Pru?"

I thought for a moment about mentioning Wrong Way Willie.

How would Kurt react to hearing that I had a ghost living in my shop and home? That might spook him, so to speak, so I decided not to divulge that little aspect of my life. "I think you're the best one for this assignment, Kurt."

Our main courses arrived, and Kurt became engaged in cutting and chewing. We had completed the longest conversation of our short, *sort-of* relationship. Progress.

After he completed every smidgeon of steak, baked potato and corn, he wiped the corner of his mouth, and a satisfied smile crossed his lips. I hoped one day that same look would appear from being close to me rather than a steak.

As the waitress cleared the plates away, I noticed Jake Yalley and Sally Midge Cunard stroll into the diner. They saw us and came over.

Sally Midge held out her left hand. "Notice anything different?"

Kurt stared at her hand. "Liver spots?"

"No, silly something else." She waggled her fingers.

Kurt looked closer. "Clean fingernails?"

He wasn't getting it so I jumped in. "Beautiful ring, Sally Midge."

"Isn't it though." She gave Jake a hug. "He popped the question, and I said yes."

Kurt furled his eyebrows. "What question?"

"Jake and I are engaged."

Kurt scratched his ear. "Oh."

"We thought we'd stop and get hot fudge sundaes to celebrate. B-better than champagne."

"That's what my granny always says. To quote, 'Liquor is quicker but fudge makes you budge.'"

"Your granny is a w-wise woman." Jake took Sally Midge's arm.

"Big event in two days," Sally Midge said. "I trust you'll be attending."

"What's that?" I asked.

Sally Midge gave a satisfied smile. "Bart's funeral. Come join the celebration."

I didn't think someone should act so cheerful over a funeral, but I guess Sally Midge had had enough of Bart. No one had mentioned the funeral to me before. Hmm. Might be a good opportunity to see some of the suspects in action. The murderer might want to attend to see the result of his or her handiwork. "When and where?"

"St. Gadfly's at two PM. Let's go order those yummy sundaes, Jake."

"I'll plan to attend. As Granny says, 'Be there or be in a chair.'"

Sally Midge waved her ringed hand one more time. It gave off a blue sparkle. "We'll see you later."

They departed to find another booth.

We ordered pie, apple for him and cherry for me. I loved pie. Good thing I didn't eat it very often or I would turn into a blimp. Then I'd never catch Kurt's eye.

After we both consumed our dessert, I suppressed a burp and put my hands on the table. He dropped his napkin next to his plate. Then his eyes met mine.

My heart beat a staccato.

He moved his hands toward mine. Would this be the moment?

I waited in eager anticipation.

Then his cell phone jangled. Rather than grasping my hands, he reached in his pocket, pulled out the offending device and put it to his ear. "Kurt here."

He listened, and his eyes narrowed. "Got it. Right away." He stood. "There's a fire at the Thompson place. Have to go." He dashed off without so much as an apology, a suggestion on how I would get home or a backward glance.

Oh, well, I could use the exercise of an after-dinner walk home. He had left me with one item—the bill. Good thing I had cash from sales during the day.

Chapter 23

THE NEXT MORNING, I AWOKE, wondering how the firefighting had gone for Kurt. I could see him racing to the blaze, rushing in to save women and children, carrying a heavy fire hose and dousing the flames. Then I put my hand to my cheek. Fires were dangerous. I hoped nothing bad had happened to him. I thought of calling him but then decided it would be best to wait for him to contact me. I would not be a pushy woman. Then again, I might wait forever. Deciding not to debate the point any longer, I set to work.

I puttered around the shop all morning. Two prospective customers arrived right after opening, and one actually bought a mobile and a sculpture. Money was flowing, the economy was rebounding, life was good. Sort of. Yeah, me and my *sort-of* boyfriend.

With no other buyers in sight, I went into the workshop to craft a few new creations. I fashioned a mobile out of some of the driftwood I had found at Moonstone Beach and glued some moonstones onto a gnarled piece of wood. I spilled a bottle of beach rocks, and they tumbled to the floor. At the sound, Spools came running to help, skidded on the rocks and crashed into a spool of fishing line I had stupidly left on the floor. He spun around until he had succeeded in getting tangled.

"How do you do that?" I reached down and detached him from the fishing line. While this was going on, Boopsie guarded the front of the store by snoozing. Wrong Way Willie stopped by periodically to ruffle the curtains.

After completing another sculpture, I stepped back to admire the morning's work, and the phone rang. I answered to hear Kurt on the line.

"Sorry I had to leave so abruptly, and I forgot to pay. I owe you another dinner."

That sounded promising, but I would stay calm and cool. "I was worried about you. Did everything go okay at the fire?"

"No one injured. Most of the house was destroyed, but the only occupant escaped. Apparently old Mr. Thompson fell asleep with a cigarette in his hand. Set the rug on fire, but he woke up in time to limp outside. Man, those old wood houses can burn quickly."

"I'm glad you're safe."

"I had to get close to the flames, but the bunker gear protected me. I have one other thing to mention."

"Oh?"

"I thought over what you said and decided to see if I could learn more about the murder. I stopped by Detective Moriarty's desk this morning..."

I waited, but he said nothing further. "Don't keep me in suspense."

"I didn't see anything useful, but I had a chance to speak with him..."

Good old Kurt. Didn't complete many sentences. "And?"

"He didn't have Nate Dupres on his suspect list. Now he does."

"Good work. That's progress."

"Yup. That old boyfriend of yours should be investigated."

From his forceful tone, I detected a note of jealousy. Hey, maybe that would force his hand, so to speak.

"I enjoyed our dinner... before you had to leave."

"Me, too, Pru."

He was turning into a poet. I waited to see if there would be a further invitation, but nothing followed. I imagined him sitting there thinking of a steak dinner. I decided I would have to take the initiative. "Given that we're working together to find the murderer, you and I should schedule a time to debrief on our investigation."

"Yeah, good idea." The tone of his voice had perked up. "I could stop by your shop when my shift is over today. Say around six."

"I'll be here. I bet you're tired with the fire last night and work at the police department today."

"Not a problem. I don't need much sleep."

Ah, the first personal thing he'd shared with me.

We signed off. My ploy had worked. We might see each other on a more regular basis because of the murder investigation. Whatever it took.

*   *   *   *   *

The afternoon brought a few more customers, and interspersed with these, I completed two more sculptures and a mobile, which allowed me to replenish my stock from sales over the last two days. I walked through the display area, arranging sculptures for best viewing.

Then I sat down and gave Spools a chuck under the chin. He eagerly accepted the attention.

I used this break to think over my list of suspects. Jake Yalley and Sally Midge didn't waste any time getting engaged after Bart died. They appeared pretty wrapped up in each other last night at the diner. Either of them could have eliminated Bart, but neither seemed like killers to me. As the result of Kurt's help, maybe Detective Moriarty would get after Nate. That would keep both of them from bothering me.

My thoughts were interrupted by the phone ringing. Would it

be Kurt again or some customer interested in purchasing a dozen sculptures?

"Driftwood Creatives. Pru Pendergast speaking."

No one replied. Was this one of those obnoxious robocalls? I prepared to hang up when a metallic voice came over the line. "Stay out of what doesn't concern you. This is your last warning."

"Who is this?" I shouted.

The line went dead.

"Rats." I returned the receiver to its cradle, then picked it up again and called Detective Moriarty. It cut over to voicemail. I called the main police station number and asked the receptionist to page Moriarty. After five minutes, he answered, and I explained that I had been threatened.

"Another diversionary stunt, missy?"

"Don't missy me. This is serious. I expect you to pay attention when a citizen receives a menacing phone call. It could be the same person who killed Bart Cunard."

"Okay. Okay. Repeat the exact words you heard."

I did, and I could hear a pencil scratching. At least he wrote them down unless he was only working on his shopping list.

"Tell me again what the voice sounded like."

"It was electronically altered. Had a metallic sound."

"You didn't recognize it?"

"No. I don't know any robots."

"Don't get snippy, missy."

"Don't be patronizing, Detective."

"I'll be as patriotic as I want to be."

Great. This was the detective charged with tracking down the killer? I would definitely have to solve this case myself.

Chapter 24

AFTER GETTING OFF THE PHONE with the detective, I slumped into the easy chair in my work area. What a bummer. Having to put up with Moriarty when he should be out finding the real killer. Sometimes I wondered why I had moved back to Omnipodge. Then I remembered all Granny had done for me and my opportunity to run my own business. *Suck it up.* I would have to learn to deal with Moriarty and his incompetence.

The curtain swished.

"What do you think of that bozo detective, Willie?"

The curtain clumped up and drooped.

"My sentiments exactly. Say, maybe we should continue your reading and writing lessons."

The curtain danced.

"Good. Let me get the sheet pan of sand." I set it out on the table. "Do you remember what we went through last time?"

The word "YES" appeared.

"Good. I want you to practice writing the names of the suspects in Bart's murder. Then if you see any of them coming in my shop, you can let me know."

Wind swirled through the sand, and he scrawled another "YES."

We went through the names and this time he even spelled Larry with two Rs. Willie was a quick study. We spent a good two hours practicing until I was ready to move on to a new subject.

"I can't imagine that you never learned this before, Willie. I guess you never felt it was very important. Did anyone ever offer to teach you before?"

Three lines and a circle formed "NO."

"Let me go through the list again and this time you tell me if you suspect them or not. First, Bea."

A small "YES" then a small "NO" then another small "YES."

"Okay, you're kind of ambivalent to her. Nate?"

A huge "YES."

"Okay. I'm with you. He's one of my top candidates."

We proceeded through the list. Willie, like me, hadn't eliminated anyone, but besides Nate, Larry was also his top person of interest.

"I'll have to keep poking at the people on my list. Kurt is also helping me. It's good to have an inside man at the police department."

I heard the front bell jangle, and who of all people but Kurt stuck his head through the curtain separating the retail area from the workshop.

I gave him what I hoped was my good-things-could-happen-if-you-got-to-know-me smile. "I was thinking about you."

He gave me his aw-shucks grin. "I was thinking about you, too. I got off my shift early and thought I'd stop by."

"Come on in."

He ambled over to where I sat in front of the sheet pan of sand. I thought of Sally Midge and her offer to do a séance. I wondered what Kurt might think of my ghost writing or maybe I should call it ghost texting.

He furled his brow. "You wrote "YES" in that pan?"

"Oh, yeah. Something I do when I need to think."

He peered more carefully. The sand swirled and "NO" replaced the "YES."

Kurt's jaw went slack. "You do magic tricks. That's really cool, Pru."

"Uh… yeah. One of my hidden talents."

"Can you do that again?"

The sand rippled and another "NO."

Kurt laughed. "Awesome."

I couldn't remember the last time someone had used that word. I decided not to risk anything else with Willie and Kurt. I didn't think Kurt would understand Willie. Maybe when our relationship had progressed a little further. "Let's go in the kitchen. I should be able to round up a snack for you."

"Great. I'm starving."

I found a package of Oreos and poured him a large glass of milk. He happily munched while I watched the kitchen curtain twitch. Kurt was too absorbed in the cookies to notice anything around him. I clenched my teeth. He would have to become more observant if he expected to become a police officer. Speaking of which, I decided to ask, "How's your studying coming for the police officer exam?"

"Gut." He chewed and swallowed. "That book is really helping me. I think I'll be ready for the next time the exam is offered."

I sighed. My *sort-of* boyfriend and his quest.

"You doing anything tonight, Pru?"

Did he intend to ask me out again? "I'm going to take a trip to collect some more driftwood and rocks in a little while. I like beachcombing at the end of the day. Then an evening of reading."

"That's good that you'll be out of the house for a while and then returning."

I craned my neck to look at him. That was an odd thing to say. "How about you?"

"I… uh… will probably be studying for the police officer exam." He smacked his right fist into his left hand. "I'm going to pass the exam. I really am." He reached for another Oreo.

I considered eating a cookie myself, but with Kurt's eager

munching I didn't want to deprive him of any extra energy. Also, given how he tore through the package, I wouldn't risk getting my fingers chewed on, although finger nibbling might be kind of romantic in a weird sort-of way, but then again, he was my *sort-of* boyfriend.

After demolishing half the package of cookies, Kurt wiped crumbs from his mouth. "I stopped by Detective Moriarty's desk right before I left the police department."

"Find anything useful?"

"Yeah. He's checking on your old… uh… boyfriend, Nate Dupres. He had noted that Nate couldn't account for his presence at the time of Bart's murder." His eyes lit up. "That could be really important."

Interesting. Detective Moriarty had listened to what I told him. Progress. "A definite clue worth following up on."

"Yeah. I'll have to discuss it with the detective tomorrow."

I held my hand up. "Whoa. You don't want him knowing you've been snooping around his desk."

"Oh, yeah. Good point, Pru."

He had a long way to go before he'd be ready to be a police officer. I never had to lose sleep over Kurt being the conniving type. That would be up to me.

"You going to Bart's funeral tomorrow?" I asked.

"I don't think I'll be able to take off. I have to work until five."

"I should stay in the shop, but I want to see if anything new turns up. I bet Detective Moriarty will be at the funeral, checking out everyone. That might be a good time for you to peruse his desk again."

"If I can't get to the funeral, I'll do that instead. I have my break at two thirty. We make a good team, Pru."

I blushed. "I think so too, Kurt."

We looked in each other's eyes, and he reached for my hand.

My fingers tingled.

I watched as his hand moved to within inches of mine when my attention was diverted by a retching sound. I raced through the curtain into the main part of the store to find Boopsie proudly guarding a hairball.

I put my hand on my hips. "Bad timing, Boopsie."

She licked her paw and yawned. So much for romance when you have a cat.

Chapter 25

AFTER KURT LEFT WITHOUT ASKING me out (and I wasn't going to hint any more), I packed up my beach bag with several plastic bags and went to where I had chained Mopsy to the lamppost between my shop and Jake's. I fastened the bundle to my handlebars, tightened my helmet and putt-putted toward Sandy Beach, the closest place for driftwood hunting.

I enjoyed this time of day as the sun dropped toward the ocean. I'd have a chance to see it sink below the horizon, remembering those good metaphors that my science teacher in fourth grade had assured me were completely inaccurate. I didn't care about the scientific correctness of the Earth turning rather than the sun sinking. Patooey on factual details.

My mind wandered for a moment until I realized that I needed to focus on the road. Mopsy could easily be overlooked by aggressive drivers particularly as dusk approached. I turned onto Beach Road and heard an engine gunning behind me. Swiveling my neck, I saw a large black SUV heading directly toward me. *Uh-oh.*

I jammed my handlebar to the right, clamped on the brake and tumbled into the grass alongside the road. I hit hard but fortunately the ground was soft enough to cushion my fall. I had a brief glance at the back of the SUV. *Check the license plate.* I only caught the letter "A."

I stood and dusted myself. No blood, No bruises. Mopsy appeared no worse for wear, other than a new dent where she had hit a rock upon landing. I shook my fist in the direction of the disappearing car. "I'll get you… you sucky undesirable vehicle." Well, what do you expect from a frazzled female?

I took out my cell phone and called Detective Moriarty to report the incident, reaching his voicemail. I asked him to call me ASAP. He was probably following some irrelevant clue. Hopefully, he'd check messages soon. Even then, I wondered if he would return my call. No telling.

My cell phone made a plaintive beeping sound. My battery was low. I hadn't noticed that I needed to charge it. Oh, well. When I got home, I'd take care of that.

I wasn't going to let that yahoo SUV driver disrupt my driftwood collecting expedition. As they say, you have to get back in the saddle after a tumble, so I did.

Not another car in sight as I continued my short journey. I came to the parking area for Sandy Beach and chained Mopsy to a tree. Then a short climb down the trail to the sand. I removed my tennis shoes and let my toes wiggle in the cool sand.

Waves broke against a rocky point, and the sun hovered above the sparkling water. A seagull slowly floated over the ocean, tilting its wings in the gentle breeze. I could have painted a picture except my art skills beyond driftwood creations ran between dismal and atrocious. We all had to find our creative niches.

Only a few footprints dotted the sand below the high tide mark. I followed the line of debris, discovering several acceptable pieces of driftwood. These found a home in my plastic bag. Next, I picked up an undamaged clam shell and a water polished red stone. I pictured this turning into a laser and shooting a red beam to zap the black SUV into smithereens. Wishful thinking.

I continued to collect flotsam and jetsam, although technically that should be floating wreckage or items jettisoned from a ship. As mentioned, I didn't bother myself with these technical details. If a hunk of wood looked interesting, I didn't care where it came from. Gnarled, misshapen, disfigured, twisted—all fit in my category of collectibles. Hey, maybe that could be the name for a new rock group—GMDT.

After I had accumulated a plastic bag full of ocean treasures, I sat on the sand to watch the sun and ocean collide. Again, not accurate, but so what?

No clouds or fog banks blocking the view, I awaited the possibility of seeing a green flash, the elusive event when the last remnant of sun disappeared. I steeled my gaze so as not to blink at the crucial moment and stared intently. There, the sun had vanished. Spots dappled my vision but nothing green.

Only once had I seen a green flash, at least I think I had seen it. That time I actually saw all kinds of colors from overdoing the sun staring. Some people thought the green flash a mythical occurrence, but Granny had reported seeing it numerous times, and she wasn't one to fabricate stories.

I stood, stretched my arms and waved a goodbye to the glow on the horizon, before picking up my bag of goodies and heading back up the trail. From the top of the cliff, I gazed one last time at the ocean. I loved living near the sea. I'd never want to become landlocked inland. No, siree. I was a coastal gal and proud of it.

I stashed my bag of ocean delivered presents, fired up Mopsy, turned on her lights and headed back toward civilization—if you could call Omnipodge civilization.

A quarter of a mile before reaching home, Mopsy sputtered and her engine died. I tried starting her again. No dice.

"Now what?" I had filled her with gas recently and that should have lasted for another month. Then I sniffed. I could smell gasoline. I looked down and saw a bubble of liquid on the outside of the gas tank. Apparently, our tumble had punched a small hole in the tank and the gas had leaked out.

My cell phone rang. Could someone on the Auto Club hot line be a better psychic than Sally Midge and be calling me because of my emergency? I answered to hear, instead, that Detective Moriarty had returned my call.

"I want to report that a black SUV tried to run me off the road."

"This is getting pretty repetitive, missy. You trying to distract my investigation?"

I clenched the phone. "Listen, carefully, Detective. Someone is out to get me. I have a piece of information for you. There's a letter "A" in the license plate. And it was definitely a California plate."

"That doesn't help a whole lot."

"It should give you something. Can't you search your vehicle database thingy? There can't be that many black SUVs with the letter "A" on the license plate."

"Probably not more than a hundred in the state."

"Check it out."

"You have anything to confess to me?"

"I confess that I'm getting pretty fed up with your negative attitude."

"Get used to it."

The connection died. I couldn't tell if he had hung up on his end or if my cell phone had died first, because my battery had definitely gone kaput.

I stared at my phone. Resisting the urge to fling it into the road, I took a deep breath. Anger wouldn't serve any good purpose. Maybe Moriarty would follow up and maybe he wouldn't. It was still up to me to move things forward on this case. And where was I? Still at square one.

No confirmed suspects, no identification for the black SUV, nothing.

I pedaled Mopsy back without any engine assist. Hard work since I wasn't used to this form of manual labor. Mopsy would have to visit Ralph's Repair Shop the next day.

By now, darkness had descended. Not that it really descended or ascended, but so what? It was dark.

After chaining Mopsy to a lamppost, I headed to my door, the siren call of a left-over ham sandwich in the fridge beaconing to me. My mouth watered. I realized I hadn't eaten anything for hours.

I reached for the door handle, and the door swung opened. I shivered. I had left the shop locked.

Chapter 26

I TIPTOED THROUGH THE DOOR. THE floor squeaked. I jumped but remembered it was only the loose floorboard from the earlier resident tearing it up to look for Willie's imaginary gold. I turned the light on. No intruder in sight.

"Hello?" My voice came out as squeaky as the floorboard. "Boopsie?" I checked the pillow. No cat in sight. "Spools?" No fishing line-entangled dog appeared either.

This wasn't good.

I stepped into my workshop and grabbed the largest piece of driftwood on my table. Armed, I scanned the area. "Willie?"

No curtain swishing or letters appearing in the sheet pan of sand.

Was my haunt sleeping upstairs? I didn't know if I wanted to go up to check.

Should I call 9-1-1? Maybe that would be the wise thing to do. I reached for my cell phone and then remembered it had died. Besides, I could never get reception near my store.

Next choice—the land line. I went over to the counter where the phone rested. It wasn't there. My foot hit something on the floor. I reached over and picked up the phone. No cord attached. *Uh-oh.* I gulped. That could have been Spools. He'd done that trick once before when he became tangled in the cord and ripped it off the phone and wall jack. Or it could be an intruder making sure I couldn't seek help.

What to do?

Then the lights went out.

I resisted the urge to run out the front door screaming. No. I wouldn't be a shrieking female. Obviously, the circuit breaker had gone out. I'd have to go into the basement to reset it.

In the pitch black, I felt my way into the kitchen and located my flashlight in the cupboard. I turned it on.

A weak beam blinked. Another battery ready to die.

I flashed the faint glow toward the basement door.

It was ajar.

I knew I had left it shut. Willie's wind wasn't strong enough to open that door, and certainly neither Spools nor Boopsie had learned how to open doors.

This wasn't good.

I knew I should leave, but I couldn't give up. I squared my shoulders. With the flashlight in my left hand and the driftwood club in my right hand, I pushed the basement door fully open with my shoe.

It creaked loudly.

I shivered. What was down there?

I put my right foot on the first step. Another loud creak.

Pausing to listen, I thought I heard the sound of heavy breathing. I tilted my ear. No, nothing.

I put my left foot on the next stair.

"Creak."

I jumped.

My motion jiggled the flashlight. The dim beam went out, and I didn't have any spare batteries.

That turned out to be the least of my worries, because I heard a whoosh of air and the basement door slammed shut behind me.

What had I gotten myself into?

My chest seized with fear. Forward or backward?

The lights flashed on.

"Surprise!" came a chorus of shouts from the basement floor.

I looked down to see a crowd standing there in party hats holding a banner proclaiming, "Happy Birthday, Pru."

I let out a loud breath. Because of the murder investigation, I had forgotten it was my birthday.

Granny stepped forward and blew a tin horn. "We're here to help you celebrate, Ladybug."

I put my hand to my breast to still the rapid beating. "Did you plan this, Granny?"

"Sho' nuff. Come on down and have some birthday cake. A cake in time saves nine."

I staggered down the remaining stairs and set down the dead flashlight and piece of driftwood.

Granny wrapped her arms around me. "Bet you didn't expect this."

"You can say that again."

"I bet you didn't expect this. We snookered you good. While the cats away, the mice have a field day."

Herb dashed over and embraced me. "Happy Birthday."

I looked around the room. The other shopkeepers were there: Bea Potter, Flo Florrest and Jake Yalley with his arm around Sally Midge. My heart beat faster again. And Kurt stood there with a goofy grin on his face. He waggled his fingers at me.

Boopsie pranced over and gave me a fuzz-by followed by Spools racing around. I noticed he had the missing phone cord wrapped around his paws.

Then my gaze fell upon a table covered with a bright pink paper tablecloth and containing plates of cookies, bowls of potato chips, drinks and a large cake.

Granny went over and lit the candles on the cake. Then she signaled to me. "Don't stand there gawking. Come blow out the candles. Just don't spit in the breeze."

Everyone sang a dissonant, "Happy birthday to you…"

I wiped away a tear. "Aw. What a great bunch of friends."

Granny held up a knife. "Make a wish."

I looked toward Kurt, registering my wish, took a deep breath and blew out the candles. Maybe I would get my wish.

Then the candles sputtered back to burning again.

Everyone cheered.

Granny held her fist in the air. "Gotcha with the trick candles."

I guessed I would have to work harder to get my wish.

"Granny, how did you know I would come down here?"

"You're predictable, Ladybug. When Herb tripped the circuit breaker, I knew you'd try to be the independent woman and come turn it back on. Then we waited quietly."

"Although I almost giggled when Jake tickled me," Sally Midge tweaked Jake's cheek.

"I guess I should have spotted Bessie in the parking area, Granny."

She pointed to a pair of walking poles resting against the basement wall. "Nope. I walked over. I wasn't going to risk spoiling the surprise."

I heard loud stomping on the stairs and flinched at the sight of Nate Dupres arriving.

I glared at him. "What are you doing here?"

"I heard there was a party and stopped by to wish you Happy Birthday."

"Okay. You've done it. Bye."

He grinned. "Is that any way to welcome your old boyfriend?"

Herb stood erect and thrust out his chest. "You want me to throw him out, Pru?"

"No, we don't need to disrupt the party." I gave a resigned sigh. "Have some cake, Nate. Then you can leave."

Granny cut the cake, and everyone had a piece.

I took a bite and relished the delectable peppermint flavor. "You made my favorite, Granny."

"Yup. With my secret ingredient. Honey. I know you love honey, Ladybug. It's bees you can't stand."

Kurt furled his brow. "You don't like bees?"

I shivered. "They scare the bejabbers out of me."

"You allergic to bee stings?" Kurt asked.

"No. A bee stung me when I was two years old, and ever since I run whenever I see one. I hate bees!"

I didn't realize how loud I had shouted.

The room became silent, and everyone stared at me.

Heat rose up my neck. "Enough of that. Eat up."

Everyone munched and chattered. I received a round of hugs, except for Kurt who only waved and grinned at me. "I was given the assignment to get you out of the shop, but you said you were going driftwood collecting so I notified your grandmother to get everything ready."

"Thanks, Kurt. It was quite a surprise."

Nate mingled with the others. Every time he moved toward me, I disappeared in another direction. I might have let him stay, but it didn't mean that I wanted to talk to him. What a dipstick.

Unfortunately, in the small space Nate finally cornered me. He put his hands against the wall, I was trapped. "We need to talk, Pru."

"No thanks."

Granny marched over. "Is he bothering you?"

"Yes."

Granny grabbed one of her walking poles and whacked Nate. "I believe in doing unto others until they get their comeuppance. Out."

He stepped away from the wall, and I used the opportunity to move out of his reach.

Granny went into a fighting stance and raised her walking stick again. "Haya!"

Nate's mouth dropped open, and then he hightailed it for the stairs.

As his footfalls receded, Granny set the pole against the wall again and dusted her hands together. "The walking stick is mightier than the sword."

A round of applause erupted from the other partygoers.

After I finished my third piece of cake, I pulled Granny aside. "How did you get in here?"

"You must have forgotten, but you made an extra key for me."

Then I remembered what I had thought of before. Someone had entered my store to kill Bart. Could that person have a key to my shop and residence as well?

Chapter 27

I AWOKE THE NEXT MORNING WITH a headache. I had overdosed on honey-infused cake the night before. I was the girl who couldn't say no—when it came to Granny's cake. A good stiff cup of black coffee did the trick. My head responded by reverting to only a dull throb.

First order of business—attend to Mopsy. She was a little sluggish as I pedaled to Ralph's Repair Shop. Ralph greeted me with a huge smile, obviously realizing money would flow from my bank account into his. "What is it this time, Pru?"

"Hole in the gas tank."

"No problemo. I have a spare tank in inventory that I can install this morning."

"You actually have the right part in stock?"

"Of course. I've stocked all the parts you could use." He ticked off on his fingers. "You've already needed a new fender, front wheel, back wheel, carburetor, starter, brakes. It was only a matter of time before you would have to replace the gas tank."

Was I that predictable or that accident prone?

"When can you have it ready, Ralph?"

"By lunchtime."

I walked back to my shop, calculating that I had spent all the money I'd earned in the last two days. That Spring Break rush had better be good.

Boopsie greeted my return with a deluxe hairball. That cat could cough up more hair than she had on her body. I stared at what she had done. Fortunately, I didn't try to read anything into it like Sally Midge had tried to do.

Spools came out of the workshop in his usual tangle of fishing line. No matter where I stored it, he found a way to get into it.

"Are you going to give me trouble this morning, too, Willie?"

The curtain bounced up and down.

"Maybe you picked up some new clues during my birthday party?"

The curtain swished back and forth.

"What good are you anyway? You're supposed to help me solve the murder."

Our conversation was interrupted by the door bell jangling, and a family of four entered. Two boys who I estimated to be six and four jumped up and batted at a mobile.

"Don't touch that," the pregnant mom shouted.

Like any kids their age, they ignored her until the dad stepped over and pulled them away. The boys immediately picked up driftwood creations.

"Oops," the older one said as he dropped the piece to the floor. Several imbedded stones popped out of the wood.

"Oops," the younger one said as he threw his piece of driftwood down. It split in half.

The mom picked up the pieces and set them on the counter. "Not very durable, are they?"

I glared at the two monsters. Maybe this would be a good remedy for my ticking biological clock.

After the family left the store without offering to compensate me for the damage and without buying anything, I resisted the urge to put a hex on the mom to have quintuplet boys.

I retired to the workshop to repair the damage, gluing new stones in place and selecting a new piece of driftwood to replace the split piece.

With no other customers, I worked for a while with Willie on his reading and writing in the sheet pan. He had become quite proficient at writing the names of the suspects. We sounded out a few words and he wrote, "HAPY BRTDAY."

"Aw, Willie, how sweet. I'd give you a hug if you had any form."

He drew a smiley face in the sand.

"Where did you learn that? Oh, I guess you've been watching me on the computer."

I looked at my watch. Time to go retrieve Mopsy and meet Herb for our scheduled lunch.

*   *   *   *   *

Mopsy purred as I drove away from Ralph's. In addition to the new gas tank, she had received a bath, one of Ralph's free courtesy services. You wouldn't find something like that in Los Angeles.

After attaching Mopsy to a lamppost, I sauntered in to the diner to find Herb in a booth, holding a menu.

I slipped into the other side of the booth. "Why are you looking at the menu? You know everything here by heart, and there are never any new items."

He made a shushing sound and whispered, "I'm watching Larry Ludwick and your ex-boyfriend at the table across the room."

I started to turn, but Herb grabbed my arm. "Don't look. They have some sort of intense conversation going on."

"I didn't notice them when I came in. I wonder what those two conniving so-and-sos are up to?"

"They've been talking Italian, you know, waving their arms for the last five minutes. I wish I could hear what they're saying."

"Whatever it is, I'm sure they're up to no good." I slunk down in the booth. "As long as Nate doesn't spot me. I had enough of him crashing my birthday party last night. That lizard liver."

"Whoa, Princess. You and your cussing. You do have a way of attracting them."

I groaned. "Don't remind me. If only Kurt showed more interest."

"He'll get there. I saw him watching you last night. He only needs a little encouragement."

"Like with a cattle prod."

Herb giggled. "Oh, Princess. You have a way with words."

We ordered, and I kept out of sight as much as possible. My burger and Herb's salad arrived, and I felt the grease coursing through my arteries to dilute the sweets from the night before.

"Have you picked up any new clues to help solve Bart's murder?" I asked.

"Nope. But Detective Moriarty came by my shop and sniffed in all the jars. In addition to accusations about the murder, he hinted again that I must be hiding marijuana in the shop." He snickered. "Got his nose in a jar of cayenne and had a sneezing fit. Served him right."

"Maybe I should buy some from you to put in my shop for the next time he comes to harass me."

"I'll be happy to make a donation for that purpose."

We bantered for five minutes, and then Herb put money on the table for his share of lunch, before excusing himself to get back to his shop. I knew I should do the same, but with Larry and Nate being together, I had another idea. I wondered if Larry Ludwick might be the owner of a black SUV. I scooted around to the other side of the booth and employed Herb's trick of holding up a menu so I could watch Larry and Nate. They still engaged in an animated conversation.

The waitress stopped by. "You want dessert?"

"Uh… only looking. Nothing right now."

Shortly, Larry and Nate stood. I took money out of my purse to pay for my portion of lunch and waited for my targets to leave.

Then I raced to the door and saw Larry and Nate go in opposite directions.

I followed Larry. Sleuth Pru in action. He went around the corner, and I pursued or as Jake Yalley would say Pru-sued.

Larry strolled another block and climbed into a red Corvette.

So much for my theory on the black SUV.

Chapter 28

BACK IN MY SHOP, I had a customer come in and buy two mobiles. I could afford another lunch or two.

At one thirty, I placed the "be back" sign in the window and called out to Willie. "You're in charge for a while. I have a funeral to go to."

I felt a breeze pass my face in response. With Willie, Boopsie and Spools, I didn't know what condition my place would be in when I returned.

I slipped on black slacks, a black blouse and black pumps. I now appeared appropriately somber to attend Bart's service.

Mopsy provided a quick ride for me, and I arrived to find a large black hearse parked in front. The letters on the side proclaimed our local mortuary, "Reese's Peace." I entered the church with my best serious expression plastered on my puss. An attendant I didn't recognize handed me a program, and I found a seat next to Herb in the back pew.

"Long time no see, Princess."

"Back at you. You scoping out all the suspects?"

"Everyone is here. And our favorite detective." Herb pointed to the row ahead of us on the other side of the aisle.

"He fits right in. He looks like a mortician, anyway."

I scanned the audience. In the front row, Sally Midge wore a black dress with a black veil and rested her head against the shoulder of Jake's black suit coat. Spaced around the church sat Bea, Flo, Larry

Ludwick and Nate Dupres. Then my heart sank. No Kurt. As he had surmised, he apparently couldn't get off work from the police department. The one person I wanted to see.

Oh, well. I could be in detecting mode rather than flirting mode this afternoon.

After Bette Midler's "Wind Beneath My Wings" played over the sound system, the minister came up to the altar and held his arms out. "Please stand and sing hymn number two-twenty-four."

By the time I opened the hymnal and found the right page, half the song had been completed. Not that it would have done me any good with my voice. Herb gave me a disgusted glance when I finally belted out the last verse. Friends were supposed to be understanding of minor flaws like not being able to carry a tune. At least no one tried to kick me out of the service.

The minister then proceeded to recount Bart Cunard's life, mentioning the things he had done for the town of Omnipodge. I wondered if he was referring to some other Bart Cunard than the one I knew. Nothing about being a money grubbing, sexist pig and harasser of his tenants.

Oh, well. I guess I could forgive a few good words at the end even if Bart didn't deserve them.

Finally, the minister said, "Please stand to pay tribute to this stellar member of our community."

No one stood. I poked Herb in the ribs and leaned over to whisper, "There's the appropriate tribute."

The minister cleared his throat. "Please... uh... stand to sing hymn three-twenty-six." This time people got to their feet.

I mouthed the words to prevent any further damage to Herb's tune-sensitive ears. He responded with a smile and nod. Friends do these small favors for each other.

The minister then asked if anyone wanted to make a tribute to the departed. I certainly wouldn't, other than muttering to myself,

"Good riddance."

Again, no one stood. Finally, Sally Midge rose and went up to the altar microphone. "Bart was once a good man. Too bad he turned into such a slug." Then she sat down. There weren't even any gasps. Everyone agreed with the last part of her statement.

No one else ventured up to say a word so the minister declared the service over and invited everyone to join a reception in the church basement. We filed out and down the stairs to find a table covered with veggies, fruit, cookies and apple juice. No one would get drunk and rowdy at this wake.

"Let's split up and work the room," I whispered to Herb. "See if we can pick up any good scuttlebutt."

He saluted me. "Right-o, chief detective."

I watched Larry Ludwick and Nate Dupres converse in the corner. Hadn't they had enough time together over lunch? Finally, Nate walked toward the snacks, and I slunk through the crowd to avoid him. I approached Larry.

"I didn't know you and Nate were such good friends."

He eyed me warily. "Not friends. He's doing some work for me."

I tried to imagine what that might be. Rough up some tenants who weren't paying? Harass people who didn't want to sell out at rock bottom prices?

"Anything new on what will happen to the Omnipodge Village Center?"

"It will keep running as it has for the time being. But things could change in the future."

"How so?"

"There could be other uses for the property."

I gulped. "Are you not going to renew our leases?"

He gave me a steely stare. "I didn't say that. Stay tuned."

Great. I regarded Larry closely. He struck me as someone who wouldn't think twice about killing if it improved his financial position. I spun on my heels and went over to speak with Bea.

"Have you heard that Larry Ludwick might do something different with the Omnipodge Village Center?"

Her eyes widened. "No. That doesn't sound good."

"He's now majority owner. I just spoke with him, and he dropped a hint of making some changes but didn't elaborate."

"I'll have to look into that as well. On a more pleasant subject, will you be at the cooking class tomorrow night?"

"I wouldn't miss it. I need whatever help I can get. What's the subject?"

"Desserts."

"Yum." Maybe if I could bake cookies, pies and cake I wouldn't have to resort to Oreos the next time Kurt came over.

I heard a loud "whap." Looking in the direction of the sound, I saw Nate holding his cheek and Sally Midge stalking away.

I followed Sally Midge who went to the snack table, grabbed a glass of juice and guzzled it.

"What happened?" I asked.

Her eyes flared. "That Nate Dupres made an inappropriate comment."

"Sounds like him."

At that moment Detective Moriarty slithered up to us. "How are my two favorite suspects?"

"How's our favorite incompetent detective," Sally Midge replied. "Have you arrested anyone yet?"

"Any volunteers?"

Sally Midge's nostrils flared. "I hope you're doing something to find the real culprit rather than bothering us."

"Oh, I think I'm on the right path."

Sally Midge threw the paper cup in the trash and sashayed away.

"You have a real knack for making friends, Detective," I said.

"I'm not paid to make friends. Do you have anything to confess?"

"I confess that I'm getting mighty tired of your inane comments."

I turned my back on him and went over to speak with Flo.

"That Detective Moriarty," I said.

"I know what you mean. No results. Only accusations." Flo leaned closer to me. "But I'm worried. Another skein of Vicuna has disappeared from my storage area."

"Have you seen anyone back there?"

"That's the problem. I never let anyone go into the back of my store and I keep the door locked when I'm not in the shop."

"Does anyone have a key?"

"Not that I'm aware of."

My gut clenched. There was something going on with keys around the Omnipodge Village Center. "Maybe it's time for us to change our locks."

Flo nodded. "That's a good idea. I'm going to call a locksmith right away. Let's see if the other shopkeepers want to change their locks as well."

Chapter 29

TRUE TO FLO'S WORD, I had only returned to my shop and changed the sign to "open" when a short man sporting a thick black moustache and carrying a black bag appeared on my doorstep. When I said short, I meant short. He couldn't have been over four foot eleven. I first thought he might be a doctor making a house call until I remembered that that never happened any more. He introduced himself as Lucian the locksmith. It had a ring to it.

He rekeyed my front and back doors and within fifteen minutes handed me two keys. "All hunky dory. Forty bucks."

I paid him from the cash register, and he proceeded to Jake's shop. He had a busy rest of the afternoon ahead. Not a bad occupation. Forty dollars for fifteen minutes of work. But he had travel time and overhead like any small business person. The emphasis on small.

I entertained Willie with some reading and writing in the sheet pan and even had a customer stop by to purchase a mobile, allowing me to recoup the cost of the locksmith. If I could stop incurring unexpected expenses and have a few more customers, I might be able to pay the upcoming month's rent. With Bart gone, I still didn't know exactly how that would work. Would Larry Ludwick, as the majority owner, be coming around to collect? I'd have to see what transpired.

After closing the shop for the day, I heated up canned ravioli, careful not to burn it. Fortunately, I didn't become distracted and served myself a steaming bowl. Boopsie and Spools sat on the floor with such baleful expressions that I put a few pieces of ravioli in two bowls and placed the treats on the floor. They eagerly shared my meal. Fortunately, Willie only needed to eat invisible ghost treats. My day after birthday party. I only wished Kurt would knock on my door, but no dice.

I washed my dishes and set them in the drainer. As dusk descended, I became restless and decided to take a ride out to the bluff and enjoy the last glimmer of twilight and watch the stars. Knowing this was a dangerous time to be on the roads, I turned on Mopsy's lights and putted away.

I kept a keen eye ahead and in my mirror to be prepared for any traffic. It was easy for a fast-moving car to overlook me. On the outskirts of town, I saw a pair of bright lights approaching me. I pulled over to the side of the road to be careful and watched as a black SUV roared past. I spun quickly to try to catch a license plate.

I could only make out an "A" and an "N." Could be the same vehicle I had encountered before. This time it didn't see me and try to run me off the road.

I let my heart rate settle and continued my journey along the cliff road. I pulled over and pushed Mopsy behind a bush where no one would notice her. Then I sat on the bluff overlooking the ocean. I had missed my chance to see the green flash, but I watched a few clouds along the horizon reflect the last faint pink of sunlight. As it became dark, I lay on my back to try to spot the first star. I saw an emerging object a hand's length above the horizon. Must have been Venus. As it became darker, true stars emerged. I lay there contemplating my miniscule existence in this vast universe.

I must have dozed for a while because, my eyes blinked open, and I couldn't see any stars any longer. I heard a rumble of thunder and the wind blew through my hair. I sat up and rubbed my eyes. Then a loud howl pierced the night.

I shivered. A wolf? Then a scream. It came from the beach below the bluff. I should have ignored it and headed home immediately, but if someone was in danger, I had to do something. I jumped to my feet and headed to the wooden stairs that led to the beach below.

I put my foot on the first stair and it creaked loudly. It reminded me of my basement stairs. I lifted my feet carefully and descended, keeping my hand on the wooden railing but being careful not to collect any splinters.

When I reached the sand, I noticed a faint glow around the bend where the cliff face jutted out onto the beach.

Should I investigate? My stomach told me no, but I had come this far. I shuffled through the sand and peered around the cliff.

A bonfire burned with a group of college kids sitting around with bags of chips and marshmallows on sticks over the flames.

I let out a whoosh of air and then joined the group. They offered me s'mores, and I gladly accepted since they were favorites of mine. With my fingers gooey and my sugar fix in place, I sat to listen to them tell ghost stories.

As they broke into couples and disappeared to different places along the beach, I thanked the remaining twosome for the treat and excused myself. As I trudged back to the stairs, I wondered if Kurt and I would ever come to the beach at night, go off into the darkness and…

Things had a long way to progress before such an occurrence with my *sort-of* boyfriend.

Mopsy had waited patiently for me and started without a whimper. We putted back to civilization with not so much as a black SUV encounter or a leaky gas tank.

With Mopsy chained to the lamppost for the night, I sauntered to the front door of my shop/residence. As I reached for my new key, I noticed a piece of paper wedged half way under the door. I bent over and picked it up. In the dim light I read, "Stay out of what doesn't concern you."

Before you could say, "threatening note," I had the key in the lock, dashed in and slammed the door behind me. Bracing myself against the wall, I turned on the light to find everything in order—Boopsie asleep on her pillow and Spools standing in the middle of the floor, wagging his tail, which trailed fishing line.

Making sure I had the bolt set, I pulled out my cell to call Detective Moriarty. As usual, no bars. I reached for the landline and punched in Detective Moriarty's number, which had become imbedded in my frazzled brain. To my surprise he answered.

"I received another threatening note," I said breathing heavily.

"One of your stunts?"

"No. Someone left a warning note under my front door. You should come take a look."

He snorted. "Okay, okay. I'll be there in ten minutes."

The ten minutes grew to twenty, but finally he knocked on my door. Being cautious, I shouted, "Who is it?"

"Detective Moriarty."

The tone of voice convinced me he was authentic.

I let him in and showed him the note I had set on the counter. He went over and looked at it before putting on a latex glove and depositing it in a paper bag. I guess he was taking me seriously.

I tapped the counter. "I have one other piece of information for you."

"You're full of it this evening."

I ignored his comment. "I saw a black SUV again. This time I checked the license plate and picked out both an "N" and an "A.""

"You've got to be kidding me. You called me out here, and that's all you have?"

"It may be more than you've found."

He glared at me but jotted a note without any further snide

comments. Progress. Then he snapped his notepad closed. "Probably nonsense, but I need to follow any clues."

Hmm. That meant he didn't yet know who the murderer was. I didn't know if that was bad or good for me.

Chapter 30

THE NEXT MORNING BROUGHT SUNSHINE and a new outlook on life for me. No sense sulking and making everyone around me miserable. I would be positive, do my part to contribute to the welfare of the universe, smile and be cheerful. With that resolved, I changed into jogging shorts, put on my tennies and decided I'd start my day with a little exercise. Nothing like running to get the juices flowing and to take a step toward good health. I went into the front of my shop and stretched, touching my toes and holding for a minute, then bending my hips.

I pictured myself gracefully loping along the beach, long strides leaving firm impressions in the sand, the smell of salt spray and the wind twirling my hair. I could almost hear the theme song from *Chariots of Fire*.

What I really heard instead was buzzing. What the heck was that? I realized the sound came from outside, so I opened my front door. "Yikes!" I slammed it as fast as I'd opened it. A beehive with a swarm of angry residents rested on my doorstep.

I broke out in a sweat. The thing in the world that most scared me was a single bee. You can imagine my response to a whole hive within striking distance. I bolted my door. I didn't know what good that would do, but I wasn't going to take any chances. Then I checked every window to make sure they were tightly closed.

My hands shook as I reached for the phone to call 9-1-1. I dropped the receiver and had to steady it with both hands, which presented a problem in punching in the digits. Finally, I freed one hand to try to accomplish the task. It took me two tries to hit the required buttons.

"What is the nature of your emergency?"

"There's a beehive right outside my door. I can't go out. I'm trapped. I need assistance. Help."

"Please stay calm and give me your name and address."

For a moment I couldn't remember my name. Then it came back to me. I took a deep breath, and with all the mental acuity I could rally, I recited my name and address.

"We'll have someone there shortly."

I wondered how long shortly would take. I paced back and forth while Boopsie and Spools stared at me as if I were nuts.

Around bees I did go nuts.

Finally, after what seemed like hours, I heard a siren. As it became louder, my tinnitus kicked in, and I covered my right ear with my hand. Finally, the siren stopped. I peeked out through the curtains to see a fire truck pull into the parking area. Then two large men in bunker gear trudged toward my shop.

I looked more carefully. One was Kurt! My hero had come to rescue me. In spite of my predicament, a warmth spread through my chest.

They stopped before reaching the beehive and conferred. If it had been me, I would have hightailed it to the next county, but my hero and his companion didn't shirk from their responsibility.

To my dismay they turned and returned to the fire truck. Had they abandoned me? I was tempted to get on the phone and call to complain.

They fiddled around in the truck for a few minutes, and to my relief trudged back toward me. They wore thick gloves, had masks on and carried a tarp. They threw the tarp over the beehive and carried it away.

I could imagine the hoard of angry bees circling the two heroic firefighters. They placed the tarp-covered object in a compartment of the truck and drove away. I waited. I looked out the window and didn't spot any errant bees. Still, I had no intention of venturing outside. So much for my early morning running plans.

I pulled the curtains wide open and positioned myself on my stool looking out the window. I saw no bees fly by. A good sign. I figured I might be able to go out my front door within a week.

Fifteen minutes later Kurt's pickup truck pulled into the parking area. He sauntered to my door and knocked.

I opened it a crack.

"Are all the bees gone?"

"Yup."

I resisted the urge to run into his arms, but I would wait for him to make the first move, the big lug.

He shuffled his foot. "You okay, Pru?"

"A little shaky. I hate bees."

"You mentioned that before. Do you know how the beehive got here?"

"No clue. Someone has it in for me." Then I remembered the birthday party. I had told everyone there how much I detested bees. Had one of the murder suspects decided to threaten me? I mentally reviewed my list of suspects. The only one who wasn't at my birthday party—Larry Ludwick.

He was the one I most wanted to be the bad guy, that is besides Nate, who had been at the party, uninvited.

"Come on in. You must be hungry after risking your life to get rid of the bees. I can fix you a cup of instant coffee and make some toast."

He regarded his Mickey Mouse watch. "Only for a few minutes. I have my shift at the police department coming up."

We went into the kitchen, and I put two cups of water in the microwave to heat and dropped two pieces of bread in the toaster.

"What did you do with the beehive?"

He scratched his arm. I wondered if he had been bitten but then decided he was nervous. "We took it into the woods on the north side of town and set it on a log. The bees flew around like crazy. Then we skedaddled."

I liked that fire fighter term—skedaddle. "Remind me never to go into the woods where you left it."

"You sure don't like bees, Pru."

I was tempted to reply, "You can say that again," but I didn't want him to say it again as he was apt to. Instead, I looked into his brown eyes and almost became lost. "Thank you for saving me."

He smiled, and I took a step toward him. Maybe he would put his arms around me. Should I make the first move and throw myself against him? I had no time to take action because my attention was diverted by a scraping sound, and Spools dashed into the kitchen with fishing line attached to a piece of driftwood trailing him.

I bent down to untangle him. "How do you get into these predicaments?"

He had outdone himself, and it took me five minutes to free him.

"Pru, there's something's burning," Kurt announced, his firefighter instincts on high alert.

I sniffed. Burnt toast. The dang toaster hadn't popped when it was supposed to. I pulled the lever and two charred pieces of toast popped up.

I threw them in the sink and opened the microwave. The water was hot in the two cups. I put in the instant coffee and stirred. Success—I hadn't ruined the coffee.

We sat at my dining nook table and sipped our brew. The moment had passed of progressing to a hug. I hugged my cup in silence.

Kurt finished his coffee, smacked his lips and stood. "Off to work."

"Thanks again, Kurt."

He waved and departed.

I had been a woman in distress and didn't even end up in his arms. This relationship would require more effort.

Chapter 31

I GATHERED MY TROOPS TO TRY to figure out what to do. There they were: a cat, a dog and a ghost (I had to assume Willie was present). What more could a girl ask for?

I could put up with a black SUV, Detective Moriarty's snide comments and even a dead body in my shop, but a beehive outside my front door was another matter. I had to get to the bottom of this latest development.

I regarded Boopsie who sat on her pillow nonchalantly licking her paw. Other than coughing up hairballs, she was useless at giving any warnings. "Boopsie, you need to start earning your tuna. I want you to pay more attention to anyone sneaking around outside."

She yawned and sneezed. So much for my first ally.

I stared at Spools.

He looked up at me with his sad droopy eyes.

"Some watch dog. You didn't even bark to let me know someone had snuck up to my front door."

He panted and wagged his tail.

I let out a resigned sigh. "Willie, I guess it's up to you and me to figure out what happened."

A breeze ruffled my hair.

"Come on. Let's go do some writing."

I marched into the work area and smoothed out the sand in the sheet pan. I assumed Willie had followed me. I hoped to get more out of him than I had with the two useless animals I fed and housed.

"Let's go over anything you might have seen last night. First of all, I've suspected for some time that you can't go outside. Is that correct?"

The letters "YES" appeared.

"That's too bad. Otherwise, I could station you as a watchman. Okay, were you asleep in the spare bedroom all last night?"

"NO."

I perked up. "Maybe you saw something?"

"YES."

"All right. Now we're getting somewhere. Did you hear anything?"

"NO."

"Knowing how snoopy you are, you must have looked outside. Did you happen to peek through the curtains?"

"YES."

"Did you see someone?"

"NO."

I thought for a moment. With Willie's limited writing skill, I had been playing twenty questions with him. Maybe there was another way. "Willie, can you draw a picture of what you saw?"

"YES."

"Good. Go ahead."

The wind swirled the sand smooth and then a curve appeared and slowly a picture emerged. I leaned over and looked at it. "I can't figure out what you drew. It looks like an upside-down turtle."

On the side of the sand came the upside-down word, "NO."

I realized that Willie had been writing from the other side of the table. I turned the sheet pan around and saw the distinct outline of a car. "That's it. You saw a car in the parking area."

"YES."

"Could you tell what color it was?"

"YES."

Now we were making progress. I looked around the room. "Make something move that's the color of the car you saw."

For a moment nothing budged. Then the lid of a small black cardboard box that contained red polished rocks flapped.

"I'll be darned. You saw a black car. I bet it was the black SUVs that tried to run me off the road."

I thought of calling Detective Moriarty to report this. Then I realized my predicament. I could imagine the conversation with him asking me who had seen the car and me explaining that a ghost had. Right. No way would I bring that up. He'd send me to the loony bin.

I wished I could confide in Kurt, but he might also think I was nuts, and I didn't want to jeopardize our extremely slow-evolving relationship.

Only one other person to turn to. Granny.

I picked up the landline and called. She answered and voiced her delight at hearing from me.

"I have a little problem," I said.

"I'll help take care of the baby when it comes."

"Not that kind of problem."

"Darn. I want to be a great grandma. Good things come to a woman who has waited tables. Get with it, girl."

"I need to get married first."

"Pooh. You can have a kid first. Make love not warplanes."

I groaned. "You're not being helpful, Granny. My problem is that someone left a beehive in front of my shop last night."

"Not a big deal. Call the fire department."

"They already came and removed it. My problem is I'm trying to find out who left it. I had a conversation with Wrong Way Willie—"

"Cool. He's talking?"

"Not that kind of conversation. I've been teaching him to write in a sheet pan."

"How can you write in a sheet pan? Don't go getting senile on me, Ladybug."

This conversation wasn't going the way I wanted it to. "I filled the sheet pan with sand, and Willie writes in the sand."

"Why didn't you say so? That makes sense. How's his spelling?"

"He's actually illiterate, but I'm teaching him."

"I'll be danged. I knew you'd make a good teacher. What's your problem or are you going to palaver all day?"

I squeezed the receiver with all my might. There were times like this when I wanted to wring Granny's neck. "It's like this. Through answering yes and no questions and drawing a picture, Willie indicated he saw a black car last night when the beehive was left. I can't call the police and tell them that a ghost saw the car. I think it's the same car, a black SUV, that tried to run me off the road twice."

"You and I need to form a posse, Ladybug. I'll cruise around in Bessie and see if I can spot the SOB. You should also take Mopsy out for a spin. Between the two of us we can track down the perp. Hell hath no fury like a woman scourged."

Chapter 32

AFTER A MORNING OF WOMANING the shop and selling a few driftwood creations, I called to consult with Granny again.

"Did you and Bessie find the black SUV this morning?"

"Nope. We made the rounds. Close, but no cigarette. I thought I had spotted it once but it turned out to a black hearse. I was ready to run it off the road when I realized my mistake. Good thing. It would have put a dent in Bessie if I had done that."

"I'm going to give it a try."

"Running it off the road?"

"No. Seeing if I can find it."

"Go get 'em, Ladybug. But be careful. This thing is a two-edged street. You need to find the SOB but not get hurt yourself."

"I'll be careful." I signed off and squared my shoulders to convince myself of my bravery. Still, as Granny always said, I had moths in my stomach.

I closed up over lunch and grabbed my helmet. Mopsy seemed in good spirits as she putted past the post office and up Main Street. Not a black SUV in sight. I turned on Maple and passed Ellie's Elegants, resisting the urge to window shop for a dazzling gown. I couldn't afford one and didn't have anywhere to wear it to, anyway. Unless I could get Kurt to ask me to the Omnipodge Ball in June. I pushed aside thoughts of evening wear and of reluctant *sort-of* boyfriends. Besides, I was on a mission.

We cruised on with no success. I checked my watch and decided to stop for a quick hot dog at Doggie Dogs. With a lump in my stomach, not from sadness, I continued to putt through town. I vowed to give it another fifteen minutes before heading back to the shop. I could only do so much and still run a business.

As I passed Hank's Hardware, I spotted a black car in the parking lot. I pulled in and came to a stop. Sure enough, a black SUV. It had an A and an N in the license plate. Jackpot! I pulled out my pen and pad and wrote the full license number down. I was getting somewhere.

Back at the shop, I prepared to pursue the license number when a customer entered. After she perused the store for half an hour, she bought a mobile. Money was flowing again. With no other customers in sight, I returned to my mission.

Now, I could report the license plate number. Then a concern nibbled at the back of my scheming brain. Would Detective Moriarty actually follow up or would he dismiss this as another of my "diversionary stunts?"

I couldn't risk a harassing encounter and lack of action. I had to find a way of tracing the license plate number.

Another idea occurred to me. I called police dispatch. A female voice answered.

"May I speak with Kurt Whelan, please."

"One moment."

I waited, and then Kurt came on the line.

"Kurt, this is Pru. I have a favor to ask."

"I'm not supposed to take personal calls on this number," he whispered.

"This isn't a personal call. This is police business. I want you to check a license plate for me."

"I shouldn't do something like that. I'm only a dispatcher."

"But you could get into the database, I bet."

"Yeah."

"Think of this as a practice exercise to prepare for the next police officer exam. Test your skills."

There was a pause the line. I tweaked the phone cord like a fisherman. I had him hooked. Next, I had to reel him in.

"I don't know."

"Think of the attention you'll get when we crack this case. You'll be a shoe-in to become a police officer. Give it a shot."

Silence again. Then a sigh. "I guess."

"Attaboy." I gave him the license plate number. "Check on this. It may be the person who left the beehive and tried to run me off the road. I'm convinced it ties into the murder. You and I will get to the bottom of this. Why don't you stop by my place after work, and you can give me the information then."

We signed off. The wheels of crime-stopping were turning.

The afternoon went slowly. Three people entered the store, but only one bought anything. I eagerly awaited Kurt's arrival. I didn't know what I anticipated more, seeing his handsome, smiling face or the information he'd bear.

Finally, at five thirty my *sort-of* boyfriend appeared. He handed me a sheet of paper. "Here's what I found."

"I hope it didn't cause you any trouble."

"Nope. I borrowed an unused computer." His eyes lit up. "You were right, Pru. It gave me a chance to learn more."

I looked at the sheet of paper expecting to find Nate Dupres as the owner, but it had the name of Samuel Jenkins and an address in Los Angeles. Who the heck was Samuel Jenkins, and what was he doing in Omnipodge?

I had a new clue to pursue. Once again, Pru the poet. I looked into my *sort-of* boyfriend's eyes. "How can I ever thank you, Kurt?"

He lowered his chin and scrapped his shoe. "Aw shucks."

I decided this might be my chance. I stepped toward him with my arms ready to embrace him.

At that moment a swirl of wind kicked up dust from the window sill.

"Ouch." Kurt's hand went to his face. "I have dirt in my eye. I better go get it washed out. I have special drops for this at my place."

"Wait, I can look at it."

He turned and dashed out the door.

I watched the retreating figure as he stumbled toward the parking lot, climbed in his pickup and drove away.

I slammed the door. "Willie, was that necessary?"

The curtain bounced up and down.

"I want you to stay out of my love life. Will you promise not to interfere when Kurt is here?"

Nothing happened and finally the curtain slowly bobbed up and down.

I shook my fist at the curtain. "Now you stick to your promise or else." A meaningless statement. I didn't know what I could do to threaten Willie. How the heck do you punish a ghost?

Chapter 33

I SLUMPED INTO A CHAIR. HERE I thought I could cook dinner for Kurt to try to win him over. On second thought, that might have done more harm than good, given my track record. Maybe after tonight's cooking class when I learned how to make desserts. How could a big hunky guy resist cookies and cakes and pies? I pictured a dessert buffet where I served the most delectable treats to my *sort-of* boyfriend. But first I had to develop some basic pastry skills.

I could also continue to help Kurt prepare for the police officer exam. That would give me another reason to be with him. After enough time together, maybe a spark would ignite. I never had to worry that he'd become too aggressive like Nate Dupres. Still, I wouldn't mind a little attention. Our time apart didn't seem to be working with him. It wasn't living up to Granny's saying of abstinence makes the heart grow fonder. Kurt needed something to catch his attention. Maybe a Taser or pepper spray. Oh, well. My primary goals right now consisted of getting Detective Moriarty off my back, tracking down the murderer and eliminating the black SUV threat to yours truly.

I looked at my note with the name of the owner of the black SUV. Samuel Jenkins. I could do a little research. I fired up Lappy, my laptop computer, and waited for the whirring to complete and the screen for my password to pop up. I entered "wooddrift." Simple and something I could remember but hopefully no one else could figure out.

After my slow internet connection came alive, I Googled on the name Samuel Jenkins and found a number of pictures and references to Facebook pages. I went on Facebook and searched for his name again. One lived in Iowa, another in Seattle and a third in Los Angeles. Could this be the guy?

I regarded his picture. Smarmy. What would he be doing in Omnipodge, assuming this was the right Samuel Jenkins? I viewed some pictures he had posted. In one he had his arm draped around a blond bimbo. She definitely had some ass…ets. Another picture showed Samuel J. holding up a bottle of Michelob with some of his drinking buddies. Then a third picture caught my attention. Bingo. There he stood next to a black SUV.

Detective Pru had made some progress.

I scrolled through his postings, glad he hadn't restricted them merely to friends. No way would I want to risk sending him a friend request. I hoped there would be something mentioning that he had come to Omnipodge. Nope. Only some dumb jokes about people going into bars. His interest in movies tended toward shoot 'em ups and gangster flicks. Probably wasn't into reading poetry.

Next, I checked LinkedIn. I found a reference to him with the same picture as on Facebook with a listed current occupation of used car salesman. What more could I expect? Samuel Jenkins, used car peddler, now in Omnipodge and running sweet young ladies off the road. Well, not so young anymore.

I returned to Google to look for other references. No published books, no Nobel prizes, nothing but a link to a used car dealership in Hollywood. Selling used cars to the stars. Had he taken an extended vacation?

What to do?

In spite of my earlier decision, I reconsidered and called Detective Moriarty. He answered. At least he was accessible.

"I have some new information for you, Detective."

"The confession?"

"No. Much better. I've located the owner of the black SUV that tried to turn me into road kill."

"I'm all ears."

I pictured two-foot-high ears on the sides of his face. Back to reality, I told him the name and license number."

"How'd you track down the owner?"

"I have my ways."

"You hacking into databases you shouldn't?"

"Nope. Find this guy and grill him. I know you're good at asking lots of questions."

"Yeah, like why you're still trying to pull me away from my investigation."

"Right. Go locate Samuel Jenkins and his black SUV. This could be tied to the Bart Cunard murder case. Bye."

This time I hung up on him. Oh, it felt good. My fingers tingled. Next step, grab a quick bite to eat before going to the cooking class.

I figured a grilled cheese sandwich was in order. I couldn't possibly ruin that.

I put a piece of American cheese between two pieces of bread, buttered the outsides of the sandwich, set the burner to medium and put the sandwich in a frying pan.

I watched carefully, flipped the sandwich and pressed the spatula against the top to make the bottom sizzle. Beautiful. A golden brown. Nothing to this cooking gig. I should buy myself a toque. A pleasant aroma of browning bread tickled my nostrils.

The phone rang. I ran into the other room to answer. It was Kurt.

"Are your eyes okay?"

"Yeah. I found my eye drops in time. Sorry I had to rush off. Uh… could we get together tomorrow after work to review for the police officer exam?"

A study date! "Sure. I'll be here. Come over any time."

"I can do it at five thirty."

"Perfect. Bring your eye drops, just in case."

I hung up picturing us huddled over *Police Officer Exam for Dummies*. He had explained to me the different sections of the National Police Officer Selection Test. I would help him with mathematics, reading comprehension, grammar and incident report writing. I wasn't super with numbers but could handle the basic arithmetic that a storekeeper required and assumed I could coach Kurt accordingly. Reading and grammar would be a piece of cake for me, and we could work through the requirements to write a coherent police report. I could see us sitting side by side, my fingers tapping an important paragraph in the book, leaning toward each other, getting closer and closer and then—

I smelled something burning. I raced into the kitchen to find smoke circling the ceiling. I took the crisp, black grilled cheese sandwich out of the frying pan and dropped it dark side up on a plate.

I wondered why my smoke alarm hadn't gone off. It was in the hall to the workshop. I looked up at it. The green light wasn't on. I would need to replace the battery.

But right now, I had something else to do. By scraping the black side of the sandwich, I was able to salvage it. I gobbled it down, not consuming too much charcoal.

When I finished, I washed my dishes and noticed the curtain over the sink jiggling.

"Hi, Willie. Kurt's coming over again tomorrow after work. I want you to be on your best behavior. Agreed?"

Nothing for a moment and then the curtain sagged slowly up and down.

I guessed that was as good a commitment as I would get out of Willie.

Chapter 34

WANTING TO GET TO THE cooking class early for a change, I dashed over to Bea's Bookstore, and to my surprise, I was the first to arrive.

Bea turned from shelving books. "You're actually early for a change."

"I know. I made a special effort to get here on time."

She put one more book on the shelf. "There. I'm ready."

"New shipment?"

"Yes. I decided to shore up my self-help section. After Kurt Whelan recently bought *Police Officer Exam for Dummies*, I decided to order more books in that series. I even have one for you."

She selected a book and slapped it into my hand. "Here you go."

I gawked. *Cooking Basics for Dummies.* Heat surged up my neck. I tried to regain my voice to make a comment and then realized something. If this could work for Kurt, maybe it would help me as well. "I'll take it."

I thumbed through my new Bible. Chapter One would teach me to cook with confidence. That's what I needed. I was the master, not the lowly vegetables and meat.

Chapter Four covered boiling, poaching and steaming. That would be better than my usual burning, swearing and crying.

Chapter Six would lead me into braising and stewing. Much better than my usual bruising and screwing up.

In Chapter Nine, I would learn about the amazing egg. The

amazing egg had only led to breaking and shell pieces in a bowl in the past. I pictured myself dancing with Humpty Dumpty and making all sorts of luscious omelets.

Chapters Fifteen and Sixteen had ten herbs and spices I should know. I knew one Herb, and I'd get him to help me with this part of the book. If I could tutor Kurt, there was no reason why Herb couldn't do the same for me. I was on a roll. In fact, I'd even be able to bake rolls. I imagined the variety of successful culinary delights.

Finally, Chapter Seventeen would teach me to think like a chef. You betchya, Red Ryder. That was the goal.

I was on my way to a whole new world of cooking success. Watch out, Julia Child. Here comes Pru Pendergast, chef extraordinaire. Prepare your taste buds. I was ready to make a statement.

I gave Bea a hug. "This book is perfect for me. Thank you."

She let out a breath. "I'm glad you feel that way. I thought you might be insulted by the title."

I laughed. "I can't pretend I'm a good cook. I definitely need the assistance. I hope to make some progress on desserts tonight."

Then my other mission took over. "But since we have a few minutes before class starts, I thought you might have some new insights regarding the murder."

She stared at me. "Meaning?"

I shrugged nonchalantly. "I don't know. I'm talking to everyone to see if there are any new clues. Detective Moriarty hasn't arrested anyone yet. We're suspects, and maybe one of us has picked up something that would help."

"Nothing new that I've noticed. No one bought *Garroting for Dummies* before Bart met his demise. What about you, Pru? Any idea how the murderer got hold of some of your driftwood for the garrote handles and how the killer and Bart entered your shop?"

I shook my head. "No brilliant ideas yet. But I'm glad I changed my locks."

"Me, too. I don't want anyone sneaking into my bookstore at night." Then she chuckled. "You never know what they might read."

"I wish we could have this all behind us."

Bea ran her hand over a book lying on the counter. "Moriarty needs to get off his bum and take care of this."

"That's the trouble. None of it makes any sense. Sure, no one liked Bart, but to resort to murder? Do you know a man named Samuel Jenkins?"

She crinkled her nose. "Doesn't sound familiar. If you'll excuse me for a moment, I need to get a few last things set up in the kitchen."

She left me to browse. I made a quick pass through the mystery novel section and then spotted a book lying open on a table. I bent down to check it. *Uh-oh.* It had a picture of a garrote. In spite of Bea's blithe comment about *Garroting for Dummies*, had she read this book and used the skills described? One more tidbit to noodle over.

My thoughts were interrupted when the doorbell jangled. Jake and Sally Midge walked in together followed by Herb and Flo.

Bea reappeared and announced, "The troops are arriving. Let's go into the kitchen."

"Blah," I muttered to myself. Nothing useful from Bea, other than the suspicious book in her store. A number of the other suspects had assembled, but I still had no useful information. My investigation skills ranked almost as low as my cooking ability. Maybe there was a dummies book for private investigators.

I'd have to keep my eye on everyone, but my task of the moment— learn to make desserts.

Bea covered the essentials of flour, milk, sugar and eggs—good products on my list. I didn't have any gluten or lactose intolerance or diabetes or cholesterol problems. I could handle the measuring and mixing side of recipes pretty well. Other than breaking eggs.

To try out the basics, we practiced with chocolate chip cookies.

Yum. I could hardly wait. I loved melted, gooey chocolate in crisp firm cookies. The problem, my cooked dough ended up gooey on one side, burnt on the other with the chocolate chips hard as rocks inside.

Bea took a taste of one of my cookies and spit it out. "Phew. What did you do to this, Pru?"

"I followed your directions. Apparently, the oven and I had a little disagreement."

"I'll say."

I looked around at the cookie sheets from the others. They had perfectly formed chocolate chip cookies. Why couldn't I achieve the same results? Was there a conspiracy? Was everyone out to get me?

No. They could bake, and I couldn't.

We next tried peach cobbler. Equal lack of success for yours truly. My peaches ended up looking like liver and the cobbler like a burnt corpse.

Bea shook her head in disgust. "I watched everything you did. How in the world did the cobbler end up so atrocious?"

I forced back a tear. "I don't know. I did everything you said."

We had one last item for the evening. Chocolate cake. No one could ruin that. No one did except for me. For some reason my cake ended up like a layer cake with white and black streaks and tasted like salty pork.

"You have an amazing knack for destroying good recipes, Pru," Bea said. "In our next war, the army should hire you out to cook for the enemy."

I sucked on my lip. It tasted better than anything I had cooked during the class. My problems started when I got near anything that produced heat. Like people who lacked a green thumb and killed their plants, I had this scorching effect on food.

"Is there a remedial class?" I asked expectantly.

"I don't know if tutoring or anything would help. Maybe you should give up trying to cook."

I suddenly stood erect. No. I would not admit defeat. I grabbed my *Cooking Basics for Dummies* and dashed out of the bookstore. I would overcome this momentary defeat. As Granny said, I may have lost the destroyer, but I could still win the battleship.

Chapter 35

I AWOKE SOAKED IN MOISTURE THE next morning with a memory of a dream still lingering in my half-awake brain. I had fallen into a vat of dough. I had struggled to climb out, clambering over the rim only to plunk down on a conveyor belt. My arms and legs became glued tight, and I couldn't move. The conveyor belt carried me into a giant oven. The heat seared my face, but my body seemed protected by the dough that had accumulated. I emerged from the oven and discovered I looked like the gingerbread woman. Then I found myself floating on a raft in the middle of the ocean, and giant sharks appeared with jaws spread wide to take bites out of me. The first one missed, but the second one aimed right toward me. That's when my addled brain decided to discontinue the film and woke me up.

Didn't I have enough problems during waking hours? Why'd I have to suffer through frustrating dreams? I was supposed to have calm, flying dreams where I floated through a beautiful meadow with wildflowers everywhere and prancing fawns and trickling brooks. I deserved a peaceful rest from the problems of the day. Who needed vats and ovens and shark attacks?

I stumbled out of bed and mixed a cup of instant coffee. My one cooking skill. I could still heat water in the microwave. Whoop dee do.

Boopsie and Spools kept getting under my feet until I fed them. No way were they going to wait patiently. I provided generous dollops of cat and dog food, mixing their favorites— Fussy Feast covered with sprinkle cheese and Doggy Dynamite slathered in chicken noodle soup. Then I watched the two ingrates gobble their meals, before continuing with my morning preparations—a quick shower and a good brushing of my hair.

Ready for whatever fate would throw my way, I regarded my new cooking book. My will power of the night before had vanished. I shoved it aside. I didn't want to look a piece of fish or a potato in the eye. Later for cooking. I needed to pursue my other futile hobby—investigating the murder.

Before the official opening of my shop at nine, I headed to Flo's, the other source of deadly garrote material. She hadn't opened yet, but through the glass door I could see her organizing some yarn. I watched as she removed skeins from a box and put them in selected places on a shelf.

I rapped, and she came over to let me in.

"What can I do for you, Pru?"

"I'm kind of down after my cooking disasters last night and need to talk. Mind if I come in?"

She gave me a hug and offered to fix me a homemade sweet roll. I declined. I didn't need to be reminded that others could cook and I couldn't.

I cleared my throat and launched into my other subject. "In addition to my cooking problems, Bart's murder still concerns me."

"Me, too."

"And you and I play a key role in that our materials were used to cause the death. That's made us suspects."

"It really disturbs me that some of my Vicuna is missing. With the locks changed, I haven't lost any more."

"I haven't had any intruders lately either. Does the name Samuel Jenkins mean anything to you?"

Flo shook her head. "No. Who's he?"

I could either play coy or be direct. I decided on the later. "He owns a black SUV that tried to run me off the road several times."

"Have the police arrested him?"

"I've told our illustrious Detective Moriarty about him but don't know if there have been any results yet. Moriarty hasn't been exactly forthcoming with information. You pick up anything new?"

She looked over her shoulder as if someone might be eavesdropping. "One peculiar event happened last night after our cooking class." She looked around her shop again.

I wondered if there were hidden cameras or bugs. She had me antsy. I started peering over my shoulder. I saw only yarn.

Once she seemed assured of no spies, she continued. "I overheard Jake and Sally Midge arguing. They were going at it hot and heavy for two people who only recently became engaged. She was accusing him of doing something despicable, and he ranted that she should be more understanding."

Wow. I tried to imagine this scene if I had encountered it. "Could it be that Jake murdered Bart?"

"I don't know. They divulged no details. Both were pretty angry. They literally shook their fists at each other. And this from two people who usually act quite calm and peaceful."

"Did they come to blows?"

"No. They showed some restraint. But after a final verbal barrage, they stomped away in opposite directions."

"Oh, boy. That doesn't sound good for their relationship. All is not sunshine and light in the world of the soon-to-be newlyweds."

"That's for sure."

Now I had another line of investigation to pursue later that day. But that would have to wait. I tried a few more questions with Flo, but she had no further useful information for me and started getting defensive, so I decided it was time to cut my losses. As Granny said, you can't squeeze milk from a turnip.

Flo's phone rang, and she went behind her counter to answer. While she talked, I wandered around the store and poked my hand into several bins of colorful yarn. In the third one, I encountered something hard. I lifted it out. A piece of driftwood. *Uh-oh.* Could this be a clue that Bea had taken some driftwood and used it to construct a garrote?

She hung up the phone, and I quickly stashed the piece of driftwood where I had found it. I wasn't ready to confront her. I'd have to think this over.

I needed to get back to my shop. I could imagine the mob of customers who were going to select today as the one day to buy driftwood creations. They would be there lined up to grab every mobile and sculpture in sight.

Not so. No one waited outside even in a line of one, and no one showed up the rest of the morning.

I busied myself with making a few more creations in my workshop and practicing writing with Willie. His penmanship was improving. We even added a few words to his vocabulary, including car, intruder and run. If my snooping got me in trouble, I would need any ghostly assistance possible.

Maybe eventually Willie could also help Kurt prepare for the police officer exam. Once I had taught him a good number of words, he could share some of his several centuries of experience. That is if I had the guts to inform Kurt of Willie's existence. On the other hand, maybe Kurt would become jealous if he knew I lived with a ghost. I could argue both sides of this all day long. Enough.

Then my mind returned to finding a book on garroting in Bea's store and discovering a piece of driftwood in Flo's yarn. Suspicious, but of my neighbors, I would still put my money on Jake as a more likely suspect. By eleven, I decided to display the out-of-the-shop sign and stopped to see Jake. Maybe I could wrestle a confession out of him like Detective Moriarty was always trying to do with me. But I'd have to be careful. If he was the killer…

Chapter 36

I STOOD LOOKING OUT THE FRONT door of my shop as sun reflected off a puddle formed by a maintenance worker hosing down a section of sidewalk. I had to plan my conversation with Jake carefully. I couldn't come right out and say, "I think you killed Bart to free things up with Sally Midge and you were caught arguing last night with her about your dastardly deed." That's exactly what I wanted to say, but would have to find some more subtle way to broach the subject if I expected results.

Detective Moriarty wouldn't worry over such niceties, but then again, he hadn't produced any meaningful results yet. Maybe I would snoop around Jake's shop for a while, as if I were pricing tennis bracelets or some other absurd item I couldn't afford. Then when the time was right, I could start up a different conversation and slowly direct it to the subject of interest. I could be Pru Pendergast, silver-tongued inquisitor. That had a ring to it. Yes, that would be my approach.

Before I could take a step outside, something soft stroked my ankle. I looked down to see Boopsie rubbing against my leg. "Are you helping me build my courage?"

She rubbed again, and I heard a loud purr.

"Oh, that's it, you want food."

I reset my priorities and went to replenish her food dish. Never confuse affection with hunger around cats and dogs. I also added some food to Spools's dish. He came over, happy to partake in a meal.

With my companions sated, I prepared to leave with renewed resolve to confront Jake in a cautious manner. Before I opened the door, a breeze whistled through my hair.

"Are you going to give me moral support as well, Willie?"

The curtain jiggled up and down.

"Good. I can use it."

Now ready, I locked my door and marched next door, peered through the large plate glass window into Yalley's Jewelers and spotted Jake at the table in the center of the store, his loupe to his eye inspecting a ring. I steeled myself for my entry, ready to catch him unaware. Then I swept in like the Japanese attacking Pearl Harbor on December 7, 1941.

Before he even looked up and forgetting my vow to bring the subject up carefully, I blurted out, "Did you kill Bart Cunard and get into an argument with Sally Midge last night because of what you did?"

He dropped his loupe and blinked at me. "Huh?"

"You heard me." I shook my right index finger at him. "You were seen having a heated conversation with Sally Midge last night."

"H-how can someone see a conversation?"

"You know what I mean. You and Sally Midge had an argument last night. Your body language indicated highly-charged emotions."

"Yeah. S-so what?"

I had lost the initiative. I should have paid more attention to my World War II analogy. After all, Japan lost the war. "Um… like me, you're a suspect in the murder. You have a motive because of your relationship with Sally Midge—"

His eyes narrowed. "You leave S-sally Midge out of this."

I winced. Was I off base? Could Jake be covering up for Sally Midge? Had I stepped in it?

I took a deep breath. "Okay. Let me start again. Since Detective Moriarty is constantly harassing me, I'm trying to find who killed

Bart. I've also raised the ire of someone in a black SUV who has tried to run me off the road, and someone has been leaving me threatening notes and killer bees. I want my life back with no one after me. That's why I'm talking to the other suspects to see what they've learned, clear myself and solve this mystery. End of story."

"Okay, b-but you come in here loaded for bear." He grinned. "I simply couldn't bear it."

I groaned. Even when confronted, he resorted to his dumb jokes.

"And y-you making accusations. That's no better than what you claim Moriarty has done to you."

I gave my best petulant pout. "Sorry. But you did have a heated argument with Sally Midge last night, and she accused you of doing something awful. I naturally assumed that bad thing was killing Bart."

Jake picked up his loupe and twiddled it in his fingers. "We argued over where we would live. I th-thought it would be good for us to move to Los Angeles so she could get away from anything to do with Bart and his death. She said she had no interest in moving away from Omnipodge. That was the crux of our argument. I feel really bad about it, so I don't need any lectures from you accusing me of killing Bart."

I hung my head. "Sorry. I wish I could make up for it by buying something today, but I'm low on funds myself."

He grinned. "I g-give credit."

"I give credit where credit is due myself, but I have to watch my expenditures until after the Spring Break rush. Simple as that. If you didn't kill Bart, who did?"

"I thought you had, Pru. After all, it happened in your shop with your d-driftwood."

"Why does everyone keep saying my driftwood? There's driftwood covering miles of beaches around here. Nothing that ties me to it."

"O-other than yours being the only shop that has driftwood in it."

"Okay, we both made bad assumptions. You didn't argue with Sally Midge over killing Bart, and I didn't do it with driftwood. There's also Vicuna yarn that someone stole from Flo's shop. Someone put this together in a very intricate plot."

"S-someone with good craft skills?"

"I resent that."

"Y-you're the one who started the accusations, not me."

I looked toward the ceiling wondering what I had got into. "Okay. Let's declare a truce. I acted out of line. You can accuse me of being an emotional female."

"Like S-sally Midge last night."

"Right. Put us in the same bucket if it pleases you."

His phone rang, and he stepped over to the counter to answer. I used the opportunity to stroll around his store and try to regroup. I had certainly blown this interrogation. Pru Pendergast, foot-in-mouth specialist.

In my current mood, not even the dazzling diamond engagement rings appealed to me. They only reminded me that I had such a long way to go with my *sort-of* boyfriend, Kurt. Would we ever reach the point of considering a long-term relationship that a ring might signify? Or for starters, a present of some less expensive and less significant form of jewelry? How about a charm bracelet or a necklace with an artificial stone? Get a grip, girl. That guy hadn't even held my hand yet. And our big dates had been going to the diner. Talk about slow progress. What a dilemma.

Jake continued to be absorbed in his phone call. He had his back to me so I slithered to the end of the display case and parted the curtain that led to the back of his shop. The first thing I saw was a stack of boxes. Something was stuck between a couple of the boxes. I looked more carefully. A small ball of Vicuna yarn. Hmm. Very suspicious to find this in the back of Jake's store. Then I peered behind the boxes. The sight caused me to gasp. Sally Midge lay unconscious on the floor.

Chapter 37

I PULLED OUT MY CELL PHONE. Interesting. I could get reception here, why not at my shop? I punched in 9-1-1 and reported that we needed medical assistance at Yalley's Jewelry. Would I need to administer CPR? My heart raced. I had taken a CPR class a year ago. We had learned to push on the victim's chest to the beat of the song, "Staying Alive." The instructor told us if we did it correctly, we would break some ribs. Could I do it for real if I had to? Would I have enough guts to push on Sally Midge's chest hard enough to break her ribs?

I dropped to the floor and felt her neck. A pulse, and Sally's chest heaved. She was alive and breathing. I patted her cheek and whispered. "Sally Midge. This is Pru. Can you hear me?"

She moaned but didn't open her eyes. What had happened to her? Then fear gripped my chest. Had Jake done something to her? I checked her head. No bruises. I looked around the floor. No blood. She hadn't been shot, stabbed or bludgeoned. Had she passed out? I sniffed. No gas or fumes.

I listened. Jake continued his conversation, unperturbed. Did I want to alert him to my finding Sally Midge?

I whispered again, "Sally Midge, did Jake do something to you?"

Her breath caught and returned to normal breathing. No answer.

I patted her cheeks again.

She smacked her lips but didn't wake up.

A siren wailed in the distance. It became louder, causing my tinnitus to go berserk. I peeked out through the curtain and saw Jake still on the phone. He appeared completely oblivious to anything other than his phone conversation.

Then two EMTs burst into the store. I stood and waved to them. "In here. Come quickly."

Jake's jaw went slack. "W-what's going on?"

I pointed an accusing index finger at him. "Something's happened to Sally Midge in your back room."

He flinched. "What's sh-she doing there?"

"That's a very good question."

By this time the EMTs had turned Sally Midge on her side. She coughed, started making sounds like Boopsie and disgorged a flow of liquid onto the floor. The EMTs lifted her onto a stretcher.

I followed them out of the shop, while Jake stood transfixed.

I trotted along as Sally Midge groaned.

"What happened?" I asked.

"I took sleeping pills." Then she conked out again.

I tried to convince the EMTs to let me ride with them, but they weren't buying, so I dashed back and unchained Mopsy to follow them to the hospital. In my turmoil, it was amazing I didn't have an accident. Good thing. I might have ended up sharing a hospital room with Sally Midge.

I fidgeted in the waiting room and kept asking any passing nurses if they had any information on Sally Midge. After an hour, I was given a room number where I could visit her. She had been settled into a semi-private room with a curtain drawn between her and an elderly snoring woman. I plunked down in a chair beside the bed and took her hand. "How are you doing, Sally Midge?"

A faint smile appeared on her face. "Much better."

"You said you took sleeping pills."

She nodded. "Dumb thing to do. I was so mad at Jake. I snuck into the back of his shop and downed the pills."

"Did you intend to kill yourself?"

"No, I only took enough to look that way. I wanted to get back at Jake."

I squeezed her hand. "It might have been some time before he noticed you. I happened to be snooping and saw you on the floor."

"Thank you."

"Did it have to do with the argument you had with Jake last night?"

She nodded. "We argued over money. I had given him a loan, which he admitted putting into a bad investment. He said he was trying to build a little nest egg for us, but it backfired. I rightfully got pissed. He told me I should be more understanding because his intentions had only been to provide for us. I went stomping off."

Whoa. That was a very different story than Jake had told me. "Not something to do with moving to Los Angeles?"

She looked at me as if I were a bug from outer space. "No, why would you think that? It was only financial problems."

As Granny would stay, something was rotten in the state of Belgium. Either Sally Midge or Jake had misled me. Which one and why? Could one of them be the murderer and made up a story about the argument the night before? Sally Midge appeared to be coming around. I heard a noise and realized it was the sound of an un-tuned power lawnmower, probably cutting grass in nearby Omnipodge Central Park.

Sally Midge smiled at me. "I'm feeling much better. Say, there's something I've been meaning to do."

"What's that?"

"Use my psychic powers to figure out who murdered Bart."

I refrained from rolling my eyes. "Don't worry about that. You need some rest."

"No, I want to help the investigation." Sally Midge closed her eyes and let out a deep breath. "Yes. I'm getting some vibrations. I can hear something. It's saying very clearly, 'Pru, Pru, Pru, Pru.'"

Her eyes shot open. "Could you be the murderer?"

"No, Sally Midge. This is the second time you accused me of killing Bart. You're only hearing the sound of a lawnmower."

She cocked her head to the side. "Could be. You're sure you didn't do away with Bart? I wouldn't hold it against you."

"Wasn't me. Why don't you get some rest?"

Sally Midge yawned. "I guess you're right." She closed her eyes again and fell asleep in moments. No further pseudo-psychic proclamations.

I left her to recover.

What to do?

I could confront Jake again.

Mopsy and I putted back to Omnipodge Village Center. I stomped up to Jake's store. A sign indicated closed for the day.

"Rats." Where had he disappeared to? He hadn't come to the hospital while I was there. Was he skulking around town somewhere?

I hopped back on Mopsy and cruised the streets.

Within fifteen minutes I spotted him at the florist's shop. I pulled to the curb and dashed inside.

He had just paid for a dozen roses. I stormed up to him. "I spoke with Sally Midge, and she said your argument was over money you had unwisely invested, not some hokey story of moving to Los Angeles.

I got ready for an argument, but he only looked at me with sad eyes. "S-sally Midge is right."

"Why'd you lie to me?"

"It wasn't really a l-lie. We had discussed moving several weeks ago. I didn't want to admit to anyone else what a dumb investment I made. That's all."

"You expect me to believe that?"

"You can believe w-whatever you want, Pru, but I need to go visit Sally Midge at the hospital."

Chapter 38

I RETURNED TO MY SHOP TO consider life, the universe and everything. Willie ruffled my hair, and I didn't even bother to smooth it out. In addition to not making many friends, I was having a bad hair day.

There was only one thing to do when in a funk. Go see my best friend. Leaving Willie in charge of Boopsie and Spools, I set the sign on my door to indicate I'd be back in an hour. If any customers had tried to come in my store today, they might give up for good. It couldn't be helped. I needed some friendship therapy.

I found Herb puttering around his shop, dusting and arranging jars and cartons.

"Hello, Princess." Then he stopped and stared at me. "You look like you lost your best friend, but that's me, and you haven't lost me."

I tried to squeeze out a forced smile, but it must have appeared more like a grimace because Herb put his hands on his hips and said, "Don't give me that look. I'm trying to help."

"I know. I know."

He opened his arms. "Come tell Uncle Herb your problems."

I sank into his embrace. If only it were Kurt welcoming me.

He pushed me away at arms' length and looked into my blurry eyes. "Don't get all weepy on me. You know I can't deal with that." Tears began to pour out of his eyes. I grabbed two tissues from his counter so we both could dab our eyes.

He pointed to two stools. "Take a seat and start at the beginning."

I sniffled and gulped back another tear. "Everything is falling apart."

"It can't be that bad. You still have me."

I managed a wan smile. "That's true. And I appreciate your friendship. I'm afraid I've damaged some other relationships this morning."

"Not with Kurt, I hope."

"No. I haven't seen him. That's another problem." I wiped my eyes again. "The trouble with Kurt is nothing's happening."

He patted my hand. "The big clunk will come to his senses."

"But I don't know when. The main trouble is my investigating the murder has put me at odds with Jake. And then Sally Midge took an overdose of sleeping pills. I don't know. Everything is going wrong."

"There, there. It'll work out. What happened with Jake?"

"It goes back to last night. Flo encountered Jake and Sally Midge having an argument. She told me about it this morning. I jumped to a conclusion that it must be over Jake having killed Bart Cunard. I confronted him, and he gave me his version of the fight with Sally Midge. Later after Sally Midge woke up from her pill overdose, she told me a different story. I went back to Jake, and he admitted that Sally Midge's version was correct. Every time I try to investigate, I make things worse."

"This sounds like a soap opera."

I nodded. "After my last encounter with Jake, he took off to see Sally Midge. I don't know if they'll keep fighting or reconcile."

"That's their problem, Princess, not yours."

"You're right, but I ended up in the middle of it, and I feel bad about it. And on top of that, I found a book on garroting in Bea's store last night, a piece of driftwood in Flo's yarn and a ball of Vicuna yarn in Jake's shop today. I have evidence that everyone I know and like could be the murderer."

"Except for me, Princess."

I snuffled. "That's true."

Herb reached for a tissue and discovered the box was empty. "Wait a moment. Let me get a new box." He disappeared into the back of his shop.

I took a moment to wander around. I picked up a jar of thyme. Would I ever be able to use herbs and spices correctly in my cooking?

Herb returned and handed me a tissue out of a new box. "Any good news?"

I gave a loud honk and threw the tissue in the wastebasket. "I've tracked down the black SUV that tried to run me off the road. It belongs to a man named Samuel Jenkins. Ring any bells?"

Herb scrunched up his forehead so that it looked like a wrinkly prune. "No, but tell me more."

"He's a used car salesman from Los Angeles. His car is here in Omnipodge, but I don't know what he's doing here or why he's after me."

"Are the police doing anything?"

"Detective Moriarty knows, but I don't have much confidence in him, given his lack of results in solving the murder."

Herb pursed his lips. "I know. He's still accusing me of the murder and of selling illegal drugs."

I snuffled again. "And on top of everything else, my cooking is a disaster. You saw what I did last night."

"I hate to say it, Princess, but cooking may not be your thing."

I slammed my fist down on his counter. "I'm not going to admit defeat."

Herb held up his hands in a defensive posture. "No violence please. I admire your gumption, but, frankly, your cooking... um... sucks."

In spite of myself, I giggled. "I bought a new book from Bea titled *Cooking Basics for Dummies*. It might be able to help me. There are even two chapters on spices and herbs. I thought you might go over those with me."

"I'll be happy to try."

"I can't ask for more. Would you spend a few minutes with me on it?"

"As you can see my shop isn't exactly hopping with customers at the moment. Go get it."

With something constructive to work on, I returned to my shop, checked to make sure that my three residents hadn't done any damage, grabbed the book and scampered back to Herb's. I had a mission.

I opened the book to Chapter Fifteen on the ten or so herbs I should know and pointed to the list in alphabetical order starting with basil. "Since you're the only Herb I know, why don't you introduce me to your relatives?"

"It's very simple. I'll show you what they look like and describe how they're used. All you need to do is pay close attention."

I saluted. "Yes, sir, Chief Instructor."

"Now basil. Its scientific name is *Ocimum basilicum*. It originated in India over five thousand years ago. It's added at the end as cooking can destroy the flavor. Specific uses include…"

He continued to expound, and my eyes glazed over.

"Pru, are you paying attention?"

I jerked my head up. "Huh? I think I dozed off."

He rapped me on the knuckles. "How are you going to learn if you don't listen?"

"I think I'm a visual learner. Show me some basil. That will be more meaningful to me."

He stepped over to a jar. "Almost empty. Would you dash into the storage room and grab the box on the first shelf on the left. It's labeled 'Basil.'"

To wake up I needed to move anyway. "Be right back."

I entered his storage area and scanned the shelves. All this stuff. How would I ever learn which leaves and twigs to use for which dishes?

I located the box he had mentioned and started to move it, when I bumped the shelf. Something fell to the floor. I didn't need to cause any damage here.

Looking down at what had fallen, I winced. It was a garrote made of Vicuna yarn and driftwood.

Chapter 39

I GAPED AT THE GARROTE ON the floor of Herb's storage area. *Uh-oh*. Was Herb trying to hide something? My heart sank. Even my best friend had a clue linking him to the murder. I had a real dilemma. Should I accuse my best friend of murder? Should I call Detective Moriarty? Maybe I could casually mention to Herb, "Oh, by the way, you have a weapon similar to what killed Bart."

Nothing felt right. I couldn't ignore it. I had lost my appetite for any cooking lessons.

"What's taking you so long?" Herb shouted.

"Um… we have a little problem."

"I hoped you didn't spill anything."

"That's not the problem, although something fell to the floor."

He stood in the doorway. "You knocked something over?"

"Not exactly." I pointed. "When I reached for the basil, this dropped off the shelf."

He bent over to look and then put his hand to his cheek. "Where did that come from?"

"My question as well."

"You don't think… I've never seen this before."

"I don't know what to think."

Herb's eyes widened. "Someone must have planted it there. I know it couldn't have been you, Princess. But who?"

I wanted to believe that was this wasn't Herb's handiwork. I thought back to when I had tried to get him to help me with my driftwood creations. My incompetence at cooking was only matched by Herb's lack of dexterity in handling driftwood. He couldn't even connect fishing line to driftwood pieces to make a mobile. I couldn't imagine him actually crafting a garrote out of yarn and driftwood, and I didn't want to believe he had hidden the garrote here. Had someone been planting clues to implicate other shopkeepers? I'd have to think this over.

"Has anyone been in your shop this morning?" I asked.

"Only Larry Ludwick and Nate Dupres. They came in together to purchase some spices."

"Could either of them have gone into your storage area?"

Herb thought for a moment. "It's possible. I received a phone call from Carl's mother. She checks in with me once a week or so. With Carl gone…" He gulped loudly. "She considers me her surrogate son. I turned my back on Larry and Nate and went behind the counter to have more privacy. I didn't pay any attention to them for five minutes."

I knew what I had to do. "All right. You call Detective Moriarty and have him come collect the garrote. Maybe he can find some fingerprints on it."

"He'll probably arrest me."

"Tell him I found it. That way he'll want to talk to me before he does anything. In the meantime, I'm going to make a little call on Larry Ludwick."

"Do you think that's wise?"

"Probably not, but I've got to get to the bottom of this."

"Shouldn't Detective Moriarty do that?"

"We can't count on him. I'm off." Before Herb could argue with me, I dashed out the door and raced to where Mopsy stood, working on her tan.

As I putted toward Larry's office, I suddenly realized I didn't have any coherent plan of attack. Confront him and ask why he left a garrote in Herb's storage room? Right. As if that would work. No, I had to have some other starting point. He and I had discussed the future of the Omnipodge Village Center. I could begin there.

After finding a patch of grass next to a lamp post where Mopsy could rest her tires, I entered Larry's office and told the receptionist that I had urgent business with her boss.

She looked up from filing her gold nails that matched her hair and the gold **lamé** blouse she wore over a very enhanced portion of her anatomy. "And the nature of your business?"

I gave the plastic Barbie my most endearing smile. "An important real estate transaction that will be of interest to him."

That passed muster, and I waited ten minutes before being ushered into a conference room with a shiny mahogany table. Sheez. It was large enough to fill up my whole shop. I turned down the offer of coffee, and waited another five minutes before Larry slithered into the room. He sat across the table from me.

"Are you getting into the real estate market, Pru?"

"I'm considering it. It depends on what happens with the Omnipodge Village Center. I thought I'd check in with you. I need to find out if our leases will be renewed or not. If not, I'm thinking of becoming a Realtor."

"You're here to see me about a job?"

"Not necessarily. I'm trying to understand my options for the future."

He leaned back and laced his fingers together. "I'm sorry to report that you may have to consider that change in career or else relocate to another retail location. I'm planning to tear down the Village Center and build a high-rise apartment building."

"What!"

"It will be a much more lucrative use of the land. Simple as that."

"What will happen to my cottage?"

"It'll be torn down like all the others. Maybe I'll even find Willie Woburn's gold when we dig under your cottage."

I wanted to punch him in the nose, but I held my temper. I needed to get some other information first.

"And how soon will this take place?"

"The leases run out over the next three months. Everything should be ready to begin demolition by the end of the summer."

Demolition. Then it struck me. What would happen to Wrong Way Willie, if his house got torn down? Larry had to be stopped, but how could powerless me accomplish that? Unless Larry had committed the murder. Then he could be locked away for the rest of his life.

I took a deep breath, ready to pursue one of my next questions. "I've seen you and Nate Dupres speaking. Is he an employee of yours?"

He forced a smile. "Mr. Dupres is doing contract work for me."

"And the nature of that work?"

"It's confidential."

"Do you know Samuel Jenkins?"

He stared at me. "Who's that?"

"His black SUV tried to run me off the road. I thought you might be acquainted with him."

He gave a dismissive wave of his hand. "I have no idea who he is. I have another meeting. Is there anything else?"

"Yes. Why did you leave a garrote in Herb Hanover's shop?"

"Huh?"

He looked genuinely surprised at my question.

"After you and Nate visited Herb's store today, a garrote identical to the one used to kill Bart Cunard showed up. It appears to have been left to incriminate Herb. I think you did it."

He stood. "Get out of my building. I won't stand for this. I could sue you for making such a false accusation."

I stood as well. "Only if it's false. If it proves to be the truth, you might have other legal problems."

He came around the table, grabbed my arm and propelled me toward the door.

I stumbled, regained my balance and brushed his arm away. "I can get out by myself, thank you."

I barged past him and through the reception area without so much of a nod to his plastic receptionist.

Chapter 40

WITH MY HEAD HELD HIGH, I attempted to navigate the remainder of the lobby of Larry Ludwick's building. In fact, it was held so high that I could only see the ceiling tile, which I noticed contained little black specks as if someone had thrown darts at them. My inattention to where I was going caused one little problem. I ran smack into Nate Dupres.

He caught my arms and held them fast. "Whoa. You look like you're a filly on the run, Pru."

Given my feisty mood, I wrenched my right arm free and smacked him in the chest with my hand. "What are you doing here?"

Be backed off a step and winked seductively. "The better question is what are you doing here?"

"You answer first."

"I'm not going to play your little games, Pru. I have an appointment with Larry Ludwick."

I gave him the onceover. He wore a dark blue suit, white shirt and a red power tie. To this conservative attire he had added shiny black wingtips. He even had a neatly folded white handkerchief tucked in his jacket pocket. His combed black hair shone from hair goo. Not his usual form of non-sartorial splendor. "Does your presence here have something to do with the contract work you're doing for Larry?"

He blanched. "What do you mean?"

"Oh, I don't know. Probably something that indicates you're up to no good with Larry. For starters, I assume you're in on trying to put shopkeepers in the Omnipodge Village Center out of business."

He put his finger under his collar and tried to loosen it. "Ah… I don't know what you mean."

I wagged my fingers at him. "Oh, yes you do. Larry told me all about it. He's going to let the leases run out, kick us out and build an apartment building. That doesn't sit well with the current leaseholders, including me."

Nate shrugged. "Could be."

"What's your role in this despicable plan? You look like a wannabe consigliore although you lack the legal education. You his enforcer or something?"

He dusted off his sleeve as if a cootie had dropped on it. "The nature of my work is confidential."

"Right. As in harassing people. I know you're up to no good. Who is Samuel Jenkins?"

He looked at me as if I had escaped from the planet of the apes.

"Don't give me that look. I want an answer."

"I have nothing more to say to you." He tried to push past me.

I shuffled my feet to the side to block his progress. "Not so fast, I'm not finished with you."

"That's rich. You've been nothing but negative to me since I arrived in Omnipodge. I thought you'd be friendlier."

"If you expect friendly, you can start with the truth." I crossed my arms and gave him the Pru evil eye. "Samuel Jenkins?"

He tried to act casual and shrugged his shoulders, but it came off more as a twitch. "I have no clue who Samuel Jankins is."

"It's Jenkins, and I think he's working with you and Larry Ludwick."

He shot his cuff and looked at his watch. In spite of the spiffy suit, he still wore a Timex rather than a Rolex. "I'd like to continue this conversation, but I'm late for a very important meeting." He tried again to move past me, but I was having none of it.

"Who killed Bart Cunard? You, Larry or this Samuel Jenkins?"

Now I noticed fear in Nate's eyes. He practically knocked me over as he ran through the lobby and disappeared up the staircase.

My ex-boyfriend was connected to nefarious dealings. What to do? I couldn't call Detective Moriarty and tell him my suspicions. I had no proof, and he'd only accuse me again of a diversionary stunt. I could return to Larry's office and hang out, but that would probably earn me a bum's rush from the security staff.

Instead, I headed out the swinging doors and stopped to stare up at the building from the walkway in front. Somewhere in there resided a secret that connected the murder and the black SUV. I vowed to get to the bottom of it.

In the meantime, what else could I do?

If Nate or Larry departed, I could tail them. No, they'd notice me putt-putting behind and could lose me in an instant at Mopsy's slow speed.

Still, it wouldn't hurt to watch to see if one or both of them left in the near future. The building was fronted by a small plaza with several benches. I selected one that faced the doorway and sat down to watch. The sun had become blocked by another fog bank, and an onshore breeze whistled over my arms, giving me the shivers, but I held my place for thirty minutes before deciding that I hadn't come prepared for a chilly spring day. I would be cold enough riding Mopsy back to my shop. No sense getting hypothermia.

Giving in to the inevitable, I glanced one last time at the building, not finding any large banners admitting guilt, I freed Mopsy and started her. As I weaved my way through the parking lot, something large and black caught my eye off to the left. I veered in that direction and screeched to a stop behind a black SUV. I set Mopsy on her kickstand and approached it warily. No one was inside. I circled the vehicle, peering in each window to see if I could find anything incriminating on the seats. Only a blank notepad, a Snickers wrapper, an empty brown paper bag and a chewed number two pencil. Then I looked in the back. Was that what I thought it was? I peered more closely. A number of dead bees. *Uh-oh.*

Looking at the license plate, I verified the same numbers and letters I had seen before.

The plot thickened.

Maybe I should let the air out of the tires, so the car couldn't leave to threaten me anymore. I pivoted to check around the parking lot. Nope. Wouldn't work. Too many people and cars coming and going. I wasn't sneaky enough to get away with that maneuver.

I had only one other choice, as much as I hated the thought of it. I pulled out my cell phone to call Detective Moriarty. It clicked over to voice mail. I wanted to speak with him in person, but I couldn't stay here with my teeth chattering either. "Detective, this is Pru Pendergast. I've located the black SUV I previously mentioned to you. It's in Larry Ludwick's parking lot. Go check it out."

I signed off. Would he do anything?

Then I returned to my shop, wondering how this would play out.

Chapter 41

BACK IN MY SHOP, I reopened for an hour with nary a customer in sight. With no dollars flowing my way, I closed for the day. The only consolation—Kurt would be stopping by.

I fed my beasts, who only expressed their gratitude by gobbling up every scrap and crumb.

I made one driftwood creation, but my heart wasn't in it. My lack of investigative results nagged at my tummy. I considered drowning my sorrows in M&Ms but was too despondent to even go into the kitchen.

Fortunately, I was saved by a knock at the door. There stood Kurt, a book under one arm and a sagging daisy in his clenched fist. "For you, Pru."

"Aw, you shouldn't have." I retrieved a vase, put in a splash of water and dropped the stem inside. This deserved a place of honor on my mantel. After it dried out, I could press it and put it in my memory book. Right alongside a picture of Kurt and me holding hands if that ever happened.

He set the book down on my table, and I noticed it was *Police Officers Exam for Dummies*. "Uh, Pru, are you ready to help me study for the exam?"

Our study date. "Sure, Kurt. How much of the book have you covered?"

"I skimmed through it. There's a lot of stuff there. I need to practice the sections that will prepare me for the Police Officer

Selection Test. I've been working the math exercises, and they're not too hard. You want to quiz me?"

"Sure. Let me take a look." I read through the math section. It was pretty basic. I retrieved a pad of paper and some pencils. "Okay. I'll make up a question for you. If a burglar took two cell phones valued at a hundred dollars each, a three-hundred dollar television and a fourteen hundred dollar laptop, what was the total amount of all items stolen?"

He stuck his tongue out the side of his mouth, looked up at the ceiling for a moment and wrote $1900 on the paper.

"Correct." I should have given him a kiss as a reward, but that would have been too forward of me.

I posed several other problems, which he aced.

"I think you're set on the math portion of the test. Let's move on to reading comprehension." There were several exercises I had him do. He missed one, but correctly answered the other questions.

I saw several definitions that I thought he should become familiar with. I pointed to the book. "Have you read these yet?"

"Nope."

"Go through them and we'll discuss them."

He hunkered down and ran his finger through the page. "Okay. Ready."

"What's the definition of murder in the first degree?"

He grinned. "Like with Bart Cunard. Intentional and planned."

I gulped. "That's correct. Using a garrote couldn't be accidental or unplanned. Murder in the second degree?"

"Intentional but not planned."

"Voluntary manslaughter?"

"Taking a life unintentionally, like during a crime of passion."

I gave him a high five. Our own crime of almost passion— we had made skin contact. We proceeded through involuntary manslaughter, which he nailed.

I closed the book. "You hungry, Kurt?"

"Yeah."

"I could whip up something."

A look of panic crossed his face. "How about a bowl of cereal?"

"I can handle that." Which I did without spilling a drop of milk or knocking the raisin bran off the counter.

I joined him, and we munched away.

"Seconds?" I asked. "Or I could fix you toast."

"Another bowl will be great."

It was obvious he didn't want to risk me doing anything with heat involved.

After putting the empty bowls and spoons in the sink, we returned to our study date.

I flipped forward to the grammar section and quizzed him on complete sentences versus fragments. He needed a little work on this but after a few examples consistently made the distinction.

On to reading and writing incident reports. I read though comments made by the authors of the book. "It says here to be sure to use complete sentences in writing an incident report on the exam, Kurt."

"Yeah. I think that's what tripped me up last time." He gave me a great big grin. "Now that you've explained complete sentences to me, I shouldn't have any trouble."

We tried this out on several examples, and he seemed on track.

"I know you're going to pass the next time you take the exam."

"You really think so, Pru?"

"You're solid on the four sections. Once you get through that we can work on the physical and oral exams."

"I'm in good shape so the physical won't be a problem. I could use help on the oral part."

"We'll take that on after you get through the written exam."

The phone rang, and I answered to hear Granny on the line.

"When are you going to try some of your cooking skills on me from the class you're taking, Ladybug?"

"Um… maybe tomorrow night at six?"

"Terrific. I'll be over lickety-split tomorrow. How are things with that boyfriend of yours?"

"Uh… Kurt's over here right now."

"Ooh, wee. Something hot going on?"

"No, I'm helping him study for the police officer exam."

"I'd expect you two to be studying something else."

"Granny!"

"Invite him over tomorrow as well. I need to check out this hunk of yours more closely."

"I don't know."

"Do it, or I'll disown you."

I could never win an argument with Granny. "Okay."

"Tell him to be there or be around." She clicked off.

I returned to the table with Kurt. "How'd you like to come by tomorrow at six for dinner?"

His face went through a series of expressions from happy to concerned and back to happy. "I guess so." He checked his watch. "Uh, Pru. I was going to meet some of the guys at Benny's Bar. You… uh… want to join me?"

Wow. A follow-on to our study date. I tried to act calm but instead blurted out, "Sure. You betchya."

We hopped in his pickup and drove the half-mile to Benny's. The place was hopping and for good reason. Half price drink night. I scanned the room. Herb sat at a large table with Flo, Bea, Jake and Sally Midge. The whole gang had shown up.

Herb spotted me and waved us over.

"I know you planned to join some of your firefighting buddies, but are you okay sitting down with some of my friends first?"

"Sure, Pru."

What a guy. He grabbed two chairs, and my Village Center clan made a place for us at the table.

"F-fancy seeing you here," Jake said in a clipped tone. He still wasn't over our little confrontation from earlier in the day. It was good to see that Sally Midge had fully recovered.

Kurt ordered a beer, and I asked for a soft drink. Booze and I didn't get along very well, and I couldn't risk it on my first bar date with Kurt.

Jake put his arm around Sally Midge, and she leaned against him. Apparently, all was peace and light again with the engaged couple. Jake even launched into his horrible puns. "I've been th-thinking a lot about the hereafter." He tweaked Sally Midge's chin. "What am I here after?"

Everyone groaned. Sally Midge elbowed him in the ribs, and Jake sat back in his chair with a satisfied smile on his face.

The mood was broken when Larry Ludwick and Nate Dupres entered the room. The chatter at our table ceased.

Nate came up to me. "Good to see you, Pru."

"Not reciprocated, Nate."

He shrugged.

Jake shook his fist at Larry Ludwick. "What's this I hear that you're not going to renew our leases?"

Larry smiled, unfazed. "Business is business."

I didn't want to get in the middle of this. I stood. "I need to use the restroom." I dashed off.

After splashing water on my face, I returned to find the debate still going on. Finally, Larry said, "Let's go find a seat at the bar." He gave Nate a shove in that direction.

"Good riddance," Sally Midge shouted to their backs.

They didn't bother to respond.

"Can you imagine the gall of that man," Flo said. "He's as bad as Bart. Bart may have been a pain in the backside, but he didn't try to kick us out. We need to organize a protest." She raised her fist in the air. "Power to the people. Occupy Ludwick Realty."

I suddenly felt thirsty. I gulped down the rest of my drink and stuck out my tongue. It tasted yucky. It probably had been sitting in the heated air too long.

The others continued to debate the demise of Omnipodge Village Center. I followed the conversation for a few minutes. I felt very tired. My stomach gurgled, and I belched. "'Scuse me." My head lolled to the side. Then all went black.

Chapter 42

A HAZY MIST CIRCLED OVER MY head. Pulses of warm air shot out of the ground. It reminded me of the time I went with my parents to Yellowstone Park when I was ten and we visited the geysers and bubbling pools. I watched one plume go up a hundred feet. I tried to clap my hands together, but they didn't move. Something covered my body. I shook from side to side but couldn't rid myself of what felt like a heavy blanket. I coughed. The air. Something was wrong with the air. A foul breeze struck my face, over and over again. I tried to wipe my face, but my hands still wouldn't move. My hair blew forward into my face. My eyes shot open. I took a deep breath and coughed. Smoke!

A blanket covered my whole body. I removed my hands from under the cover and discovered I wore slacks and a blouse and not pajamas. My own bed. I coughed again. More smoke wafting in through the partially open window. A strong breeze smacked me in the face. Willie. He had woken me.

I rubbed my eyes and coughed a third time. Smoke. A fire. I needed to get out of here. I jumped out of bed and raced down the stairs. I could see flames outside the kitchen window. I grabbed the fire extinguisher mounted next to the refrigerator and dashed out the back door. Flames leapt from the woodpile stacked alongside the cottage. I reached in my pocket, found my cell phone. No bars. When would the cell tower recognize my small, but important to me, area for cell coverage? Then I remembered I had good reception at Jake's store and dashed next door to see a full set of bars. I punched 9-1-1. As soon as the operator answered, I shouted, "Fire at Driftwood Creatives in the Omnipodge Village Center!"

Then I dashed back, released the pin on the fire extinguisher and began spraying the fire. I aimed where I could see the base of the flames on the woodpile. It didn't look like the flames had yet moved to the wooden wall.

I kept pressing the handle until the foam had been expelled. I shook it one last time and dropped it on the ground. I thought next of going inside to fill a bucket with water.

I took a step toward the door but stopped. In the distance I heard sirens. My tinnitus crackled in time to the wails. Then I saw flashing lights. A fire engine raced into the parking area. I waved frantically and shouted, "Over here."

Two firefighters came running. The fastest one had a familiar brawn. Kurt. He had an axe in his hand.

"Wood pile, fire," I said with a gasp.

Kurt knocked the smoldering wood pile away from the house. His companion held a fire extinguisher, which he shot against the side of the house.

"Are you okay?" Kurt asked.

I shivered in the cool night air. "I think so. I woke up smelling smoke and then discovered the woodpile on fire."

The other firefighter announced that he would check to make sure nothing was burning inside. I slumped to the ground, rested against the side of the cottage and rubbed my forehead. "I don't remember anything after going to Benny's Bar with you last night."

"Yeah, you passed out. I never saw anyone do that on one soft drink."

"That's never happened to me before. And after I passed out?"

"I drove you home."

"How'd I get into my bed?"

Even in the low ambient light, I could see Kurt's cheeks redden. "I… uh… got your key out of your purse, carried you up to your room and covered you with a blanket."

How romantic. He had touched me or my clothes. And I had missed all of it. "Rats."

He made a crossing motion with his hands. "Don't be upset. I didn't do anything improper."

This time I only thought, "Rats." Instead, I said, "That's not it. I have no problem with you having taken me up to my room. I'm upset that I passed out and then this fire happened. Do you think it was arson?"

"We'll have the fire investigator come check in the morning. Without someone setting it, I can't imagine how a fire started here, though. No lightning strikes, no electrical problems I can see. It would take some kind of accelerant to set wood logs on fire, particularly after the fog we've had lately. Let me take another look."

He poked at the scattered logs with his axe. "What's this?"

Still shaking, I raised myself to my feet and stepped over to the scattered pile of logs, some blackened with soot.

Kurt pointed. "Right there, but don't touch it."

I bent over. Some charred material. I peered closer. *Uh-oh.* Smoldering yarn. I leaned over farther as a pungent aroma caused me to sneeze.

"Did you get a good look, Pru?"

I straightened. "Yeah. Burnt Vicuna yarn."

I felt a wave of nausea course through my stomach. Someone had deliberately tried to burn down my shop and home.

I kicked at a log that Kurt had dislodged from the woodpile. It skittered to the side, revealing a wrapper. I peered more closely. Snickers. Like I had seen in the Black SUV.

I looked toward the parking area. No cars. Only the fire engine.

"Kurt, did you happen to pass a black SUV on the way here?"

"Nope. No traffic. Why do you ask?"

"As you know, I've had trouble with someone driving a black SUV. I thought he might have been in the area."

Then the scene from the bar last night pulsed through my smoke-filled brain. The drink. Something had been wrong with the drink. It had tasted funny. The realization struck me like a kite in a lightning storm. Someone drugged my drink and set my place on fire. And Vicuna yarn might have been used to start the fire, just like used in the garrote that killed Bart Cunard. And I might have died in the blaze if I hadn't awakened in time. Then I realized who had saved me. "Willie," I mumbled.

"Will he what?" Kurt asked.

I was tempted to tell Kurt about Wrong Way Willie, but maybe this wasn't the best of times. "Um… the other firefighter who went inside. Will he be out soon so I can go back to sleep?"

"He's inspecting the whole building. He should be done in a few minutes."

Kurt and I stared into each others' eyes. I took a step toward him, ready to fall into the arms of my hero, when loud footfalls caused me to peer to the side.

"Here's the fire chief," Kurt announced.

"Rats."

"No, his name is Randy," Kurt said.

Kurt and Randy put their heads together, and, shortly, the other firefighter emerged and joined the confab.

Meanwhile, I stood in the cold with no hero to console me and keep me warm in his large, strong arms.

The three broke their huddle like a football team ready to score the next touchdown.

"We'll be on our way, Pru," Kurt said.

"Thanks for coming and saving me."

Red shot up his neck. "All part of the firefighter's job."

I thought he might move toward me, but Chief Randy tapped him on the shoulder. "Let's get back to the station. You need to fill out the report."

Kurt saluted, gave me a feeble wave, turned and headed toward the parking lot.

My hunky hero. Here and gone.

Since none of the other shopkeepers lived in their stores, no crowd had gathered to watch the action. Once the fire engine drove out of sight I went inside and locked the door.

Then I remembered that I had never replaced the batteries in my smoke detector. Good thing I had Willie. I immediately raided my battery drawer, took a stool over and climbed up to put in a fresh battery. Now, I had double coverage. A smoke alarm and a ghost.

Chapter 43

SPEAKING OF A GHOST, I called out, "Willie are you here?"

No response.

"Willie, you can't possibly be sleeping after all the commotion. Let me know you can hear me. Are you here?"

This time the curtain wiggled back and forth.

I put my fists on my hips. "Funny man. Let's go have a talk using our writing surface." I marched into the workshop and smoothed out the sand in the sheet pan. "First of all, did you see Kurt bringing me home last night?"

A big "YES" appeared.

"Did anything happen?"

I leaned over to see a "?"

Willie's use of punctuation had improved.

"Okay. What I mean is this. Uh… when Kurt took me upstairs was there any hanky-panky?"

"NO."

I didn't know whether to be happy or sad. "Then what did he do?"

"OUT DOOR."

"Hey, you're getting the hang of writing. Good job. All right. After Kurt tucked me in bed, did he leave?"

He drew a smiley face.

"Next question. This is the biggie. Did you notice anything right before the fire started?"

I waited for a moment. Then the sand rippled and the words "BIG BLAK CAR" appeared.

I corrected his spelling. "The black car showed up, I assume in the parking area."

"YES."

"Did you see who was in the car?"

"NO DARK."

"I'm impressed with the words you've learned."

"GUD TEACHR."

I again showed him the correct spelling. "Keep working on your writing. You're really getting the hang of it."

He drew a hangman's noose with a stick figure.

"Good one. Did you hear anything?"

"STRIK MATCH."

"Wow. You have good hearing to pick up someone striking a match. Too bad you can't go through the walls to see outside."

"KANT."

"Anything else you can think of?"

"NO."

Once again, we were back to the black SUV. Apparently, the driver had started the fire. We needed to nail that bastard. I shook my fist. "Samuel Jenkins, you're going down!" We only had to find him. I still couldn't figure out what a used car salesman from Los Angeles was doing in Omnipodge, much less harassing me and maybe trying to kill me.

After pacing around the room for a moment, I returned to the sheet pan. "Okay, Willie. We're going to brainstorm. I'll tell you what I know about the suspects and see if you have any ideas."

"OK."

"My prime suspects are Larry Ludwick and Nate Dupres. They are working together in some way though I haven't gotten a clear picture of how. And Samuel Jenkins's black SUV was in Larry's parking lot. I saw a Snickers wrapper in the car and one near the woodpile tonight. Those three are somehow linked in some sort of shady dealings. I haven't put those pieces together yet. Any thoughts?"

"NO."

"You're a big help."

"TRY."

"Okay, you're trying. I shouldn't be so critical. I guess I'm still upset over the fire and all. Next, we have Jake Yalley and Sally Midge Cunard. Flo overheard them fighting, and they've acted squirrelly since then, although they seem to be back together. Thoughts?"

"JELUS."

I showed him the right spelling. "Jealousy could have played a role. Jake certainly wanted Bart out of the way. And soon after he's dead, Jake pops the question to Sally Midge. One or both of them could have taken care of Bart. That leaves no Bart hanging over the marriage. And I found some Vicuna yarn hidden in the back of Jake's store. All incriminating."

"RITE."

I smoothed the sand and again showed the correction. "Next are Bea, Flo and Herb. They had reasons to hate Bart and were in the area at the time of the murder. Bea had a book on garroting, Flo had a hidden piece of driftwood like the garrote handle, and Herb had a hidden garrote made of Vicuna yarn and driftwood. I can't imagine any of them being murderers. Do you think one is a killer?"

"MAYBE."

"You're right. I can't eliminate them yet." My heart sank. "No way could I see Herb using a garrote." Then I perked up. "Or someone could have planted those clues, as Detective Moriarty is always accusing me—a diversionary stunt."

"CUD B."

"That completes my list. Anyone else you can think of who had means, opportunity and motive?"

"YES."

I arched an eyebrow. "Really? Who?"

"PRU."

I sputtered. If I had false teeth, I would have spit them out on the floor. "Give me a break, Willie. You think I'm the murderer?"

"JOK."

"But not a funny one. I need your serious assistance. I want you to keep an eye out for any suspicious people or activities."

"I I."

It was obvious Willie wanted to keep up with Jake in telling dumb jokes. At least with a ghost, I could hide the sheet pan and not have to listen to him.

"Willie, I thought you might have become a homeless ghost, if the arsonist had succeeded in setting a fire."

"NEED HOM."

"Me, too. Speaking of home, there's another threat we have. Larry Ludwick wants to tear down the cottages in the Omnipodge Village Center to build an apartment complex. That would be terrible."

"SAV HOM."

I gritted my teeth. Willie was right. I had to find a way to save his home. "One last thing. Will you stay up and keep a watch to make sure no one else tries to burn us down?"

"YES."

With my ghostly watchman on duty, I retired to my bedroom. What could I do to prevent Larry Ludwick from destroying our shop and home? A thought popped into my head, like one of those cartoon light bulbs. That might work.

I fired up my computer and began Googling. I found the web

site I wanted and downloaded a form. Tomorrow I would mobilize my neighbors. We had a way to fight Larry Ludwick after all. I dropped into bed to try to get a few hours of fitful sleep.

Chapter 44

AFTER TOSSING AND TURNING FOR several hours, I finally fell asleep at daybreak, and wouldn't you know it, I had finally drifted into dreams that didn't contain images of fire, smoke, killer bees or black SUVs when my peace and quiet was interrupted by a loud pounding on the door. A breeze ruffled my hair, and I knew Willie wanted me to get up.

"Why don't you answer the door, Willie? Aren't your powers strong enough to blow the door open?"

The breeze swirled my hair again and then pulsed back and forth across my face as if someone was slapping me.

"Okay, okay. You can't open the door, and you want me to. I get it, so back off."

The breeze ruffled the curtains, and they jounced up and down.

I threw on a robe and slippers, stumbled downstairs, pulled open the door to find Detective Moriarty and another man standing there. This guy looked almost as hunky as Kurt, had a cute Errol Flynn moustache and wavy brown hair. He filled out a large parka very nicely. *Stay focused.*

"I understand you had a little fire here last night," Moriarty said.

"Someone set a fire, but fortunately I woke up and extinguished it in time. Then the firefighters arrived to make sure it was completely out."

The guy I thought of as Errol stepped forward. "You say someone set it. What makes you think that?"

"And you are?" I inquired.

He bowed. "Errol Kent. I'm a fire investigator."

Wow. His name really was Errol. And his last name of Kent reminded me of Clark Kent of Superman fame. My own superhero fire investigator here to find out what happened. If Kurt didn't get with it, maybe…

I pulled myself back to reality. I would stay true to my *sort-of* boyfriend even if nothing much had happened with him yet. "To answer your question, one of the firefighters, Kurt Whelan, who responded to the emergency call, found some burnt Vicuna yarn mixed in with the logs of my woodpile that had been set on fire. Detective Moriarty will recognize the significance of that fact."

Errol gave Moriarty a questioning glance.

Moriarty crinkled up his nose as if he had encountered a pile of rotten vegetables. "Same kind of yarn involved in a murder investigation."

Errol pulled a small camera out of his jacket pocket. "Show me the woodpile and burnt yarn."

I padded out the door and around the side of the building to the destroyed woodpile. I located the blackened yarn, damp from early morning fog, and pointed. "There it is right where it fell after the firefighters knocked apart the burning logs."

Errol bent over and inspected the mangled yarn. He snapped pictures from several different angles. Then he put on rubber gloves, removed a paper bag from his jacket and deposited the evidence inside. "Now if you two will give me a moment, I want to check the area."

I glanced down where I had seen the Snickers wrapper before. It wasn't there. I wondered if it had blown away or if someone had come and removed it. I shivered. The arsonist might have returned to the scene of the crime. Good thing Willie had stayed on guard. I wouldn't have wanted a home invasion or another fire.

"Let's go inside, Detective," I said. "I have a few things to pass on to you that will be useful."

"Anything in regards to you pulling this to distract me, missy?"

"No, but if you listen carefully, I have some useful information for your murder investigation."

I stomped back through the open door and didn't even turn to see if Moriarty followed me. Fortunately, he did.

I sat on my counter stool and let him stand.

"Several things you should be aware of, Detective. First, someone drugged my drink at Benny's Bar last night."

"Sure you didn't imbibe too much?"

"One soft drink was all I had. One of my friends took me home. Then I was awakened by the smell of smoke." I wasn't going to mention Willie for obvious reasons. "I called 9-1-1 and did my best to use my fire extinguisher to extinguish the blaze. Interestingly, a black SUV was seen in the parking area right before the fire."

"And who can verify that?"

I gulped. How could I answer without getting into the Willie situation. "I… uh… happened to glance out the window."

He raised an eyebrow almost to his hairline. "In the dark, with your house on fire, you spotted a black SUV? Doesn't sound credible."

"That's what was there. By the way, did you find the black SUV in Larry Ludwick's parking lot like I told you?"

"No. It's not my top priority."

"But it well could be the murderer's car. Don't be so nonchalant."

"You trying to run my job for me, missy."

"No. Only a suggestion." I wanted to mention the Snickers wrapper, but with the evidence gone that would only lead to another harangue from Moriarty. "I think Larry Ludwick, Nate Dupres and Samuel Jenkins who owns the black SUV are connected in some way. Might be a good lead for you."

"Yeah, to take me away from figuring out how you committed the murder."

I jumped off the stool and stormed over to Moriarty. "I can answer that for you. I didn't. Nate Dupres is working in some capacity for Larry Ludwick. Larry wants to terminate the leases of shopkeepers here in the Omnipodge Village Center. He's now majority owner of the Village Center. And with Bart Cunard out of the picture, Larry can do exactly what he wants. I don't know how Samuel Jenkins is connected, but his car is definitely involved."

"None of that indicates Nate Dupres or Larry Ludwick are murderers."

"Larry certainly benefits from Bart being out of the way, and Nate has been harassing me. He could have staged the murder to cause me trouble."

"You sure have a way of pointing to others when the murder took place right here in your shop."

Ignoring his comment, I decided to take the initiative. "Did you find either of their fingerprints here after Bart was killed?"

"I'm not going to share details of an investigation with you, missy."

"Is that because you don't have any details?"

We glared at each other but were interrupted when Errol stuck his head in the front door. "I'm finished. I've taken the pictures and collected the evidence I need."

"Let's get out of here." Moriarty pushed his way past me and out the door.

"Nice meeting you, Errol. Have a good rest of your life, Detective."

Errol gave me a pleasant smile, spun on his heels and followed Moriarty toward the parking area.

I closed the door only wishing someone would garrote Moriarty.

Chapter 45

THE REST OF THE MORNING brought me a smattering of customers. I made two important phone calls, one to Sacramento and the other to make arrangements to reserve a meeting room at the Omnipodge Community Center for the next evening to discuss Larry Ludwick's plans to close the Omnipodge Village Center. I also filled out the form I had printed the night before. I took a break in the middle of the day to make the rounds with my neighbors to assemble the troops for the next evening against the dark lord and the forces of evil. I would be there loaded for bear and any other animal.

Finally, I had to rush out to the supermarket to buy supplies for the dinner I'd be cooking for Kurt and Granny. As I scanned the aisles, I got the shakes. What could I prepare that would bring a smile to Kurt's face, meet Granny's standards and be something I could serve without poisoning either of them. Only one choice—mac and cheese.

Back at the shop, I brought in a few more bucks in the afternoon and then closed early to prepare for my big dinner event. I carefully set the small table in my dining nook with a clean white tablecloth and three places using my special gold-ware utensils, goblets, cloth napkins and Spode china. Kurt might not notice, but Granny would surely give me style points for the effort.

I debated whether I should prepare the food ahead of time and keep it warm or wait until my guests arrived and then cook. I decided on the former so I could have everything ready and not have to be too hassled.

First, I cut up lettuce, tomatoes and avocado to make a large bowl of salad, which I set on the table. I didn't want to risk making homemade dressing, so I poured some store-bought ranch dressing into a bowl and set this on the table. Then I boiled water in a pan on my electric stovetop, dropped in the macaroni and set the timer for ten minutes. Having learned from my earlier experiences when I became distracted, I watched carefully so that when the timer went off, I immediately removed the boiling macaroni and dumped it in a sieve in the sink. Then I returned the macaroni to the pan, mixed in cheese, milk and margarine. I took a taste. Delish. This would definitely pass muster.

Finally, I uncorked a bottle of sparkling cider.

Giving everything a final check, I decided I was ready for my guests.

This would be a filling meal for Kurt, and I knew Granny liked comfort food so she would approve.

I had a few minutes before my guests arrived. I wanted to keep the mac and cheese warm, so I set another burner to low and put the pan on top so it wouldn't get cold. At that moment Boopsie came charging into the kitchen holding her catnip mouse. She rolled over on the floor and batted her toy into the air.

Aw, how could I ignore cuteness like that? I gave her a scritch under the chin, and she rewarded me with a loud purr.

Not to be left out, Spools ran into the kitchen with a tangle of fishing line following him. He skidded to a stop when he saw Boopsie and bashed into my leg. He caught me by surprise, and I fell against the stove, catching myself by reaching out my hand, fortunately not to the hot surface.

"Okay, guys. You have to be on your best behavior. We have company coming."

Boopsie ignored me, preferring to rub her face against her toy. Spools regarded me with his sad eyes. Then he tried to scratch his ear, but his paw was too tangled to reach.

I bent over and untangled him, allowing him to take care of his itch.

There was a knock on the door. I rushed through the workshop, dropped the tangle of fishing line on my workbench and opened the door to find Kurt standing there in a clean blue long sleeved shirt holding a box of chocolates in his hand.

"Aw, Kurt, you shouldn't have."

"I know you like dark chocolate."

He did pay attention. Before I could take the box or close the door, Granny came stomping up the walkway with her walking poles going full tilt. "Hold your ponies, I'm here."

"I can see that."

She eyed Kurt up and down. "Not bad." She grabbed the box of chocolate out of Kurt's hand and tore the plastic wrap off. She smacked her lips, removed a piece of chocolate and popped it in her mouth.

"Granny, those were for me."

"Hold your watermelon. I needed some quick energy after my hike over here. You don't want me passing out from low blood sugar, do you?" She gobbled one more piece and then handed me the box. "I'm ready for some chow."

I led my guests to the table I'd set.

Granny arched an eyebrow. "Looks good. What kind of vittles did you fix?"

"It's a surprise."

Granny rubbed her hands together. "I love surprises."

Kurt sucked on his lip. I didn't think he looked forward to a surprise.

I filled the three goblets with sparkling cider, and Granny wasted no time in helping herself to some salad while I excused myself to go fetch the main course.

When I entered the kitchen, I smelled something burning. *Uh-oh.* I raced to the stove and saw my previously beautiful mac and cheese turning brown and sticking to the pan. My heart sank. How could this have happened?

I removed the pan from the stovetop. Then I noticed the problem. The burner was on high. I had definitely set it to low. Then I remembered. When Spools had knocked me off balance and I flailed my arm, I must have bumped the knob and changed the setting.

At that moment Granny shouted from the dining room, "What are your intentions with my granddaughter?"

I could hear heard Kurt gasp and choke. Tough question.

No answer.

"Dog got your tongue?"

Kurt coughed. "Good salad."

As much as I wanted to eavesdrop, I had a problem to take care of—the smoldering glob of mac and cheese goo. I didn't have time to make something else. I added a little water to the mass and stirred it. It was like trying to move hardening cement.

"What's taking you so long?" Granny shouted from the dining area. "I've finished munching on leaves. I'm going to have to start chewing on the tablecloth if you don't hurry up with the main course."

Gritting my teeth, I took the wooden spoon and carved out lumps of the homemade concrete and dropped them on three plates. At least the spoon hadn't broken. I packed the mounds down with the spoon and added some sprinkle cheese to disguise the brown macaroni. With no other choice, I brought plates in and set them in front of Granny and Kurt. I added my own and sat down.

Kurt took a bite and chewed and chewed. He finally swallowed, a pained expression on his face. "Uh… good."

Granny took a bite and immediately spat it out on her plate. "Yuck. What dreck is this? It tastes like burnt cardboard."

I tried to maintain my composure, but a large tear formed in the corner of my eye and trickled down my cheek. I tried my best but couldn't stifle a sniff.

Kurt's eyes widened. "Don't cry, Pru. It's not that bad."

"It's horrible," Granny said.

"I tried," I said between sobs.

"Hell is paved with good innuendos," Granny replied.

Now I couldn't hold back the tears. I put my head down on the table. It would have been a good escape path from looking at anyone, except I didn't notice that either Kurt or Granny had served me a plate of salad, which my forehead smacked right into the middle of.

I wiped a piece of squished avocado off my forehead with the napkin and then really wailed.

Granny threw her napkin down on the table. "Don't be a sniveling wimp. Suck it up. Come on, I'll help you fix something digestible."

Chapter 46

GRANNY WHIPPED UP SOME TUNA and made sandwiches. I watched, helpless to do anything except wipe my nose. She even toasted the bread without burning it. She slapped the sandwiches together and dusted her hands. "Voila, Ladybug. Before you can shake a goat's tail, we have dinner."

"Thanks, Granny."

"Go serve Kurt his sandwich, and I'll bring in the other two plates," she said. "That man needs some real food."

I meekly followed orders. Would I ever be a fully functioning adult? Maybe I was running my own small business, but Granny had rescued me again, and I hadn't mastered the art of cooking. No, not one iota.

My *sort-of* boyfriend seemed relieved when I gave him the sandwich. He did lift the top piece of toast to check what was inside, though. I guess firefighters are taught to be cautious. Satisfied with what he saw, be dove in as if he hadn't eaten in a week.

As I munched on the tangy tuna, I watched the two people who meant the most to me. Kurt continued to be fully focused on his food. Granny licked her finger and pointed it at me. "What's happening with this murder investigation?"

I sighed loudly. "It's bollixed up. I keep thinking I've found clues, and then they don't pan out."

"Out of the pan and into the fireplace," Granny said.

"Kind of like that. And then everything I do leads to Detective

Moriarty accusing me of committing the crime."

Granny's lower lip trembled. "He isn't going to arrest you, is he?"

"I certainly haven't been able to show him who the real killer is. He threatens to lock me up for the crime every time he sees me. One of these times he may do it."

Granny slammed her hand down on the table causing the gold-ware to shake and Kurt to flinch. "I won't let that happen."

"I don't know what you can do. I'm trying my darndest to prove my innocence, but it isn't working with Moriarty."

"We'll see." Granny stood. "I have to get going. Have a hot date tonight with my snookums at Old Detectives Home."

"The guy with the moustache?" I asked.

"The very same."

"When are you going to introduce him to me?"

"One of these days. Right now, I want him all to myself." She eyed Kurt again. "I like your studmuffin, Pru."

I choked on a bite of tuna. Heat raced up my neck. I didn't know why I had invited Kurt and Granny at the same time.

After Granny left, Kurt said, "Your granny is… uh… different."

I rolled my eyes. "That's for sure. I hope she didn't embarrass you."

He grinned. "Only as much as she embarrassed you. I've never seen you turn that shade of pink before."

"I guess we're even. Let's change the subject. You want to do some studying for the police officers exam?"

"That would be great. I have the book in my truck."

He retrieved it, and we spent an hour going over writing incident reports. He had really gotten the hang of writing complete sentences. I complimented him on his progress, and he turned a shade of pink as well, which was quite an accomplishment given his tanned complexion.

Finally, he yawned. "I better head home. I'm still tired from coming to your fire in the middle of the night."

"I don't blame you. I could use some catch-up sleep."

I walked him to the front of my shop. We stood there looking at each other with the door open. He took a step toward me. At that moment, a small gray object shot alongside my shoe and into the room. "Rats."

Kurt stared past me. "No, I think it's a mouse."

And sure enough, Boopsie came alive from her pillow and charged around the room like a wildcat. Finally, the mouse decided to escape and zipped out the door. Boopsie screeched to a stop, practically on Kurt's shoe. She might be brave inside my house but never dared to venture into the wilds of the outside.

Kurt gave me a feeble wave and headed toward the parking area. Rats and double rats. Foiled again.

I watched as he drove away.

Would we ever get together for more than a study date?

I slouched inside and closed the door. I was greeted with a breeze that ruffled my hair.

"Hi, Willie. Between Kurt, my cooking and this investigation, I'm not having much success. I wish you could help me solve the murder. Then I'd have one thing out of the way rather than feeling like such a doofus. Let's go do some writing."

We adjourned to the workshop and I smoothed out the sands in the sheet pan with my hand.

Letters formed and I read, "DUFUS."

"Thanks, that's all I need, Willie."

Then the words, "B HAPY," appeared.

In spite of everything that had happened, I smiled. "Willie, you know how to make a girl feel better. Now, let's discuss the murder again."

I reviewed with him the persons of interest and what I had learned. "I'm still thinking Nate Dupres and Larry Ludwick are our two most likely suspects. What do you think?"

"NAT BLK CAR."

This was like receiving a text message from a teenager. "You think Nate is linked to the black car?"

"YES"

"That's interesting. The car is owned by Samuel Jenkins, whoever he is. Why would Nate be connected?"

"STOL BOROW?"

"Hmm. That's an interesting theory. I wish I could have an open discussion with Detective Moriarty to explore that."

"DUFUS"

"Yes. Moriarty really is. The shopkeepers are also suspects. Of those, Jake Yalley has acted the strangest. He and his fiancée Sally Midge got into a fight. She has this big rock of a diamond that he gave her."

"SPARKL"

"That's right. It does sparkle. Let's go over the events the day of the murder. I spent the morning visiting the other shops and then went out to lunch with Herb. When I came back, I found Bart's body. I figure Bart could have entered my shop since he had a master key." I snapped my fingers. "And he had been interested in the idea you had hidden gold in the cottage." I slapped my forehead. "He knew I'd be gone at lunch and must have sneaked in. But then someone killed him."

"FOLLWD."

"Exactly. Someone followed him in. But who?"

"DONT NO."

"And I haven't figured that out yet either. Any other thoughts?"

"NOT NOW"

I guess I had gone as far with my ghostly assistant as I could.

Chapter 47

THE NEXT DAY, I ROLLED out of bed, literally, because Spools jumped up and nudged me with his wet nose, and, trying to avoid the slobber, I fell out of bed. I sat on the floor for a moment, deciding if I should climb back in my warm nest and avoid the world for another hour. By then wide awake, I faced the inevitable, took a shower and dressed.

* * * * *

By the end of the day, I had sold enough mobiles and driftwood creations to buy food for a week. Talk about living hand to mouth. But, as Granny would say, a penny earned is a penny in earnest. I closed the shop, put the cash in my floor safe and fixed myself a safe dinner—a peanut butter and jelly sandwich. The only problem occurred when I dropped the piece of bread slathered with jelly. Of course, it landed jelly side down on the kitchen floor. Again, Spools raced over to help clean up. With a fresh piece of bread, I completed my gourmet meal and washed it down with a tall glass of milk. Yum. You can't beat pb&j.

Mopsy transported me to the meeting without so much as a black SUV sighting. All was well in the universe.

That is until I stepped into the meeting room.

I gulped at the size of the crowd. There sat my neighbors. Jake Yalley and Sally Midge Cunard held hands in the front row. Herb leaned toward Bea Potter, deep in conversation in the second row. Flo Florrest sat by several of her friends in the third row. My neighbors had rallied quite a group of supporters. Just then Larry Ludwick and Nate Dupres strolled into the room as if they owned the place. How had the enemy learned about the meeting? Worst of all, before I could head to the front of the room to begin the meeting, Detective Moriarty slunk out of the shadows and placed his despicable frame right in front of me.

"You ready to share your confession with me, missy?"

I let out an exasperated sigh. "You're like an old phonograph record with the needle stuck in one groove. Are you ready to do something about Samuel Jenkins and his black SUV?"

He gave me an evil grin. "Speaking of that black SUV. What makes you think it's owned by Samuel Jenkins?"

"A little bird told me."

"Your little bird is wrong. It belongs to an Omnipodge resident who is out of town. Someone either borrowed it or stole it."

I winced. "How can that be?"

"Just the facts, missy." His grin widened. "I have the evidence I need to take you in."

My heart sank. I hadn't been able to assemble the puzzle pieces to find the real murderer. I needed to run this meeting to fight for the future of the Omnipodge Village Center and not be stuck cooling my heels in the slammer.

Before I could once again profess my innocence, Granny came racing up and whapped Detective Moriarty with one of her walking sticks. "Leave her alone. She's as innocent as a newborn baboon."

Moriarty, caught off guard, ducked away before Granny could wallop him again. Once out of striking range, he said, "I should arrest both of you."

Granny straightened herself up to her full five foot one. "Leave Pru alone. You can arrest me, though. I killed Bart Cunard."

"What!" I shouted. "You did nothing of the sort."

"Yes, I did, Ladybug." She dropped her hiking poles and held her wrists out to Moriarty. "Lead me to the guillotine. I wrapped that garrote around the slimebag's neck."

Moriarty's mouth dropped open, and he blinked rapidly. "Huh?"

Granny stepped close to Moriarty and poked him in the ribs. "You heard me, doofus. I demand to be arrested."

Moriarty swiveled his neck back and forth between Granny and me as if watching a ping pong match. Again, he could only mumble, "Huh?"

At that moment, Flo shouted, "Let's get this meeting going."

Before Moriarty could emerge from his trance, Granny picked up her walking poles. I grabbed Granny's arm and dragged her toward a seat in the back of the room. "What were you trying to do?" I whispered.

"I couldn't let him arrest you."

I pushed her onto the chair. "But why did you falsely confess to a crime you didn't commit?"

"A woman is innocent until proven gullible. I had to distract the detective." Granny giggled. "And it worked."

"He's still apt to arrest both of us."

Granny hefted one of her poles. "Let him try."

"You'll be locked up for assault and battery and attacking a police officer."

"Oh, fiddle-faddle. Stop worrying. If it ain't broke, don't fixate on it. Now, are you going to get this meeting going or stand here yammering?"

I headed to the front of the room with no interference from Moriarty and looked around the room. The good news—I spotted Kurt in the audience and caught his eye.

He waved to me.

My heart fluttered. How could my emotions be so easily swayed by that big lunk? Okay, I was really thinking hunk.

I grabbed the microphone. A screech of feedback erupted from the speakers, and my tinnitus went crazy.

I held the microphone out at arm's length. When the screeching stopped, I adjusted the microphone and spoke into it, "I'm calling to order our meeting on the future of the Omnipodge Village Center."

"You tell 'em!" Granny shouted.

I cleared my throat. "Thank you all for showing up tonight to discuss this very important topic. As you know the Omnipodge Village Center consists of nineteenth century cottages with the outsides preserved to maintain their original appearances and the insides renovated for modern use.

"Rather than being torn down, these should be protected. The reason for this meeting is that a local developer, Larry Ludwick, intends to level these historic buildings and replace them with an apartment complex—"

I was interrupted by a loud chorus of boos. I held up my hand. "I share your concern over this inappropriate development. Instead, I think we should preserve the character of our community by keeping the Omnipodge Village Center as it now exists."

My statement was met with loud cheers and applause. I felt my heart race. We had local support. Maybe there was hope to prevent Larry Ludwick from kicking us out.

I went on, "In particular, the shop and home I reside in belonged to the founder of Omnipodge, Wrong Way Willie Woburn. He is a key part of our town's history, and his memory and original cottage should not be destroyed. Having lived in that cottage, I feel like I personally know Wrong Way Willie Woburn and do not want his memory lost by the destruction of the house he built. We owe it to our town and the future generations to maintain this important link to our past."

Another round of applause and cheers.

Before I could continue, Larry Ludwick lumbered out of his seat, stomped to the front of the room, grabbed the microphone out of my hand and pushed me to the side. "Let me set the record straight. I own the property and have been given city approval for the new development. There's nothing you can do to stop it." He gave his head a determined nod and handed the microphone back to me.

Rather than being disconcerted, I welcomed this statement. I gave the audience my most endearing smile. "You can see the nature of the developer who wants to destroy historic property. He has no regard for the significance of these old cottages nor for the people who run the shops today. There is one thing he has overlooked. Yesterday, I contacted the California State Office of Historical Preservation and filled out the paperwork to add the cottages in the Omnipodge Village Center to the Historical Register. By certified mail, I notified the Omnipodge City Clerk that this paperwork would be filed. There is a ninety-day period for the city government to provide written comments. I think there is enough local support to prevent this unwanted destruction of historic structures."

Again, the room exploded with cheers.

Granny grabbed her walking poles in one hand and came to the front of the room to give me a high five with her free hand.

"I didn't know you had that up your cuff," Granny said.

I put my arm around her. "This buys us some time to fight Larry Ludwick's eviction plans."

Granny took a seat in the front row, and Larry Ludwick stomped back up to the front of the room and grabbed the microphone again. "You'll all regret this."

Loud boos cascaded throughout the room.

I took the microphone back. "I think you can hear how popular your idea is, Larry. You might want to figure out a way to work with your community, not against it."

The room rattled with cheering.

Detective Moriarty strolled up to the front of the room and whispered in my ear. I nodded and spoke into the microphone. "Detective Moriarty would like to say a few words since we're assembled here today."

Moriarty took the microphone, and I stood to the side. "I know you've been concerned over the recent suspicious death of Bart Cunard."

A voice from the side of the room shouted, "Not exactly suspicious. More like a murder."

Murmurs rippled through the room.

Moriarty cleared his throat. "That's right. The… uh… murder. The good news is that I have solved the case. Since this room has all the people present who have been involved in the investigation, this is an opportune time to let you know that one of you will be arrested in a few minutes."

People began shouting and waving their arms. Amid the hubbub, I looked around the room. Police officers stood at every exit.

Chapter 48

MORIARTY SHOUTED INTO THE MICROPHONE, "Okay, okay. Let's have quiet."

It took a minute for everyone to settle down.

"As I said, on behalf of your Omnipodge Police Department I have solved the murder case. I want to give you some background. The body of Bart Cunard was discovered in the shop run by Pru Pendergast." Moriarty focused on me. His grin reminded me of a hyena. "The murder weapon consisted of a garrote made from driftwood handles. Very convenient that her shop features driftwood."

I noticed several people staring at me. I tried my best to maintain my composure but felt a drop of moisture form on my forehead. I didn't like how this was going.

"Now the garrote also contained yarn that was traced to a shipment received by Flo Florrest in her yarn shop. That made her a suspect as well."

I could see Flo visibly pale. And Moriarty didn't even know I had spotted a piece of driftwood hidden in her shop.

Moriarty continued, "The other people running shops in the Omnipodge Village Center also had grudges against Bart Cunard and were considered persons of interest during the investigation."

Moriarty paused to stare at various members of the audience.

Herb twitched. I knew how uncomfortable he felt with Moriarty spouting accusations.

Moriarty fondled the microphone with both hands. "Another interesting occurrence. On numerous occasions, Ms. Pendergast has reported a black SUV trying to run her off the road. Interestingly, no one else witnessed these occurrences."

Yeah, because they happened on deserted streets where only the driver and me were present.

"She even went so far as to report the license plate of the black SUV. It turns out this belongs to a resident of our town."

I glanced over at Kurt to see a stricken look on his face. *Uh-oh.* My *sort-of* boyfriend now realized he had made a mistake. Not the car of Samuel Jenkins in Los Angeles. He must have messed up his database search.

Now more people glared at me. I tried to keep the heat from rising up my neck but being unsuccessful, imagined I had turned beet red by this time.

"In reality, Ms. Pendergast stole this car and then reported the incidents to distract us from her real crime." He pointed an accusing finger at me. "Pru Pendergast murdered Bart Cunard."

Granny stood and shook her fist at Moriarty. "You have the wrong person, you dingbat. If you have to arrest someone, I've already volunteered, but Pru is innocent."

Everyone stared at Granny.

"Don't give me your fish eyes. You all know my granddaughter didn't kill Bart Cunard." Granny sat and shouted at me. "I told you that you should have let him arrest me instead."

"But neither of us killed anyone."

"You and I know that, Ladybug, but not the rest of these yahoos."

I looked around the room again. I saw Nate munching a candy bar unperturbed that I had been accused of murder. Herb looked as pale as Wrong Way Willie might look if he materialized. Bea had her head down. Flo sat immobile. Sally Midge and Jake held hands as if they couldn't care less about anything else around them. At that moment the light hit Sally Midge's engagement ring and it reflected a blue glint. I suddenly remembered my last "conversation" with Willie. Two past images blended together. Then it clicked. I smacked my forehead. How could I have been so dense? I should have figured this out long ago. Only one thing to do. I took a step toward Moriarty.

"Don't let her leave the room!" Moriarty shouted.

Before anyone moved, I grabbed the microphone out of Moriarty's hand. "I'm not leaving. I didn't kill Bart Cunard, but I know who did."

The room grew silent.

I took a deep breath and exhaled. "Thank you for giving me your attention. There is one accurate thing that Detective Moriarty told you. I did report several incidents where a black SUV tried to run me off the road. That actually happened. I also was threatened two other times. Someone left a beehive on my doorstep and later tried to burn down my cottage in the Omnipodge Village Center. One interesting piece of evidence you should be aware of. After the fire, I found a Snickers wrapper near where the fire had been set. I also spotted a Snickers wrapper in the back seat of the black SUV." I pointed at Nate. "You'll notice that Nate Dupres, right there, is eating a Snickers bar."

Nate swallowed the last bite and quickly stuffed the wrapper in his pants pocket.

"Nate stole the black SUV, has been harassing me and is assisting Larry Ludwick in trying to destroy the Omnipodge Village Center. In fact, it wouldn't surprise me if the black SUV is out in the parking lot at this very moment. Detective Moriarty, you can check for yourself to see the Snickers wrapper there."

Nate jumped up, knocking his chair over, and ran toward the back exit, where a police officer blocked his progress. Nate veered to the side and headed back past the other side of the audience.

Before you could say lickety-split, Kurt was out of his chair, blocking Nate's way.

Nate tried to juke to the side, but Kurt raised his arm and decked my ex with a perfect right jab. I never felt so proud of my *sort-of* boyfriend.

Nate lay on the floor stunned.

One of the police officers strode over and lifted Nate to his feet.

"If you'll check Nate's pocket, you'll find a Snickers wrapper, and as I mentioned, there will also be another wrapper with his fingerprints in the back of the black SUV, Detective Moriarty."

Nate squirmed, still being held by the large police officer.

I stared at the pathetic worm. "Nate, Detective Moriarty may also arrest you for the murder of Bart Cunard. Anything you want to clarify?"

He finally stopped fighting. "Yeah, I have something to say."

I spoke into the microphone, "Let's give him a chance to speak."

People shushed each other until it finally became quiet.

Nate limped up to the front of the room with a police officer by his side. "I stole the black SUV, started the fire and left the beehive on Pru's doorstep, but I didn't kill Bart Cunard."

I took the microphone again. "That's correct. Nate didn't murder Bart, but he has been working for Larry Ludwick. He thought that by harassing me it would play into the hands of Detective Moriarty who could only think of my complaints as diversionary tactics. Larry wanted to keep us so busy with murder accusations that we wouldn't contest his plan to raze the Omnipodge Village Center. I wouldn't be surprised if Nate, acting on Larry's behalf, planted incriminating evidence in a number of our shops such as an imitation garrote in Herb's, driftwood in Flo's, Vicuna yarn in Jake's, a book on garroting in Bea's, and threatening notes on my doorstep. Right Nate?"

He hung his head. "Yeah, that's right."

I nodded. "You can see why we wouldn't want such an underhanded developer and his minion doing anything with our Village Center."

"That doesn't clear you from the murder," Moriarty called out.

"As I said, Nate didn't kill Bart, and neither did I. But someone else in this room is the killer, and it wasn't my grandmother who confessed in order to try to save me. The real murderer had a very strong motive."

I paused.

You could have heard a pin drop.

I leaned toward the microphone. "I should have realized it sooner, but I didn't make the connection until I saw the blue sparkle of Sally Midge's engagement ring. The murderer wanted to get Bart Cunard out of the way so he'd have Bart's ex all to himself. He also stole Bart's ring and used the diamond to fashion the engagement ring for Sally Midge. There's one jeweler in this room who did all of this. Detective Moriarty, you can arrest Jake Yalley."

Chapter 49

ALL HECK BROKE LOOSE.

Chairs scraped, and people scrambled to their feet.

Sally Midge stared at her engagement ring. "What? I thought this diamond looked familiar. You used Bart's diamond for my engagement ring?" She slapped Jake. "In addition to telling bad jokes, you have the nerve to recycle a diamond from my ex?"

She seemed more disturbed over this than the fact that Jake was a murderer.

Sally Midge raised her arm to slap Jake again, but he ducked away from her and strode toward me. He pulled a gun out of his belt, grabbed the back of my hair and put the pistol to my head. "N-nobody move or Pru gets shot."

My knees quaked, but I couldn't slump because Jake had my hair in an iron grip. Once again, how did I get myself into this latest predicament?

Detective Moriarty froze. Even Kurt couldn't do anything with a madman holding a gun to my head.

Sally Midge put her fists on her hips. "You told me that gun was for target practice. You lied to me."

Sally Midge still didn't seem perturbed that Jake held a gun to my head. She obviously had very self-involved interests.

"T-target practice so I could use it if I had to." Jake pushed the gun harder against my head. "I want all the police to go to the window side of the room. Now!"

Moriarty said, "Do as he says."

Moriarty moved as directed, and the other members of the fraternal order of police followed his lead. Kurt didn't join them since he was only a dispatcher. He'd have to wait until he passed his test.

"Now everyone else go out the m-main door."

I watched, helpless, as the people in the audience, including Kurt, streamed out as commanded. I was left with the pistol to my head and no support.

Jake gave me a shove. "W-walk slowly out the door. I'm right here. No sudden moves or you get shot."

I knew to follow orders, especially from a psycho. I shuffled toward the door. No way I would make a sudden move. I didn't like guns, particularly held to my head.

Think. What could I do? Answer. Nothing. I moved as slowly as possible without making Jake mad. I felt like I was on a death march. If Jake had killed once, there was nothing to prevent him doing it a second time. For now, my saving grace—by being alive I presented a shield to prevent the police from picking him off. I continued to move as slowly as possible. I had to buy some time.

"This isn't a good idea." My voice came out in a squeak.

"I've h-heard enough from you, Pru. If you hadn't interfered, Sally Midge and I would be free to get married and move away."

"I don't think Sally Midge is your best fan right now."

That earned me a thrust with the gun muzzle.

At the door, Jake paused to make sure the police hadn't moved. "St-stay where you are." Then he guided me outside.

"We're going for a little r-ride in my car, Pru."

I gulped. "I kind of like it here."

"No way. We'll be heading to M-Mexico."

"I don't like tacos."

"Too bad. You've caused enough t-trouble."

I had to delay him some way. I stumbled, but he jerked me upright, almost turning me into a Yul Brynner. Okay, I hated to admit it, but I watched old musicals on television all the time, and *The King and I* was one of my favorites.

He marched me toward the parking lot. People congregated around the building, but everyone made an effort to stay as far away from us as possible. Kurt made no attempt to rescue me as there was nothing he could do.

We approached Jake's Buick, when I made one last attempt at stumbling. This time he lost his grip on my hair and I fell to the pavement. As I looked up, I saw Granny jump out from behind a car and clobber Jake over the head with one of her walking sticks.

His gun skidded across the parking lot as he crashed on top of me.

I let out a scream.

Kurt appeared, lifted up Jake and delivered a final knockout punch. I had been saved by the dynamic duo.

Chapter 50

AFTER THE POLICE CUFFED JAKE and led him away, Granny lifted one walking pole in the air. "We gals need to stick together, Ladybug. Blood is thicker than wine."

We hugged. I wanted to share a hug with Kurt as well, but he had disappeared with the police contingent. Oh, well. Maybe another time.

*   *   *   *   *

Three days later, the Spring Break rush hit, and to my delight, money began flowing in. I could even buy steak occasionally instead of eating peanut butter and jelly sandwiches seven times a week. Once I closed the shop at the end of the day, I counted my proceeds and locked the cash in my safe.

When someone knocked on my door, I expected it might be a late customer, but it turned out to be Flo. I let her in, and she handed me a skein of Vicuna yarn. "Here's a little present for all you've done for the Omnipodge Village Center."

Warmth spread through my checks. "Aw, you shouldn't have."

"Yes, I should. We're still in business, and after the public outing of Larry Ludwick and his nefarious schemes, our historic cottage shops will stay in business. No more apartment complex plans. With the letters and emails to the City Council, they've decided to rescind their earlier decision and turn down Larry Ludwick's request to demolish the Omnipodge Village Center."

She gave me a high five, followed by a hug.

Flo stepped back. "Well, Larry did negotiate something out of the Council. In exchange for not fighting the reversal of the original Omnipodge Village Center decision, they've approved his request to develop Lilac Acres."

"Typical of Larry. Always working a deal. He's welcome to his acres of old fish parts."

"And, Pru, you found the real murderer and lifted the suspicion from the rest of us. I didn't even realize Nate had planted a piece of driftwood in my yarn."

"Between Nate and Jake, the subterfuge caused us oodles of problems. With Detective Moriarty intending to arrest me, I was fortunate to finally put the pieces of the puzzle together."

"Now Nate is in jail for arson, grand theft auto and harassment with bees, and Jake faces a murder trial thanks to you, Pru. It's amazing what Jake put together—stealing Vicuna yarn from my shop the morning right before the murder and driftwood from yours to construct a garrote. I wonder how he learned how to build one and use it."

"He was in the army. Sally Midge made a comment one time that Jake had been involved in something other than marching around in circles. That's where he picked up the necessary skills. He learned to use string or, in this case, yarn to make a twisted cord rope. And obviously he also knew how to employ the garrote."

"And how did Jake and Bart end up in your shop?"

"Greedy Bart had a master key. He knew I'd be out of my shop over lunch and let himself in to search for Willie Woburn's supposed hidden gold. Jake also knew I'd be gone over lunch, watched and followed Bart into my store and killed him there to incriminate me."

Flo stepped to the side as Spools came racing through the shop.

"And it almost worked. All I can say is that Jake will be in prison for a long time. Besides the murder, he deserves a life sentence for the dumb jokes he told."

"Isn't that the truth." I adjusted a driftwood creation to show its best side to any entering customer. "Enough of the murder. Any news on what will happen to Jake's shop?"

A glint appeared in Flo's eyes. "Yes. Here's the latest scuttlebutt. Sally Midge has agreed to assume his lease. She's going to open a psychic reading shop."

I groaned. "That's all we need."

"Actually, it could be good for business. She'll attract a certain clientele who will shop around and buy yarn and driftwood creations. I think it will work out."

"But she's a horrible psychic."

Flo put her finger to her lips. "You and I know that, but her future customers don't. People go to psychics to hear what they want to hear. Sally Midge can handle that."

"I guess you're right."

"Got to get going. My knitting group will be gathering in a few minutes. Sure you don't want to join us?"

"Can't. Kurt's coming over for dinner."

She waggled her eyebrows. "Oh, a hot date."

The warmth spread through my cheeks again. "Only a *sort-of* date with my *sort-of* boyfriend."

"Hope it goes well." With a flutter of her fingers, she left my shop.

She was almost instantaneously replaced by Bea Potter, who stepped in and handed me a book. "Here's what you ordered."

"Thanks. Just in time."

"A present for Kurt?"

"You guessed it."

"I also want to thank you for getting Detective Moriarty off my back. And I didn't realize Nate had planted a book on garroting in my shop. Moriarty would have been all over me for that if he'd spotted it."

"We were saved further problems because Moriarty isn't a very thorough detective."

"I guess we have to be thankful for small blessings."

I nodded. "There were so many things that made all of us appear as suspects. I'm glad it's over."

"You coming to cooking class tomorrow? We'll be focused on main courses such as lamb, chicken, fish and steak."

"I've decided to think small. I'm going to concentrate on very simple meals for the time being."

Bea grinned. "Maybe a wise choice. You're welcome to rejoin us anytime you want to expand your horizons."

"I'll keep that in mind."

She departed, and in moments Herb sauntered in.

"What is this, Grand Central Station?"

Herb handed me a bottle. "Here's a thank you for solving the murder and keeping our Village Center from being torn down by the despicable developer. My special herb concoction. You can put it on eggs or meat. Gives the simplest dishes a delicious flavor."

I hugged my best friend. "You're the best."

"So are you, Pru. Getting that obnoxious Detective Moriarty off our backs. And how you figured out everything."

"Just lucky. It took me a while."

"And finding that garrote in my storage area. Your ex-boyfriend sure tried to implicate all of us. I could have been locked up."

"That's what Larry hired Nate to do. He wanted us to look so suspicious that we'd be too busy to fight the demolition of our cottages. It almost worked. And it played into Jake not being caught for the murder. Moriarty became so distracted that he never pursued the real murderer."

"Oh, oh, I have something to add." Herb bounced up and down.

"Sally Midge told me that she and Jake were going to Mexico on their honeymoon, of course, now called off. I think Jake never intended to come back to the States."

"When Jake kidnapped me, he planned to go to Mexico. Obviously, that was his escape plan all along."

Herb leaned toward me and in a conspiratorial tone said, "Here's a tidbit for you from my conversation with Sally Midge. She told me she has sworn off men for the time being. After Bart and Jake, she says she's going to focus on her psychic readings."

"And we both know how accurate those are."

"But she enjoys it." He checked his watch. "I have a date tonight. Got to get going."

I punched him in the shoulder. "You never mentioned this to me."

"I'm telling you now."

I accompanied him to the front door. "I want to hear the details."

"We met two days ago. I'll tell you all about it tomorrow." He kissed my cheek and practically pranced out of my shop.

Ah, romance was in the air.

The mood was broken by a clacking sound, and Granny appeared in full stride as she vigorously pumped her walking poles. She came to a stop in front of me. "Did you hear what that putz Detective Moriarty did?"

"No, but you're going to tell me."

"Darn tootin'. He had the nerve to take credit for cracking the Bart Cunard murder case. Everyone knows you solved it."

I put my arm around her shoulders. "Doesn't matter to me. I'm just glad that I'm not a suspect any longer."

Granny whacked one of her poles on the doorstep. "I don't suffer fools gleefully. I have half a mind to let the air out of his tires."

"No need to do anything. Jake and Nate are out of commission, and with Nate locked up, my problems with black SUVs, bees and fires are taken care of. That's what counts."

Granny turned and spat on the sidewalk. "Jake and Nate. Bah. Those two are cut from the same clothes. Useless. Whereas you and I have style in common. The applesauce doesn't fall far from the tree."

"Come on in. I have something I want to show you." I led her into the workshop and called out, "Willie, are you around?"

The curtain flapped up and down.

"Willie, I'm glad you're here. You're the one who helped me solve the murder. Our little conversations worked."

"Conversations?" She looked down her nose at me as if examining a bug.

"Granny, since you're the only other person who knows about Willie, I thought I'd show you what he can do." I pointed to the sheet pan full of sand. "Ask Willie a question and look right there."

"What's that?" Granny asked. "Are you baking beach sand?"

In the sand appeared, "RITING."

Granny gawked. "I'll be hornswoggled. Like you mentioned before, Willie can answer questions."

"Yup. You can converse with him."

Granny set her walking poles against the table and cracked her knuckles. "Okay, Willie. Time for an interrogation. Where'd you hide your gold?"

"NO GOLD."

"Dagnabbit. I heard a rumor that you really found gold and pretended to come the wrong way to Omnipodge as a subterfuge."

"NOPE."

"You really made your money by fishing?"

"YES."

They spent fifteen minutes bantering.

Granny grinned. "Don't this beat all. Conversing with a ghost. It's better than a poke in the ear."

"I don't want to be rude, Granny, but I need to get ready for Kurt. He's coming over soon."

"Okay, Ladybug. I don't want to cramp your style points. Besides, I have a hot date with my honeybunch at Old Detectives Home. Maybe one of these days we can go on a double date."

I rolled my eyes. Great. With slow-moving Kurt, that would turn him into a glacier. "Yeah, maybe some time." Like in a century.

Once Granny departed, I wrapped the book Bea had delivered in some red and white striped paper left over from Christmas. At least it didn't have any Santa or reindeer designs. The Vicuna yarn served as ribbon.

I made a pass through the kitchen to check to make sure I had the ingredients for dinner. All set. When I accidently rattled a plate, Spools and Boopsie raced under my feet. Spools had fishing line caught in his tail. I removed it. Then Boopsie coughed up a giant hairball. I should have saved it for Sally Midge to "read" but instead deposited it in the trash.

My two furry companions weren't there for affection— they expected food. I served Boopsie her Fussy Feast covered with sprinkle cheese and Spools his Doggy Dynamite drenched in chicken noodle soup. They never complained about my cooking. Too bad I couldn't get by feeding myself and guests from a can.

With my minions taken care of—wait, maybe I was the minion—I reviewed one more time my plans for the dinner I would cook for Kurt. As I had told Bea, I intended to stick with easy and simple. For tonight, it would be scrambled eggs. Guys loved eggs. This was something I couldn't mess up. I cracked five eggs into a bowl and fished out the half dozen pieces of egg shell. Someday, I might be able to crack an egg without spewing egg shell into the bowl. I added a healthy sprinkle of Herb's concoction and a splash of milk. Then I beat it with a whisk. Covering the bowl with an upside-down plate, I dusted my hands together. I only needed to cook and scramble when Kurt got here. Piece of cake. Actually, simpler since I was nowhere near risking an attempt at baking a cake.

Kurt arrived shortly and gave me a wrapped box. "Here's a present for you. I'm sorry I messed up with the license plate for the black SUV. I entered a wrong digit and got a database hit for a car in Los Angeles. Detective Moriarty put in the right license plate number and found the black SUV in Omnipodge."

"That's okay. It worked out in the end. I have something for you, too." I handed him the present I'd wrapped.

He grinned. "This is like Christmas. We're exchanging gifts."

I tore open what he'd given me. It was *Mastering the Art of French Cooking, Volume 1* by Julia Child.

"This is terrific, Kurt. It will give me something to aspire to." Like in a hundred years. "Now open your present."

He carefully untied the Vicuna yarn and removed the wrapping paper to reveal *Police Exam Secrets Study Guide.*

"Since you've mastered the other study book, it's time for the refining touch. I know you're going to pass the next exam."

"Thanks, Pru. You're the best."

I hoped he might take a step toward me, but he only shuffled his foot bashfully.

Resigning myself to the lack of progress, I told him to have a seat at my dining table while I fixed dinner.

His lip trembled, and a deer in the headlights glaze clouded his eyes.

I realized I needed to allay his fears. "How do scrambled eggs sound?"

He let out a sigh. "Safe."

"Wait here, and I'll get them prepared." I dashed into the kitchen, set the burner to medium, added olive oil to the frying pan, and waited until it had heated. Then I whisked the eggs one more time and poured the mixture into the frying pan. As it started to sizzle,

I began stirring with a spatula. I added a sprinkle of onion bits and kept stirring. It smelled and looked good.

The phone rang.

I raced into the workshop and grabbed the phone to hear, "You've won a Caribbean cruise. To collect your prize—"

I slammed the receiver down. "I hate robocalls."

"You have a problem, Pru?" Kurt called out.

"No problem."

But there was. I scrambled back into the kitchen to find something else scrambled and turning black. Removing the frying pan from the burner, I took it to the sink and carved out the black sections of egg. The remaining portion was only mildly tanned.

I served Kurt the least brown part and took the rest for myself.

We sat at the table to eat. I took a bite. Herb's concoction gave a nice tang to the eggs and helped disguise the hint of charcoal.

Kurt munched away and politely didn't say anything. For dessert I served s'mores, which he greedily gobbled down. Maybe to hide the burnt taste in his mouth. I vowed to stick only with simple desserts—the one thing I could successfully serve.

After dinner, we sat on the couch in my living room. I tried to get close to him, but he inched away every time I came closer.

I resigned myself to a slow and tortuous evolution to our relationship.

"I have a surprise for you, Pru."

I arched an eyebrow. Would something finally happen? I tried to maintain my calm and act nonchalant. "You mean in addition to the cooking book?"

"Yup. I've been taking singing lessons."

"No kidding. I didn't know you could sing."

"I didn't used to be able to sing, but I've learned one song. Want to hear it?"

"Absolutely."

He cleared his throat and launched into "I Want to Hold Your Hand."

What he lacked in tonal quality, he made up for in volume. He had a pleasant voice, but my tinnitus went crazy anyway. I refrained from putting my hand over my right ear. I didn't want to offend him.

When he finished, I applauded loudly.

He smiled, reached over and took my hands in his. I shivered. This could be the start of something wonderful.

Pru's Recipes

I MAY NOT BE THE BEST cook in the world. In fact, I'm probably one of the worst. But that doesn't prevent me from following my new philosophy of cooking things that are simple and easy. I'd like to share with all of you my best starter recipes. Keep in mind, if I can master these, so can you. Happy cooking!

To begin, we have...

Toast

Yes, toast! A sure-fire success for all ages, the emphasis on fire—that is, not overdoing it. Remember, watch the toaster. Mine gets stuck and doesn't pop on time. Talk about charcoal. Don't get distracted like I do. Here's what you need:

- Take two pieces of bread and place in toaster. Can be at room temperature or from the refrigerator. Your choice of white, wheat, rye, or sourdough. (Note: I don't recommend bagels. They get stuck in the toaster; at least, they do in mine. One time I tried this and had to use a knife to extract the burnt bagel. This also filled the toaster with crumbs.)
- Push down toaster lever.
- Wait until toast pops. See above if you have a crummy toaster like mine.

- Add margarine or butter and your favorite topping such as jelly, jam, honey, or peanut butter.
- Place result on plate, gooey side up (once in a while, I get this reversed).
- Avoid dropping on floor.
- Serve, and *voila*, you will wow your guests.

Peanut Butter and Jelly Sandwich

I love pb&j. Having lived on it through much of the winter, I can attest to its robust and economical attributes. Of course, do not follow this recipe if you have an allergy to peanuts. I don't want to be responsible for you puffing up and requiring an injection of epinephrine. Also, avoid dropping one of the pieces of bread already spread with either peanut butter or jelly before assembly. Like a cat always lands on its feet, the gooey side always hits the floor. Yuck. I'm three for three on this. If it happens after the sandwich is assembled, it's not as big a deal. You can blow the cooties off and still serve. Here you go:

- Take two pieces of bread. You can use as is or toast (see previous recipe), and as above, you can choose any type of bread you want. This even works with bagels, but you have to slice the bagel in half. If you do this, don't cut your fingers. I don't know about you, but I don't like blood in my pb&j.
- Spread peanut butter on one piece of bread. I use smooth, but some people like chunky. This is a matter of personal preference.

- Spread jelly or jam on the other piece of bread. I like apricot jam, but, again, you can go with your preference, maybe grape or peach. For the more upscale, you can use marmalade. I avoid raspberry jam because the seeds get stuck in my teeth. You could even use honey, but then it would be pb&h.
- Put the two pieces of bread together. Note: make sure the peanut butter and jelly meet on the inside. You don't want to have one or more sides with the gooey part facing out.
- Place on plate.
- Slice sandwich in half. This can be done in a fashion to produce two rectangles, or if you want to be fancy, you can make a diagonal cut.
- Serve and enjoy.

Grilled Cheese Sandwich

Here's another all-American favorite:

- Select your bread and cheese of choice (I like white bread and sliced American cheese).
- Put cheese between two slices of bread.
- Spread butter or margarine on the outsides of the sandwich.
- Heat frying pan or griddle at medium.
- Place sandwich in frying pan or on griddle.
- Now here's the important part: pay attention to the sandwich. Don't get distracted as I always do with phone calls, hairballs, or tangles of fishing line. Check periodically and, once golden brown, flip with spatula.
- Repeat previous step.

- Remove from frying pan or griddle, serve on plate, and munch to your heart's content.

Mac and Cheese

This is excellent comfort food for all ages. You can buy a package at the supermarket or, if you're really industrious, you can make the ingredients yourself, although I don't recommend making macaroni from scratch. I have no clue how to do it, anyway. What you need includes: macaroni, cheese, milk, butter or margarine, and some seasoning. Here goes:

- Put large pan three-quarters full of water on stove.
- Turn on burner. (Note: make sure you turn on the correct burner. I've waited for fifteen minutes for water to boil only to discover I had a different burner turned on rather than the one under the pot of water.)
- When water comes to a boil, add macaroni.
- Set timer for ten minutes.
- When timer dings, turn off burner and remove pan. (Note: two things to be aware of here. First, on one occasion my timer got stuck, and I forgot to take the pan off the burner. You don't want the water to boil away. It makes a real mess. The macaroni turned black and stuck like glue to the bottom of the pan. I had to throw out the pan when this happened. If you catch it when it's only brown, you may be able to salvage some of the macaroni and the pan. Second, be sure to turn off the burner after you remove the pan. I sometimes become so preoccupied that I forget this step. It might be fine in the winter, but you don't want to be heating your house in the

summer using the burner on your stove.)
- Put sieve in sink and dump macaroni into sieve. (Note: make sure the sieve is stable. One time, mine tipped over and dumped the macaroni into the sink. Second note: don't lean too close. It puts off a lot of steam and can get in your face.)
- Now the secret. Put the drained macaroni back in the pan. You don't need another pan. You can use the same one!
- Add cheese, milk, and margarine or butter.
- Stir with large spoon until creamy.
- Using that same large serving spoon, ladle onto plates. Warning: avoid dropping plates.
- Serve and fill your tummy. Yum!

Scrambled Eggs

I've tried all kinds of different ways of preparing eggs but I recommend scrambled. Hard boiled is also easy, but I always leave them to boil too long and the egg shells crack. Soft boiled for me turns out too gooey. My fried eggs end up resembling bacon with a yellow-black hat on. Poached are for rocket scientists. Stick with scrambled. Here's what you need to do:

- Take eggs out of refrigerator. If you live on a farm, you can take the eggs right out from under a chicken instead.
- Crack eggs into a mixing bowl. This is the tough step. You want to crack the egg hard enough to split the shell but not so hard as to spew it all over the kitchen counter. It takes practice to find the right touch. Too bad they don't provide practice kits.
- Remove eggshell from mixing bowl. I know, some of you

don't suffer this difficulty, but I can't crack an egg without getting eggshell in the bowl. Try to use a spoon to fish out the shell, but I sometimes have to resort to dunking my fingers into the goo. Don't tell your guests if you use this technique.

- Add a dollop of milk and season to your preference. I try to keep a low salt diet, better for your heart and all. Pepper is a must, but be careful so you don't start sneezing. No one wants a sneezed booger in their eggs. I prefer Herb's seasoning. You can order this online from Herb's Herbs in Omnipodge, California (www.herbsherbs.omnipodge.biz). (Note: in the interest of full disclosure, Herb gives me ten percent if you mention you ordered because of reading this.)
- For the adventurous, you can add onion sprinkles as well.
- Beat with a whisk.
- Put frying pan on medium burner and add olive oil. (Note one: use olive oil rather than other cooking oils. It's best for your Mediterranean diet. Note two: make sure you use a clean frying pan. Once I neglected to clean the frying pan after its last use and ended up with all kinds of yucky gunk in the eggs.)
- Pour egg mixture into frying pan.
- With spatula, stir eggs. (Note: do this carefully because when eggs are still runny, they can splash out of the frying pan and make a mess on your stove top and kitchen floor.)
- Continue stirring eggs until firm. (Note: don't do anything else during this step. If you do and become distracted or take too long, you end up with something you won't want to eat.)
- Remove frying pan from burner, put scrambled eggs on plate. (Note: follow warning issued with Mac and Cheese above.)
- Serve.

And finally...

S'mores

This is one of my favorites. Of course, I absolutely love chocolate. Well, what warm-blooded woman doesn't? Three simple ingredients for this treat: graham crackers, chocolate, and marshmallows. Although this is a favorite over a campfire, you can make these in the comfort of your own home. Note: I always get gooey marshmallow on my fingers. It's like glue! Scrub immediately. Never pick up a tissue with marshmallow-sticky fingers. Talk about pieces of shredded, stuck tissue. Here's the inside scoop:

- Preheat oven to 400 degrees.
- Place pieces of graham cracker on baking sheet.
- Put chocolate on top of graham crackers.
- Add sliced marshmallows on top of chocolate.
- Cover with other pieces of graham cracker. Note: make sure you use equal-sized pieces of graham cracker on top and bottom.
- Put baking sheet in oven and cook for three minutes.
- Remove baking sheet from oven, remove s'mores from baking sheet with a spatula, and place on dish. (Note: like with the warning above regarding stove burners, be sure to turn off your oven. I haven't left my oven on for more than six hours after forgetting.)
- Munch away.

Note: this is the complicated recipe. There is a simpler version.

Buy chocolate spread and marshmallow cream and you don't have to cook it at all! Follow the directions for peanut butter and jelly sandwiches substituting graham crackers for bread, chocolate spread for peanut butter, and marshmallow cream for jelly…

You get my drift.

Bon appetit!

About the Author

MIKE BEFELER IS THE AUTHOR of the Omnipodge Trilogy which includes *Old Detectives Home* (April 2022), *Last Gasp Motel* (July 2023), and *A Mystery Yarn* (April 2024). He has also written six novels in the Paul Jacobson Geezer-lit Mystery Series—*Retirement Homes Are Murder, Living with Your Kids Is Murder, Senior Moments Are Murder, Cruising in Your Eighties Is Murder, Care Homes Are Murder,* and *Nursing Homes Are Murder*—two of which were finalists for The Lefty Award for best humorous mystery.

Mike has nine other published mystery novels: *Unstuff Your Stuff, Death of a Scam Artist, The V V Agency, The Back Wing, The Front Wing, Mystery of the Dinner Playhouse, Murder on the Switzerland Trail* and *Court Trouble* and *Paradise Court;* an international thriller, *The Tesla Legacy;* a non-fiction book, *The Best Chicken Thief in All of Europe;* and a novella, *Coronavirus Daze.* Mike is past-president of the Rocky Mountain Chapter of Mystery Writers of America. He grew up in Honolulu, Hawaii, and now lives in Lakewood, California, with his wife, Wendy.

If you are interested in having the author speak to your book club, contact Mike Befeler at mikebef@aol.com. You can also find Mike on Facebook, and his website is www.mikebefeler.com.

www.ingramcontent.com/pod-product-compliance
Lightning Source LLC
Chambersburg PA
CBHW050156120726

47903CB00002B/652